LITTLE MISS CHAOS

Paula R. Hilton

ISBN: 1523701536
ISBN 13: 9781523701537
Library of Congress Control Number: 2016901379
CreateSpace Independent Publishing Platform
North Charleston, South Carolina

For C. J., with all my love and gratitude

Not Anyone Who Says

Not anyone who says, "I'm going to be
careful and smart in matters of love,"
who says, "I'm going to choose slowly,"
but only those lovers who didn't choose at all
but were, as it were, chosen
by something invisible and powerful and uncontrollable
and beautiful and possibly even
unsuitable—
only those know what I'm talking about
in this talking about love.
—Mary Oliver

CHAPTER ONE

Vivian

Vivian met Jake when he robbed the Dunkin' Donuts where she was a seventeen-year-old cashier in Belmar, New Jersey. She didn't find him intimidating, although she realized that her inability to hide this fact might be dangerous.

"Seriously?" she asked him after he demanded the contents of her register and tip jar, along with a large Vanilla Bean Coolatta.

"Yeah, I'd say I'm pretty serious...*Vivian*." As Jake's voice trailed off, she noted that his eyes, which were on the greener side of hazel and framed by absurdly thick black lashes, had fallen down to the name tag pinned to her pink and brown uniform. "And, Viv, I'm diabetic, so use the sugar-free syrup in my Coolatta, please."

"That fake stuff will kill you before the diabetes does," she said. Her father had been a diabetic, so she knew much about it. It became even more difficult to be afraid of Jake as she noticed he didn't look much older than she was, and she now had an image of him wincing as he took his daily shot of insulin to the belly. Also, it didn't escape her that he'd said "please" without a hint of sarcasm. "And I don't believe you have a gun."

Jake arched an eyebrow at Vivian and shoved the gun-shaped bulge inside his beat-up jacket out a bit farther in her direction.

"That's probably just your hand. Like a little boy playing robber."

"You wanna gamble on that?"

Vivian wasn't a Jersey native, but she had lived in the state for most of her life and was able to mimic the attitude she felt a person needed to survive there. Over time, she'd grown to believe that the state's brashness was her own, that she had absorbed its boldness into her character, and she valued the confidence of her Jersey self. She knew she could handle the fact that not one of her customers—who were busy staring at their iPhones or typing furiously on their laptops, most with earbuds firmly in place—not *one* of them was going to look up while she was being robbed.

What if this guy *is* crazy? she thought. What if that is a gun and I make the choice to start screaming and he takes us all down? Do I want to be responsible for the deaths of my customers? For my own? For leaving Mom completely alone? Vivian imagined herself dying in her Dunkin' Donuts uniform, in her silly, coffee-colored baseball cap. Just last week, she'd sent her college application to Princeton. She had a lot to live for, big dreams to pursue. She glared at Jake.

"I'll make your motherfucking Coolatta," she snapped.

"Language, Vivian!" yelled Sal, the resident donut baker.

"Oh, *that* you hear!" she screamed back.

"What?" called Sal.

Vivian shook her head in frustration, opened her register, and took out what little was in it, as most of her customers charged everything.

"Here you go, tough guy."

He stuffed what amounted to about 120 bucks into his back pocket. She turned her back on him to complete his order.

"I'm not giving you my tips," she said. "Now take your fake-sugar poison and *go.*"

Jake reached for his cup with the hand that was not busy holding, or pretending to hold, the gun. He put the signature Dunkin' Donuts hot-pink straw with orange stripes between his lips, and Vivian continued to stare him down as he took a long slurp of his drink with a mouth that she found aggravating and arrogant looking.

"Well, then add this to your jar," he said. "That was one great Coolatta, Viv." He threw five bucks on the counter along with a piece of lined paper. It looked as if he'd ripped it out of a Marble composition notebook. He really was just a kid too.

"Oh, and here's a threatening note, so they don't think you were the one who cleaned out the register."

"Gee. Thanks."

Vivian opened up the register again and put the five bucks back inside, glad she'd recovered something, no matter how small. Jake left with a long backward glance at her and a ding of the cheerful bell that hung from the door of the franchise.

The next day, the *Asbury Park Press* detailed the theft under the column it ran regularly, titled, That's Odd. The heading read, "Cops Seek Robber with a Sweet Tooth." The article described Jake as "a serial robber with a penchant for ice-cream stores and Coolattas." Apparently, Jake was making a habit of cleaning out cash registers at Carvels and Cold Stone Creameries, as well as Dunkin' Donuts, but not before ordering a frozen treat. The reporter also joked that perhaps the petty thief was "watching his waistline" as he tended to order only "the sugar-free options" on the menu.

After the police had been called, Vivian spoke with them and the local reporter, who did the write-up in the *APP* about the robbery. She made no mention of Jake's diabetes, not thinking a person's health was any of their business. It hadn't occurred to her then to be troubled by her compulsion to protect the privacy of someone who might have just robbed her at gunpoint.

Jake

It bothered him that he couldn't stop thinking about the cashier who'd taken a stand to keep her tips and kept her head so cool while he'd robbed her. Most people started blubbering, even some of the guys, and he'd never had time to have a drink right there in the store before, like a regular customer. Usually he placed his order, quietly made his request, got the cash, and ran. She was pretty too, that girl, even in her wacky uniform. *Vivian* was the name on her tag. Vivian. He liked the sound of that. If he ever saw her again, would he introduce himself as Jake or Jacob? Which sounded better? Which would he rather hear her say? Or should he give a fake name, in case she'd feel the need to call the police and identify him? Who could blame her? He'd cleaned out her register, *and* he'd acted like a real a dick. No, not a good start. Maybe he should try to get her out of his head right now.

He wasn't a bad guy, really. He only ripped off the places he thought were fucking up the world. Fucking up Belmar, New Jersey, to be specific—fucking up his beach, his life, his home. Along his section of the shore, people referred to Belmar as "The Runners' Beach," and Jake was an avid runner. It kept his blood sugar down and his attitude in check. His mom had gotten him into it when he was thirteen, the year before she went crazy and took off for Atlantic City, leaving him with only his father to raise him. It was as if she wanted to give him something constructive to do with all the anger she knew her upcoming exit would ignite. So running was her parting gift to him, so to speak. Gee, thanks, Mom, he often thought as his feet pounded against the boardwalk. Thanks a helluva lot.

His mom was an alcoholic, and she'd broken his heart. On their last day in the same house, she told Jake that he'd be better off without her. He told her that she was wrong, and he'd cried that day, and every night of that first motherless week, like a pathetic, snot-nosed kid. Well, never again. He was stronger now.

Jake was eighteen, so he'd been running the boards for five years. First he ran out his fears about being sick, and then he ran over his rage about his mom taking off. When both those pains quieted down a bit, he began to look at his surroundings, and what he saw created a fresh anger that energized him and fueled his criminal behavior.

The beach that had saved his life, that had been his own special piece of New Jersey, was rapidly being invaded by all the worst America had to offer, erased by places that would put him into a diabetic coma if he wasn't careful. Where there used to be a store that sold elaborate kites in the shapes of animals, from dogs and birds to octopuses and dragons, there was now a Cold Stone Creamery. That had been the scene of his first, highly satisfying robbery. Where an art shop that had displayed seashell sculptures and jewelry made by local artists once stood, there was now a McDonald's. A favorite mom-and-pop diner of the locals had been replaced by a Dairy Queen. The Dunkin' Donuts where Vivian worked? That had been a nonchain coffee shop where the owner had sold her own homemade muffins. As a little boy, Jake had frequented all these places with, yes, his runaway mom. Today, his goal was to rob every one of their shitty substitutes.

And it wasn't just the old stuff being pushed out and replaced that was wrecking everything. There was always a fresh hotel in the works or another Hooters to lure the tourists, effectively evicting much of the shore's wildlife. As someone who'd grown up on the Jersey beaches when they were more unspoiled, and who had been taught by both of his parents to do his best to help keep them that way, this drove Jake absolutely crazy. Sometimes he wondered if he should step it up a bit in the crime department, do a bigger job, make a real statement, but he was too troubled by the money aspect of it all to consider that just yet. He wasn't even sure what he wanted to do with the money that was piling up from just his small hits.

Aside from the rage that fueled his recently discovered criminal tendencies, the other thing his mom had left him was a very healthy trust fund that was to be his when he turned twenty-one. Every morning when he woke up, he thought of it, and of how he was one step closer to adulthood and freedom. No, it wasn't the money he was after.

He'd been such a young kid when he started running the boards that although all these changes had happened right around him, he'd been too lost in his own troubles to notice the gradual disappearance of the shore he loved. When he did take in the view during the early days of his abandonment, he'd only turned his gaze toward the ocean.

The Atlantic had the power to calm him. From a distance, it was postcard perfect, but when he'd used up the last of his running energy, he'd feel it pulling at him, and when he got close to it, the angry cymbal crash of its waves spoke to him, urging him to leave the safety of the boardwalk behind.

Despite its beach-umbrella and seagull-in-the-sky appearance, his experience at the shore was anything but tranquil. He'd strip down to his running shorts, leaving the rest of his gear in a sandy pile, and walk right into those waters—the rougher, the better. He made it a ritual to stand there after each summer run and let the waves beat against his back. He wasn't the strongest swimmer; sometimes the ocean would win and submerge him, but he'd get up again and again, only leaving when he was completely played out. Even on sunny days, the Atlantic often felt bitterly cold. He liked it best that way. It was good to put his thoughts on ice, amazing to escape his brain.

After meeting Vivian, Jake's Belmar Beach runs and ocean time took on a renewed sense of urgency. For two weeks, he tried to freeze the image of that mysteriously fearless girl out of his head. Forget her, Jake. Forget her, forget her, *forget her*, he told himself as the waves beat against him, all the while knowing that he had to go back.

Sonny

Jake's dad, or as everyone at church called him, Mr. Sonny, hosed goose shit off the statue of Saint Francis of Assisi and shook his head. He was fifty-two and had been Saint Catherine's janitor for three years now, daily coming into contact with the devoted, daily keeping the weeds around the azaleas down and the massive building tidy. Everyone operated on the assumption that he did this for more than a paycheck. Father Giraldi said he must have been called to the parish, drawn to do this humble but important work, because of his faith. But Jake's dad didn't believe in God, though he kept this fact to himself. Every minute Mr. Sonny spent under the watchful eyes of the statues he cleaned only served to cement his atheism firmly in place. If God existed, he thought, wouldn't he have sent a blast of wind to blow the geese someplace else? Would he really give them free reign to shit all over the patron saint of animals, for Pete's sake? The truth was, he had taken on this second job because it allowed him to work alone.

Working alone was always Sonny's definition of what made a good job. Every May through October, he was also employed as a banner pilot for Mid-Air Ads, the largest aerial advertising company in the United States. Back and forth he flew in a converted crop duster, from Sandy Hook to Cape May, trying to entice people on the beaches below to spend some vacation cash. Even though some of the other pilots moaned about how boring the job was, Sonny focused on the fact that his office window looked out on the sky. In his mind, you couldn't beat the feeling of flight and freedom, even when dragging along a sign for one-dollar shot specials at the Déjà Vu Lounge. Although it was seasonal work, Sonny looked at piloting as his main job. Flying defined him. And his janitorial work? Well, that just paid the bills, kept his feet on the ground and his head in reality.

Sonny gritted his teeth when he realized that the damned geese must have been into the berries again. Their dung was deep purple today, splattering the stone folds in Saint Francis's robe, and even the pressure of the hose wasn't removing all the stains. He went inside to the janitor's closet to get a bucket and sponge and some rubber gloves. On the way, he passed by the church's statue of Jesus, which was next on his list to wash. The geese had missed that one today, so it would be a quick cleaning. The Jesus statue was startlingly white, chosen because of the contrast it made against the church's dark granite walls. He was beautifully rendered, his face wise and kind, his strong hands held up and open in what was intended to be seen as a blessing to all. But to Sonny, it looked as if he was saying, "Haven't I already done enough for youse guys? I'm not getting involved in *this* fuckin' mess again." In his head, he always referred to this statue as "Jersey Jesus." Sometimes the thought made him chuckle, but not today.

Summer was almost over, and the anniversary of the day his wife left him flying solo with an angry son was looming. That was the one job he'd never wanted to do alone. So while Sonny was the kind of guy who had trouble remembering people's birthdays, 8/28/08 managed to hold a permanent place in his memory bank. He fucking *hated* the number 8.

The kicker was that Wendy used to be a great mom. She read with Jake all the time, took him to museums, talked with him about his feelings, got him into running. Stuff Sonny didn't like to do back then and was too damned busy to do now.

Yeah, he got that his ex-wife was an alcoholic. While she'd stuck around and tried to get better, he had endless sympathy for her. Countless were the nights he held her while she sobbed, and he listened to her long list of worries so often that he could have recited them along with her. Sonny could have easily passed the Everything-That-Is-Wrong-with-Wendy quiz with an A plus—that was for sure. So of course he got it that she feared they might be better off without her. But when she acted on all those crazy thoughts and really took off? That big well of sympathy he had? It dried up so fast it kind of shocked him. It evaporated as soon as he realized his wife really wasn't coming back. Wendy could keep writing them all those emotional letters until her fingers bled. No matter what she said, or how well she said it, his heart felt hard and dead, and he feared there was no forgiveness in it.

In three years, Jake would come into enough money to be on his own. That was the only good thing Wendy had done before she fled to Atlantic City. She came from money, and although she didn't have a great relationship with her own parents, they would usually grant her requests if they deemed them worthy. Before she left, she begged them to put her entire inheritance into a trust fund for Jake, to be his at twenty-one.

Sonny had always thought of his in-laws as distant genies, fulfilling Wendy's wishes from afar. But when they became aware of her alcoholism, they went all tough love on their daughter, freezing her access to funds she used to dip into quite freely. In the past, if Wendy's pleas rubbed them just the right way, she was able to get exactly what she wanted. Thankfully, she chose her words well one final time, and—*poof!*—Jake was given the promise of an adulthood filled with ease and the privilege of many choices. But until then, and with no more help from Wendy or her parents, they had just enough to get by.

Sonny filled his bucket with hot water and dish soap and went back outside. He put his gloved hands into the soapy water and kneeled at the sandaled feet of Saint Francis. I wish I still believed in something, he thought. He hated himself when he sank into self-pity, but some days, he couldn't help it. He had a son who had struggled with juvenile diabetes since he was thirteen and a wife who absolutely lost it and took off, leaving him with their kid's glucose monitor, insulin syringes, and his fits of rage. And to top it all off, the kid seemed be hiding something from him, some kind of big secret.

Sonny sighed heavily. He had gotten the stain out of one of the robe's folds and was moving on to the next. As he continued to scrub, he began to feel more comfortable, realizing that if there was one thing he did believe in, it was honest work. These days, it would have to be enough.

Vivian

The way Vivian saw it, long before her dad died, her mom had been heartily sick of him. She'd made no secret of the fact that being a caregiver wasn't her gift, and complained often and loudly that his illness "chained her to the house," that her own life was "passing her by." It wasn't that Vivian didn't understand her mom's frustration. She thought that perhaps her mom would have been more into taking care of her dad had he at least tried to follow the doctors' orders. But her dad had always hated orders. He refused to stop smoking and eating junk food and ended up with congestive heart failure, which the doctors had warned was one of the scariest complications of diabetes. At one point, he'd been a candidate for a transplant, but as soon as the specialist found out her dad was still smoking his Camels, he was taken off the list. The heart he could have had rightly gone to someone with the discipline to live a cleaner life. In the end, he'd also succumbed to dementia, had needed constant care, and had said things that would haunt both Vivian and her mom forever. These were the things that ran around and around Vivian's head during nights when she couldn't sleep. Frankly, there were too many of these nights, and it was during these silent hours that Vivian felt much older than her seventeen years.

The worst thing was the knowledge that if he'd been willing to give up his freedom to eat, drink, and smoke as much as he wanted, they wouldn't have had to watch him die. Their family would still be intact. Vivian knew her mom was relieved when he finally passed, because she felt it too, after the first wave of grief was over, that feeling of finally being able to breathe. She didn't begrudge her mom that relief. It was what came after that she could hardly bear.

Now that her dad was gone, Vivian found her mom's behavior both heartbreaking and a little bizarre. In the last weeks of her dad's life, her mom started pulling out old pictures from the bins of discarded memories in the basement. Photos of them as a young couple, framed in gold-leaf, now took center stage in their home— on dressers and nightstands, on coffee tables and on top of the TV, even on the kitchen counters. Vivian could not escape the images of the fairy-tale memories where her mother took her refuge.

There her parents were laughing as they danced at their wedding in New Orleans, the city where Vivian had been born. That one sat in the middle of the kitchen table like a centerpiece. There were pictures of them at Mardi Gras, her mom perched on her dad's shoulders wearing so many purple, green, and gold beads that you couldn't see her neck at all. Vivian knew much about the debauchery of Mardi Gras, having visited her birthplace many times, and didn't want to imagine how her mom had managed to get so many of those coveted necklaces. *Revolting* was the word that popped into her brain as unwanted images of her parents' youth and excess ran through her imagination.

Then there were the pictures that really messed her up, all the photos of them holding her as a newborn. She was wrinkled and pink with a shock of black hair that defied gravity and as alien-looking as most babies are in their first days. But there her parents were, shockingly young, both staring down at her as if she was the most incredible life form they had ever seen. Why her mother would want to surround herself with memories of these bright beginnings, which only worked to reinforce the tragic way their coupling had ended, was beyond her understanding. All Vivian knew for certain was that she would never tie herself to another human being for the long term. She saw how the story began and how it ended. She had no need to live yet another version of the same old tale.

Ivy

It aggravated her that she was only forty-five years old and had such a grandma name. What had her mother been thinking? Ivy? Please, the name would only suit her when she finally became eligible to ride the free bus for seniors into Atlantic City for a day of one-armed bandits and watered-down cosmos. There were times, especially since her husband passed, when she wished she was already old. She relished the thoughts of wearing a silly visor and ugly-yet-comfortable shoes, of walking around with sandwich bags full of nickels, dimes, and quarters just waiting to be gambled away. What she really wanted was to be a character, a force to be reckoned with, rather than this pale version of herself. She had felt paper-thin since her husband's health failed, and since his passing, she felt as if the stuff she was made of was not only thin, but torn. So, yes, there were times when she wished she was old enough and feisty enough and many years removed enough from the tragedy of her life to match her antiquated name at last.

"Mom?" called her favorite voice. The sound of a screen door slamming came next. "Mom? You'll never guess what happened!" Ivy got up from the king-sized bed where she'd been resting and grieving for most of the afternoon and walked down the hallway to greet her daughter. Her Vivian. So, OK, it was a name that had been around awhile too, but it seemed classic rather than outdated, and she liked what it meant. "Full of life" is how *The Best Baby Name Book (in the Whole Wide World!)* had defined it, and her whirlwind of a daughter was most definitely that.

Ivy watched as Vivian tossed her ball cap onto the breakfast bar while stepping out of her shoes, leaving them by the counter stools to trip over. Then she shook out her ponytail and stuffed the holder into her pocket, where it was usually forgotten, only to appear again in the lint bin of the dryer several days later. "Hurricane Viv" is what she and her husband had called her as a toddler. Ivy had given up correcting her long ago, as her daughter was a good kid.

Putting up with a little chaos was a small price to pay for the joy of being her mom.

"Sounds like the donut business was exciting today."

"You have no idea. Mom, you'd better sit down."

For the next half hour, Ivy sat with her mouth hanging open, while Vivian told the tale of the robbery, the juvenile delinquent she'd refused to let intimidate her, and the fact that she was ("for the first time *ever!*") the employee of the month.

"I want you to quit that job, Vivian," Ivy said quietly, her voice trembling.

"Quit? Are you freaking *kidding*? Don't you see, Mom? If I can handle that, I can handle *anything!*"

For her part, Ivy wasn't so sure. She was exceedingly proud of her daughter for her grace under pressure, but the descriptions she gave of the criminal bothered her deeply. As she learned of the boy's "dark hazel eyes," his "lopsided grin," his "arrogant mouth," and how she actually felt sorry for him, because he was a "diabetic like Dad," Ivy knew she would feel far better if her daughter vacated the scene of the crime too.

Jake

He wasn't a stalker. He wasn't, all right? He always ran the boards. So what that he no longer did it in the morning, but in the late afternoon when Vivian's shift started? So what that he'd Googled her and found out that she'd been in the paper for her "preternaturally mature" clarinet performances, both in school and out? So what that he had to look up the journalist's stupid, show-off word *preternatural* just to learn that all it meant was that Vivian was really, really good at music? Proud mother was Ivy Ellis; father, William Ellis, deceased. So what that he already knew these facts about her, without her sharing them? So what! He wasn't a stalker.

Soon after the Googling, he startled her by the Dumpsters when her shift ended at eight o'clock.

"Hey, Viv, long time no see."

Her back was to him, and he saw her stiffen with a black garbage bag still in each hand. She let the bags drop to the sidewalk and slowly turned around with her right hand now in her pocket. Jake watched as she pulled out her cell phone. It struck him that she hadn't looked scared when he first robbed her store, and she didn't look scared now. Just pissed.

"What's to stop me from calling the police?"

"Absolutely nothing."

She pressed the nine and then the first one. He heard the high-pitched beeps and then a long pause while she stared at him with her striking, amber-colored eyes, her pointer finger hovering above the digit that would end his petty crime spree.

"You deserve to go to jail. The cops told me about you. How you keep robbing places all over the beach."

"I'm not here for that."

"Then why are you here?"

Jake found he had to look away from the intensity of Vivian's gaze. Her eyes seemed to be searching him for some deep motives, but he never thought beyond the initial impulse that led him to act.

He just did whatever the hell he wanted to do. He was pissed that Cold Stone Creamery closed the shop where his mom had bought him that dragon kite he flew on the beach when he was seven, so he robbed it. He wanted to see Vivian again, so he came. He hadn't thought about how she would react, what he would say. He hoped the words that were about to fall out of his mouth would be good ones.

"To make it up to you," he said, walking over to her abandoned garbage bags and tossing them, one by one, into the waiting Dumpster.

"I hate your stupid store," he added as he slammed the enormous lid of the Dumpster shut, "but I'm sorry I did something scary to you."

Vivian's eyes flashed again. "I was never afraid."

Jake dared to grin. "Yeah, I get that. What I did would frighten anybody, but you? I've never seen anyone take it so calmly before."

"How often do you do stuff like that?"

"Whenever the urge strikes me. When I'm pissed off, I do it a lot."

"And when you're not?"

"I take a break. I'm taking a break right now, here with you."

Jake watched with satisfaction as Vivian slid her cell back into her pocket. She took off her ugly ball cap to reveal her raven-colored hair, which she shook out and let fall past her shoulders.

"It's time for me to go home now." She pulled her cell phone back out and glanced at the time. "My bus will be here any minute."

Jake pointed to his motorcycle, which he'd daringly parked right in front of the store. "I can drive you."

"That's your bike?" she said. "Figures you'd drive one of those bad-boy clichés."

"You can trust me," he said. "I'm an excellent driver."

Vivian narrowed her eyes and drummed her fingers on her arms, which were folded across her chest. "It's not your driving I'm worried about," she said, but to Jake's astonishment, she walked over to his bike anyway and climbed on.

Little Miss Chaos
Vivian was four years old. Her parents had taken her to Ocean City for a long weekend. She can remember filling her electric-blue plastic bucket with hot sand and dumping it out again, filling it and dumping it, filling it and dumping it. She can hear her parents squabbling, her mother saying, "Will, I think this whole thing is ridiculous." Then she can hear her dad's voice, high above her, saying, "Viv, it's time to go play inside." She can still feel the smallness of her hand inside of his, and the wonder of being taken into a very large, dimly lit room and then up some stairs that led to a stage. She was aware of people staring at her and smiling. There was applause, and her name was announced: "Miss Vivian Dorothy Ellis, age three, originally of New Orleans, Louisiana, but who now resides in Belmar, New Jersey!" Except the announcer dragged out the name of her newly adopted hometown, yelling, "Bel-maaaaaaar," making the place sound very important to her. There was more clapping and then silence.

She looked around her and saw that the stage was littered with cowbells and xylophones, pots and pans, forks and spoons, tambourines and drums. Then she reached out to grab one of the spoons, looking over at her dad, who nodded his encouragement. He gave her a thumbs-up from the side of the stage, and that's when it happened.

That's when she first felt the power of completely letting herself go.

Grabbing a Dutch oven pan to her right, she took the spoon and banged it as hard and loudly as she could. Instead of playing the xylophone, she shook it. Then she used her spoon to bang on each and every pot. She put the tambourine on her head, so it made noise as she moved around too. She grabbed a cowbell and shook both it and her tambourine-crowned head, and the audience erupted with laughter and applause.

Someone slipped a satin sash across her shoulders. It was Weird Contest Week in Ocean City, and she was awarded the title of "Little Miss Chaos." That day was imprinted on her memory for all time. It was the day she learned that she liked to be admired for her true self, that she liked to make noise, and that she could sometimes be a very wild and strange creature.

And it was this version of herself who climbed onto the back of that motorcycle on that fateful Wednesday evening. It wasn't the honor student. It wasn't the good daughter or the first-chair clarinetist or the dutiful employee. It was none other than Little Miss Chaos, who was flying down the interstate on the back of a strange bike with a strange boy whose name she realized she didn't even know.

CHAPTER TWO

Jake

She didn't give him her address. He would have thought she was nuts if she had. It occurred to him briefly that he really shouldn't throw stones where the topic of mental health was concerned, but that thought came and went as quickly as a wave crashing over the beach.

"So if I'm not allowed to take you home, where do you want to go?"

"Point Pleasant," she answered. "I'm in a boardwalk mood."

He heard her loud and clear. "A ten-minute drive to a place with lots of people. So, Viv, I'm getting the feeling you don't trust me."

She gave him an icy stare, but the hint of a smile played at the corners of her mouth. "Just drive," she said.

He handed her his helmet, and he made the engine roar to life as she put it on.

He gave her a backward glance to see if she was really going to go on this adventure with him and saw the determined set of her jaw, a look of serious excitement in her eyes. He noticed that she'd taken off her Dunkin' Donuts smock and tied it around her waist, revealing a white t-shirt with the words *Dare To Be Great!* He also looked back to make sure she was ready to go, as he'd waited to feel her putting her arms around him, but no, he saw she was gripping the grab bars by her seat. He shook his head and wondered if she'd ever ridden a bike before. Then he turned back to face the road, let go of the clutch, and the two of them took off into the darkening, late-summer night.

Vivian

She adored the carnival atmosphere of the boardwalk, its sparkling lights, the noise of the rides going around, the happy screams. The smell of funnel cakes was thick in the air. Their powdered-sugar scent reminded her of her visits back to New Orleans and the smell of beignets in the French Quarter, the perfume of so many daily celebrations. She and the boy who'd robbed her walked side by side like old friends. It was surreal and strange and exactly to Vivian's liking.

It seemed as if each of them was waiting for the other to break the silence. For her part, Vivian was in no hurry. Her mind raced with questions. Who were they about to be to each other? What caused this spark between them? What common ground did they share that made them silently mark each other as kindred spirits? Away from the scene of the crime, it felt as if she had known him since childhood.

They continued to stroll rather aimlessly, simply taking in all the sights and sounds and feelings that surrounded them, until they came to the slice of the boardwalk that contained the next-to-impossible-to-win games of skill that vacationers threw wads of money at due to the optimistic spirit that a break from work will awaken in even the most cynical of hearts.

Finally, it was the boy who broke the silence. "So, Viv, which one should we try first?"

Vivian had whiled away so much of her youth on the boardwalks of New Jersey that she'd become something of a master at carnival games. She couldn't wait to show off and pointed to Machine Gun, one of her specialties. In this game, the player is given a target with a red star as its bull's-eye. If any part of that star is still visible after you shoot one hundred BBs at it, you lose.

"That seems right up your alley," she said with a smirk.

"Oh, Vivian, you're going down!"

"We'll see."

She had a feeling he would do what the majority of players assume is their best bet and go all Rambo on the target. And like most guys who were used to video games, he did just that and began blasting away, while Vivian calmly took the time to shoot a few BBs at the white space on her sheet. Her goal wasn't to hit the target just yet, but to align the sight on her gun. Then, rather than starting from the center and working her way out as most players tended to do, she began shooting at one side and then chipped away at her target from the opposite point. She calmly used her technique until the star disappeared, and she was proclaimed the winner by the fellow teenager running the game. While the center of the boy's star was completely shot away, he'd left almost all of its points semivisible.

"You're a lousy shot!" Vivian laughed, after giving a nearby kid the dolphin stuffed animal she'd won.

The boy laughed too. "And you're Annie Oakley. Who knew?"

"Damn straight," she said, mildly surprised that he even knew who Annie Oakley was. She'd pegged him as street-smart only. Making a historical reference made her think that maybe he'd paid a little attention in school. With his every word, her interest grew.

He redeemed himself from his Machine Gun defeat by demolishing her in basketball, although a dad tall enough to be a member of the NBA creamed them both. But Vivian triumphed again at Break a Dish, Bushel Toss, Rising Waters, and a very silly game called Frog Bog, in which you use a mallet to launch a rubber frog from the frog-launching mechanism onto the fast-moving lily pads below. As soon as you get just one frog on its pad, you win.

During this game, Vivian noted with delight that the boy didn't even try to beat her. He just stood back and looked on in amazement as she folded her frog in half. "This lets it leap more aerodynamically," she explained. Then, she waited until there was a row of lily pads lined up three deep, before she aimed straight across.

"This way, you can overshoot or undershoot and still land a winner," she explained. Vivian was thrilled to be that winner again. Each time she scored another stuffed toy, she gave it to a child that had been playing near them, and everyone walked away smiling.

But there was one game the boy claimed to be very, very good at.

"Vivian," he said, "could you sit one out? I'd like to win you a goldfish."

She nodded, noticing that his hazel-green eyes reflected the flashing gaming lights all around them. "I'd like that," she said. "And you should know that if I did play, you'd probably beat me. My mom never wanted me to try this one, because we have a cat. She said a fish in the house would just torture poor Einstein."

"So you don't want me to win you one?" Jake asked.

"Oh, I'd absolutely love a fish," Vivian said. "I'll just keep him in my room and remember to shut the door."

"Great," said Jake, and she watched as he shelled out two bucks for twelve Ping-Pong balls. "Once a summer when I was a kid, my dad would come here with my mom and me, and he always won me a fish that would live about a year. Whenever it would go belly-up, Dad wouldn't let me get too sad about it. He'd say it was just his time and a sign that summer was here and we needed to take our annual trip to Point Pleasant. Then he'd win me a new one."

"Sounds like you have a great dad," Vivian said.

The boy's eyes looked troubled for a minute, but he just said, "Yeah, he's a good guy," and turned his attention back to the game.

"The trick is to not set your sights on one fish," he explained, and Vivian noticed his voice sounded proud. Clearly, he was enjoying his turn at being the expert. "My dad taught me to be open to whatever you can get. You've got a better chance if you throw straight down one row of bowls, because the Ping-Pong ball will bounce down the aisle, giving it more chances to land in one of them. Kind of like your Frog Bog strategy," he said.

Then he demonstrated this technique, quickly winning Vivian an incredibly large goldfish, with long, feathery fins. She noted that the boy looked relieved to be the victor in her eyes at last as he handed her the prize, which was swimming wildly in its tubular-shaped plastic bag.

"Nice job," she said. "Thank you."

"So, what are you going to name it?" he asked.

She smiled mischievously. "I was thinking that I'd name him after you."

The boy grinned back. "I'm not sure he looks like a Jake," he said.

"No, I think it suits him just fine. Nice to meet you, Jake," she said, still looking at the goldfish in the bag and addressing this comment to him.

⊨⊨ ⊨⊨

She bid him farewell at the bus stop.

"When will I see you again?" he asked.

"You know where I work," she said, and they both grinned.

Her hand brushed against his once while they waited, and Vivian jumped at the electricity she felt between them in just that slightest of accidental touches. The bus came too quickly. She climbed into it, showed the driver her pass, and took one more glimpse out the window, but Jake was already gone. She wondered what his day-to-day life was like. She wondered how much further she was willing to take this. She questioned her sanity.

But as much as she'd wanted to be crazy and speed home with Jake on his bike, she didn't want to alarm her mom. Her mom, who was still on Vivian's back to quit her job because what Jake had done had convinced her that Belmar's Dunkin' Donuts was no longer a safe place for her daughter to work. Even though Vivian brought home Ivy's favorite cinnamon-spice muffins every day in a blatant attempt at bribery, her mom was holding firm.

Vivian had been instructed to give two weeks' notice tonight, but she hadn't done what she was told. Instead, she worked her shift as usual and even accepted her manager's request that she add an extra one next week. With college only a year away, she could use the extra cash, and she hated to start all over again at some job where she'd get the worst hours because she was the new girl. With her disobedience about to be revealed, she thought it would be stupidly bad form to arrive home with Jake, whom she now regretted describing in such detail to her very observant mother.

Vivian cradled the bag that held her new pet in the crook of her arm. With their huge eyes and jumpy swimming pattern, goldfish always looked anxious to her, and this one was no exception. Yet Jake-the-Fish was very beautiful too, large for a boardwalk prize, and the way his white-tipped fins undulated gently in the water was mesmerizing. She looked forward to taking him home.

Wendy

Like a stone in her heart, she carried the knowledge that she was no longer a force for good in the lives of the people she loved. Her hands often shook, and it took all her energy to push through the self-inflicted punishment that was her day. Sometimes it felt as if she was walking underwater with everything she'd done strapped across her back, each step so heavy, which was a pretty shitty way to feel when you were a cocktail waitress at the Tropicana. Her job was all hustle-bustle and tacky glamor, and Wendy knew that at forty-four she was getting pretty old to cram herself into a bustier.

But it was a job. And due to the fact that, once upon a time, she had been a very privileged little girl, it was her first job. At least it had its perks. The after-hours drinks were half price with her employee discount.

During her self-imposed exile at the casino, she'd become well acquainted with shame, and she'd discovered it to be a peculiar thing, a definite fork in the road. The way she saw it, a person could either learn to carry its heaviness and move forward or be defined by it, stacking up more shameful deeds, one on top of the next, in a frenzy of bad behavior, thinking, It can't get any worse than this! Until it did.

When her son, Jake, was very little, three or four, he got into the habit of making any hole in his clothes or any flaw he found around the house—say, a tear in the wallpaper—bigger and bigger until the pants were so very torn they were beyond mending and had to be thrown away, or a new strip of paper had to be bought. When she asked her son why he kept picking at things until they were ruined, why he couldn't point out that something needed mending and just ask for her help, he said, "Mommy, I don't know! I just can't stop myself sometimes. Don't be mad!"

And she never was, but now she wanted to scream the same things to him and to her ex-husband, Sonny. "Please don't be mad. It's like I'm in a trance sometimes. I just can't stop!"

She had tried cold turkey. Then she'd tried AA. Then for years she tried denial, pretending she could drink in moderation, fooling everyone except herself. Yeah, she'd put on quite the good show. Now she was just trying to survive. This job at the Tropicana was a confusing thing as it served to drag her even further down while still providing a sense of relief.

Surrounding herself with other addicts as desperate as she was, all of them filled with longing for things they knew they shouldn't have or do, made her feel better, in a perverse sort of way. The most comforting thing about the Tropicana for Wendy was how the hopelessness of most of her regulars hung heavily in the air, enveloping them, thick as the clouds of cigarette smoke they were once allowed to blow inside the casino's walls, but now had to take outside. It was good not to be alone.

Ivy

She sat motionless in her chair, staring at the Audubon Singing Bird Clock on the wall above the door, an absurd gift Will had once given her as a gag after she'd complained about how often it was advertised on TV for $19.95: "Enjoy nature's sweet sounds when a different, real bird announces each hour with its pleasant, natural song!" She could hear the gratingly cheerful announcer's voice even now. Oh, how she'd *hated* that clock and how annoyed she'd been with Will when she'd watched him mount it to the wall above the door that Vivian should have walked through an hour ago. But now she knew she would leave it up as a reminder of how her late husband always tried so hard to get her to laugh, to lighten up.

Of course she wouldn't be laughing tonight. Where *the hell* was her daughter? Ten minutes after the hermit thrush gave its eleven melancholy whistles, and just as Ivy was thinking that when it hit eleven thirty, she'd get in the car and bring her home herself, Vivian finally entered the room with the usual crash of the screen door. Their cat, Einstein, a Persian with long and unruly white hair, who had been sleeping heavily on Ivy's lap, startled and jumped to the floor, flashing an offended glare at Vivian that Ivy did her best to match.

"I'm sorry! I'm sorry! I'm sorry!" she said, before Ivy could even start. "I was just having fun on the boardwalk, and I lost track of time, and I'm sorry!"

"You've made that clear," Ivy said, keeping her voice calm but knowing that the vein on the side of her neck was throbbing wildly and probably giving her away. When she was very upset, the pulse in her neck became visible. She knew the heat of her unspoken anger, from all that waiting and worry, would explode out of her if she wasn't careful. The last time that happened, Vivian had barely spoken to her for a week, and it had been too much for Ivy. Vivian was all she had left. She couldn't afford to lose her affection. She took a deep breath and tried to slow the beating of her heart.

"Why didn't you at least answer my texts?" she said, her voice still carefully controlled.

"I...I got caught up. I honestly never heard my phone."

Ivy noticed that Vivian was still standing on the doormat. She also noticed for the first time that her daughter was holding a plastic bag with a goldfish in it.

"You and your new friend are welcome to come all the way into the room, Viv."

Vivian gave her mother a weak smile. "Gee, thanks," she said. Then Einstein walked over to Vivian, staring greedily at the fish in the bag. "Scat, genius!" she told him, and he scampered noisily away.

"So tell me, what was so exciting that you lost all track of time and reason?"

"I was winning at all the games."

"You always win at all the games."

Vivian flashed her mom another smile, and Ivy noted that this one was stronger, saucier. In fact, it was her daughter's signature grin. "Yep. I was on *fire*. You would have been proud."

"I'm not proud now," said Ivy, who watched with some satisfaction as Vivian's smile vanished again. She was determined not to scream, but, by God, she would do her best to make Viv writhe a bit. "So who were you with?"

Ivy noticed Vivian's eyes as they flashed to the side of her mother's neck. If who her daughter had spent time with tonight was an approved friend, Ivy knew that Vivian wouldn't have felt the need to check her for signs of serious anger. This realization made Ivy's pulse rage even harder.

"I was just hanging with Hailey."

Vivian couldn't have chosen a better name to drop. Hailey was the teenager who worked the drive-through window at Dunkin'

Donuts. Like Vivian, she was smart and kind and focused on getting into college. But unlike Ivy's daughter, she was also extremely organized, and she would often help Vivian in her constant search for brilliant but misplaced homework assignments or car keys or tip money.

"I didn't think Hailey was that big on the boardwalk."

Vivian shifted her weight from one foot to the other, back and forth, back and forth. "Well...um...You know, summer's almost over, and she realized it was pretty lame she hadn't even been there once, so she kind of dragged me along. Then we started playing games, and I got this fish, and it was really loud there, as usual, and now here I am late, but I wasn't intentionally defying you or anything!"

Ivy stared at her beloved daughter and the big fish in the small bag, and she knew two things. First, she was absolutely exhausted and wanted to turn off the lights, so the sensor in the bird clock would shut down, and she wouldn't have to hear the summer tanager chirp its way to midnight. Second, she was absolutely certain that Vivian was lying to her. But she would get a good night's sleep before she dealt with that.

"Be home on time tomorrow," she told Vivian.

"Of course, Mom, and I *am* really sorry."

"I forgive you," Ivy said, noting how Vivian, who was quick to feel guilt, frowned a little and looked anxious at words that were truly meant to comfort her rather than make her feel worse. Once she calmed down and gave into her tiredness and her relief, Ivy really did forgive Viv completely. She so rarely did stuff like this. Yes, she was now on high alert with everything where her daughter was concerned, given tonight's odd behavior and especially since the robbery. And she was so very glad she'd talked Vivian into quitting that stupid job. Only a couple more weeks of this nonsense. But for now, her kid was home, safe, and it was late. She put her arm around her daughter's shoulders and led her to the kitchen. Just showing her that small bit of affection made Ivy's pulse return to normal.

"Now, let's find a bowl for your new pet and call it a day."

"You don't mind the fish?"

"As long as you keep him out of Einstein's sight, I don't mind."

"Thanks, Mom," said Vivian. "You're the best."

Jake

Before heading home, he flew down Ocean Avenue for another half hour, breathing in the salty air with no destination in mind. He was still full of adrenaline from his time with Vivian and needed to clear his head. Having her on the back of his bike had felt great, but it was also strange to be responsible for someone other than himself. Normally, he was an intentionally reckless driver, but with Vivian, he'd never broken the speed limit. He usually saw a yellow light as a clear challenge, a race against time, but with her, he slowed down. He obeyed every stop sign and even avoided revving his engine in a menacing way at the bikini-clad pedestrians and their significant others taking forever in the crosswalks. He had been as responsible as a teenaged thief could ever hope to be, but he wasn't in the habit of altering his behavior for anyone. Yeah, he really *did* need to clear his head.

He considered casing out the new KFC that had opened up next to Belmar Fitness last week. He kept seeing all these buff guys coming out of their workouts and then buying a huge bucket of chicken, diving right in, licking grease from their fingers, which totally cracked him up—but fuck, he was overdue for his insulin shot. His dad often did it for him, but he knew that Sonny would be asleep by now, exhausted from scrubbing out every commode at Saint Catherine's. Reluctantly, he turned down Fifth Avenue and headed home.

He used his key to let himself in the backdoor and saw that he was right. Sonny was passed out in the recliner with the TV blaring, an empty beer can crumpled in his fist. His dad rarely spent the night in the room he'd once shared with Jake's mom. From his wide-open mouth, an occasional snore escaped. Jake remembered how his mom had always worn earplugs to get through the night, and not knowing he was doing it, he smiled wistfully at the memory of the fluorescent-orange plugs in her ears in the mornings, because she often forgot to take them out. "What was that

Jake? What?" she'd ask, until he pointed out what she'd done, and she'd take them out, and they'd both laugh and laugh over their oatmeal.

The room was cold, and Jake saw that some of the windows were still cracked, letting in the late-summer air. It smelled good, so he left them open. Then he gently removed the can of Miller Light from his dad's loose grasp, took the blanket from the back of the couch, and draped it over him. He felt a pang of guilt, seeing Sonny so wiped out from another long day of trying to make life more bearable for the two of them. He knew his dad had a really heavy flight schedule right now and that there was some fundraiser bingo thing at the church, which always meant lots of extra cleanup. His dad worked while Jake played, and for some reason, they both accepted this as the normal state of things, even though it didn't make either of them very happy.

"Sorry I'm such a fuck-up," he whispered, before turning out the living-room lights.

In the bathroom, he opened the medicine cabinet and grabbed one of his disposable syringes, a vial of insulin, and an alcohol swab. He pulled up his T-shirt and cleaned a small patch of skin on his lower belly. When he'd first been diagnosed, the nurse used an orange to try to show his mom and dad how to give him injections. Wendy left the room crying, but he and Sonny sat motionless while the nurse sterilized the orange, extracted the insulin from the vial, and then pinched up the fruit's skin, injecting it at a forty-five-degree angle. *Push the insulin in slowly but steadily.* Jake still heard her voice, clinical and calm, every time he performed this task. *Put a finger on the skin near the needle before pulling it out,* she said, and Jake, imagining himself as the orange, listened and did it.

When finished, he used the swab to rub the injection site and close the needle's track. He wondered what Vivian was doing and hoped she was having a better end to the night than he was.

CHAPTER THREE

Vivian

"I met someone pretty incredible," she told her friend Hailey at work the next afternoon. She tried to keep the excitement out of her voice, because it made her feel a bit silly to be this worked up about a guy so fast, but she simply didn't have the composure right now to be matter-of-fact. Whenever she thought of her night with Jake—the bike ride, the games, his gift of the fish, the way the boardwalk lights flashed and reflected in his hazel eyes, that brief touch of his hand and the current that ran through her—Vivian couldn't help but smile in a cat-who-ate-the-canary kind of a way. Then there was also the crazy giddy matter of knowing his secret pastime, not that she approved of it, of course. But the fact that she was continuing to keep something as huge as that to herself? It only worked to add to the excitement of their beginning. She was greasing a mountain of muffin tins in the kitchen while she gushed about him, and Hailey was on a break from her post at the drive-through window. As Vivian spoke, she watched her friend pop munchkins into her mouth, one after the next, making Vivian think of a chipmunk she saw under Ivy's birdfeeder once, sucking up seeds like a vacuum cleaner, its cheeks bulging out farther and farther, as if it could never be satisfied.

"Didn't we make a pact not to get involved with anyone before college?" Hailey said, in between her mad chewing and gulping. "Didn't we agree that boyfriends were too distracting?"

"I think we agreed to that because we never met anyone who was *worth* the distraction."

"Oh, *please*," said Hailey, as she made herself an extralarge Blue Raspberry Coolatta to wash down all the munchkins. Her choice of drink made Vivian grin even wider, which seemed to annoy Hailey even more. "Princeton is *monumentally* more important than boyfriends. Why is it that I even have to point that out?"

"Agreed," said Vivian. "But I haven't let myself have any fun in years. I feel old already and burned out at seventeen. I work. I study. I practice. I deal with my mom. There's got to be more to life. Shouldn't I have some fun before I chain myself to more school?" Vivian's right wrist was starting to ache from the constant circular motion she was making with the pastry brush in her hand, greasing each and every space in each and every tin that would soon be filled by colossal amounts of muffin batter.

"Don't you want to get *into* school first before you chain yourself to a relationship?" Hailey grabbed a piece of waxed paper from the dispenser on the counter and used it to scoop up a large variety of donut holes. Vivian knew she always went for the ones in the back because they were the freshest, and sometimes Hailey even scored some when they were still warm, but this amount of munchkin eating seemed way out of control, even for Sugar Queen Hailey.

"What are you stressing about?" Vivian asked, realizing she was going to get no support from her friend as long as she was in this mood. "You know you're gonna regret eating all that junk later."

"I don't know. Everything. Nothing. Whatever." She sampled a heavily powdered cinnamon munchkin this time, chasing it down with her Coolatta. "Your new enthusiasm for men isn't helping to ease my nerves one bit."

"He's not a man yet," Vivian said, realizing that the image of Jake as a teenager like herself was what she clung to when she thought of the robberies. If she looked at him as a kid, well, kids grew up, got better, wiser, left bad habits behind. Oh, she was realizing that she had a strange combination of hopes, dreams, and excuses forming where Jake was concerned, but for now she needed to deal with this unexpected Hailey business.

"But again, I ask you, what do you have to be nervous about?"

With an exasperated sigh, Hailey threw a napkin over the remaining munchkins, squished them in her fist, and tossed them in the garbage.

"Well, that was unnecessarily violent and kind of wasteful," joked Vivian.

"OK, *fine!*" Hailey yelled. "I'm really pissed off at you! Your mom called me this morning."

Vivian had just finished greasing the last of the tins and tossed the brush into the huge stainless-steel sink with a clatter. "Oh no, what did she say to you? What did you say to *her*? I knew she didn't buy a word of my story last night, but I never thought she'd check up on me!"

Taking a deep breath, Hailey crossed her arms across her chest, and Vivian cringed, knowing that her best friend was about to let her have it.

"First, she asked me how the boardwalk was, and then she reminded me that you have a curfew, and she let me know how surprised she was that we didn't check in with her before going out like that. She wanted to know if I thought you were OK. Then she wanted to know if *I* was OK, or if she needed to speak with *my* mom. Yeah, that's all I need."

"Oh God, Hailey, I'm really, *really* sorry I dragged you into this, but I need to know...Did you cover for me? I mean, I would have covered for you."

"Except that you'll never have to because my life is boring, boring, boring."

"Hailey, come on, please, you're killing me, dragging this out. What do I have to deal with when I get home?"

"Nothing more than your mom's usual obsession with you, because I didn't miss a beat. I said the boardwalk was great and that it had all been my idea. I said I was so sorry, but since summer was almost over and senior year was going to be intense, I'd asked you to come with me to blow off some steam. I told her you were most definitely OK, as always, and that we would both be our normal responsible selves henceforth."

Vivian dared to walk over to Hailey. She wanted to hug her, but she could tell that much affection wasn't welcome right now, so she squeezed her hand instead. "Thank you *so* much. I owe you."

"And you can pay up by not getting too caught up in this guy and wrecking all our plans."

Vivian stood up exaggeratingly straight and recited the motto they had come up with in their sophomore year. "First Princeton. Then world domination."

For the first time that afternoon, Vivian was relieved to see her friend smile, even with her teeth stained a deep, raspberry Coolatta blue.

"Damn straight," Hailey said.

Hailey

She had eaten so much more than she'd meant to while arguing with Vivian. She didn't know why she kept on working with food, surrounding herself with this much temptation. She really couldn't handle it, and she wasted so much energy pretending she could that she felt completely drained most of the time. After she and Viv made up, she only had five minutes of her break left, but it was enough time to undo a bit of the damage.

She was grateful Dunkin' Donuts had a private employee bathroom. She couldn't risk doing what she had to do in a public space. "Well, it's clearly time to work my drive-through magic and get some tips," she'd told Vivian, once they were on friendly terms again, but she headed for what she thought of as her very twisted sanctuary first.

She locked the door, turned on the vent and faucet, and used the Comet under the sink to scrub the toilet. She would clean it out before and after. It made her feel less gross, less like some strange animal who had no control over her urges. It somewhat civilized the process of cramming three fingers down her throat until she brought up all the frosting and deep-fried fat she'd needed to temporarily quiet her anxiety, if she started and ended with a clean, sparkly bowl.

"Out, out, damned spot!" she'd often whisper as she scrubbed, distracting herself from the grossness of it all by thinking of murderous Lady Macbeth, whom they were writing a paper about in AP English. At least I'm not that crazy, Hailey thought. The only person I'm hurting here is me. She always brushed her teeth too, afterward. She kept a travel-sized toothbrush and paste in her purse at all times.

She shuddered as she brought up that Blue Raspberry Coolatta. Its overly sweet smell combined with the odor of the bile in her belly was truly disgusting, and everything she'd eaten that afternoon was now stained neon blue. What the hell had she been thinking, drinking that? But that was the point, wasn't it? When she was binging, there were no deep thoughts in her head. No, this smart girl's brain went on vacation in those moments. Sometimes she worried that she would die back there, that maybe her heart would give out or something before she even got a chance to flush everything away. What a gruesome way to go. What a teenaged-message-movie cliché.

So what did she have to stress about? Vivian had asked her.

Well, a helluva lot, actually. If anyone really wanted to know.

Wendy

Despite all the assholes, she was really having an amazing time tonight. She had long ago embraced the fact that as a server of cocktails, no one expected her to be particularly smart or accomplished or special in any way. In fact, people were constantly surprised that she wasn't stupid. Just a few minutes ago, there had been a French customer, a real high-rolling blackjack player, whose English was difficult to understand. Her parents had employed au pairs from France for the duration of her childhood, and she was able to take his complicated "aperitif" order and exchange a few niceties with him as well. As she walked away, she overheard an obnoxiously drunk man at the table ask, "How in the *hell* does the waitress know French?" It was fun to prove them all wrong from time to time, and she got a hundred-dollar tip from that French guy. It was turning out to be a very lucrative night, and she really *was* pretty good at handling all the assholes.

"What can I get you to drink tonight?" she asked an attractive couple, in their midthirties, at the roulette table in her station.

"Do they have cosmopolitans here?" the woman asked her boyfriend, never making eye contact with Wendy.

"I don't know," he said. Then he turned to Wendy and asked, "Do you have cosmopolitans here?"

Ah, she knew this type. The woman either thought she was a barracuda who liked to hit on her customers and that Wendy was casing out her man, or she thought that Wendy was scum and simply too far beneath her to speak to directly. Or both. Yes, she was probably being pegged as both, judging from the pinched and disgusted look on the girlfriend's face. But Wendy persisted in trying to engage her anyway. What did she care? It was yet another liberating thing to have fallen so low that what others thought of her ceased to matter. Her successful exchange with the French customer had energized her, lifting her gloom for the first time in ages.

"Yes, we do have cosmos," she said, still speaking to the girl-friend. "Would you like one?"

The woman continued to look sullen and merely nodded at her boyfriend, a quick, curt gesture.

She might as well have given me the finger, Wendy thought, try-ing hard to keep a straight face. And lucky her, she got to ask one more question.

"What brand of vodka do you prefer?"

"Grey Goose," came the clipped answer, still addressed to the boyfriend.

"She'll have Grey—" the man began.

But Wendy cut him off. "Grey Goose, yes, I don't need you to translate. Her English is impeccable. Now, what can I get for you, sir?"

That got the girlfriend's attention. She looked at Wendy for the first time, with a stare that was clearly meant to unnerve her. Wendy stifled the laugh that kept trying to escape her.

"I'll just have a Corona, no lime. Thanks." Wendy noticed a small smile playing at the corners of the boyfriend's mouth. At least she'd gotten through to one of them.

"You're very welcome," Wendy said cheerfully, this time look-ing only at the boyfriend. She could feel the girlfriend's eyes still boring into her as she walked to the bar to place their orders, but she just as deliberately ignored her as she had been purposefully trying to get her to acknowledge her presence at the beginning of their exchange.

She didn't understand women like that, she mused, as the bar-tender poured two ounces of Grey Goose into a chilled martini glass, followed by one ounce of Cointreau, a splash of cranberry juice, that delicious twist of lime, and finally, the pretty orange peel for the garnish. No, she would never understand the jealous type. When she'd been with Sonny, she'd never felt threatened by other women, not even all those tanned college girls who worked at the airport, setting up the banners he flew. They were forever flirting with him, but Sonny was a good guy, and she never doubted his loyalty. Why would anyone stay with a man she couldn't trust? Then, realizing the absurdity of her judging a woman for committing to a guy when she'd pushed such a good one away, she went back to longingly staring at the drinks that were now on her cork-topped tray.

Even though she felt full of energy and sass tonight, she couldn't wait for her shift to end, to have a cosmo or two or three of her own. Or maybe she'd just drink the vodka straight as it was speedier, despite how much she craved the sour bite of the cranberry juice, the bright taste of lime. She would numb herself and then crawl into bed, wearing one of Sonny's old shirts that she'd taken with her when she left. She wished it still smelled like him, but she'd been gone too long, and his scent had disappeared. In its absence, she usually ended up remembering how strong his arms felt, back when having them wrapped around her waist was a privilege she enjoyed every night.

Often, when the bottle was empty, her defenses annihilated, she'd think about how many women at Saint Catherine's used to look on him with approval when she, Sonny, and Jake attended services there as a family. Between those church women and the banner girls, she was sure the only way that Sonny was lacking in female companionship was if he chose to be. The fact that other women found him attractive, and didn't try to hide it, had never been lost on her. And when she was with him, she truly wasn't jealous, confident as she always was in his devotion to her. But of course she felt pangs now, knowing she'd left him to be with whomever he wanted, whenever he wanted, as was his right, the minute she ran out.

Regrets? Only that she couldn't be a better woman. She hadn't deserved Sonny then, and she surely didn't deserve him now. No, she'd done what she'd done, and there was no going back. She made her bed, and she would lie in it, but still, she would do it while enveloped in the oversized comfort of her ex-lover's shirt, remembering when she had been greatly loved and had allowed herself to love in return. The echoes of that feeling, and the vodka, would lull her into forgetfulness and sleep.

Vivian

Life was incredible right now. It was hard to believe that her senior year was on the horizon, that she had a real shot at getting into Princeton, that she was lucky enough to live right by the ocean and have these mind-blowingly beautiful dates with such a mind-blowingly beautiful boy. She and Jake never formally declared themselves a couple; they just kept coming together. Her shift would end, and there he was, leaning on the wall next to her framed employee-of-the-month photo with a wicked grin on his face, or idling outside on his bike, ready to take her someplace good. Usually, they gravitated to the shore, and today was turning out to be wonderfully usual. It was such a relief not to overthink things, to act on whims. Being with Jake was a break from the pressures of everyday life. Time spent with him, like a dream she was having while awake. She smiled as she watched him unearth a child's abandoned yellow shovel and pail from the sand.

"Should we use them?" he asked.

"Sounds good," she said, and for the next hour she and Jake were on their knees building a sand-castle city. Names from seventh-grade biology came flooding back to her—scallops, mussels, moon snails, clams, jingle shells, and knobbed whelks. Vivian used the shovel to dig for as many intact ones as she could find to jazz up the simple structures Jake was making with the pail. She used them to form doors and windows, she embellished all the roofs, and she made elaborate pathways out of the huge surf clams, linking one sand structure to the next. She also found herself laughing a lot, because Jake whistled loudly while they were making their creation. He was so carefree and happy, so in the moment. It was infectious.

After a while, Jake joined her in her decorating efforts, but he was far less particular about the quality of the shells. Where Vivian used only the best of the best, Jake grabbed broken shells and connected their jagged edges in interesting patterns. The sand houses he embellished had an abstract, mosaic look. His best find of the day, though, was a black shark's tooth.

"Wow," said Vivian, "you should keep that."

"Nah," said Jake, "you like it, you keep it. Or use it for one of the castles." So Vivian put its pointy top into the right side of one of her doors, making the flat edge stick out like a handle. Then she stood up and clapped her hands spontaneously, like a child. It delighted her, this city made from the former parts and haunts of Belmar Beach creatures. The only thing that lessened her joy was when Jake insisted on pulling out his phone and docking station from his pack, blasting Bon Jovi while they continued to expand their kingdom.

"For inspiration," he said.

"I was doing pretty well on my own, I think. Besides, it's such a cliché. Playing Bon Jovi while *at* the Jersey Shore? Please, make it stop."

Here, Jake gave her a look of mock offense, but his voice was serious. "Viv, Bon Jovi is not a cliché. Bon Jovi is an institution."

She supposed it was because she wasn't a native—that, and the fact that she'd fallen in love with the New Orleans jazz her dad used to blast daily on his old-fashioned record player. Whatever the reason, Vivian wasn't awed by the local rock god who'd become the internationally worshipped Jon Bon Jovi. She knew her tone wasn't sufficiently reverent when the topic of his band came up, and she might have been the only person in the Garden State who didn't own one of his CDs. She did have a copy of Springsteen's greatest hits, though, so she wasn't a total disgrace to Jersey. Even though he could be a hopeless romantic too, she felt Springsteen ran much deeper. She loved that line in "Born to Run," the one where the boy wanted to die with the girl "on the streets at night in an everlasting kiss." Looking at Jake's mouth, at his full lips and crooked grin, she really got that line. No, Bon Jovi had never captured her feelings in lyrics, and she felt he had no business being the soundtrack to her first real romance.

"Just put in earbuds, Jake. Is that too much to ask?"

"I'll do it," he said, "but under protest. The greatness of Bon Jovi wasn't meant to be contained." Before looking for the earbuds in his pack, Jake briefly turned up the volume. "Come on, Viv, just listen."

You say you've cried a thousand rivers, and now you're swimming for the shore. You've left me drowning in my tears, and you won't save me anymore...

"It sounds like he's eating his microphone. One more time I ask you—*please* make it stop."

But it was too late. As curious onlookers strolled by, Jake started singing along so loudly that Vivian felt heat rush to her face, and she knew she was blushing deeply. He was on his knees, his arms reaching out to her, imploring: *I pray to God you'll give me one more chance, girl!* This was followed by what Vivian found to be a crazy, wailing noise, the sound of deep and very retro hair-band pain, and Jake mimicked it surprisingly well.

Vivian dropped to her knees again and rummaged around in Jake's pack until she located the earbuds and connected them to his phone. Then she stuffed them into his ears, at last silencing Jon Bon Jovi, cupped his face in her hands and kissed him full on the mouth. She gave in to this urge because she found him intoxicatingly silly, but also, if she were honest, to shut him up. It struck her that this was an odd feeling to have when she was also experiencing their first kiss, something she'd fantasized about since that first crazy meeting. But she was much more introverted than he was, and even though she hated this about herself, the older she became, the more she cared what strangers thought, and she felt embarrassed to be serenaded on the beach. It was one thing to jump on the back of his bike, not even knowing his name, because it was secretive. Her rebellion, a private act. She could only dare to let Little Miss Chaos come out to play every once in a while, and she was no longer a child who wanted everybody's attention. No, she couldn't risk losing all control now. But the more they kissed, the less space she had in her brain to worry about the fact that she was losing her mind over this boy. In fact, after the first five minutes, she barely remembered her name.

Sonny

Jake was acting stranger than usual. At first, Sonny couldn't figure out what was different. Then he realized that the kid was simply home more than he had been in the last couple of years. Yeah, it was odd for Jake to be around long enough for Sonny to notice he was acting weird in the first place. There hadn't been as many late-night disappearances these last few weeks. Also, his kid looked really good. He was brushing his hair instead of just grabbing a gob of gel and spiking it up all over the place like some crazy sea urchin. And then there was the whistling. When Jake was little, as soon as he learned how to do it, he whistled almost constantly—while he played with his Matchbox cars, in the tub, and when he was older, in the shower. You could hear him above the running water, in every room of the house. You could even hear him over the TV. Yep, that kid was one powerful whistler.

He and Wendy had laughed and laughed when his kindergarten teacher sent home an exasperated note about how Jake whistled whenever she gave the class a paper to complete. "I keep asking him to stop it, and he claims that he doesn't even know he is doing it, which, frankly, I find difficult to believe. Mr. and Mrs. Donnely, to put it simply, your son is distracting the class from its work, and it is imperative that you speak to him about this issue."

"Ah, poor Jakey," said Wendy. "The real world is no place for a whistler."

"And I don't think he does know that he's doing it," added Sonny. "He's just a happy kid."

"That's because *we're* happy," said Wendy, running her pointer finger over a small scar on her left forearm, a souvenir given to her by a turtle she and Jake rescued from the middle of Ocean Avenue one summer day. She always seemed to touch the scar when faced with a parenting dilemma.

"Hmm…What to do? What to do?" she mused. "I think the only way to get the child to stop whistling is to make him miserable."

"Well, there's zero chance of that with you around," Sonny remembered saying. Then he closed his eyes, put his hand to his forehead, and squeezed his brow as if trying to shove the memory back into the unconscious part of his mind. Jake had long ago stopped whistling, that was for sure, and the sudden reemergence of a habit he'd had when he was the most carefree and joyful was definitely something to be happy about for a change.

He wondered if it was a girl. If so, he hoped Jake had found somebody strong, someone who would stick around for a bit, maybe see him through some of the shit he was going through. Of course he knew that teenaged romances had a short shelf life. But still...He hoped that if Jake was in the middle of one, it would bring him more pleasure than pain.

Sonny had been thinking lately about the differences between generations. When things had gotten unbearably rough, Wendy had run away. One of the reasons this shook Sonny to his core after all this time was not only because he believed he and Wendy could have weathered anything, but because of how he'd seen his parents stick together. His mom stood by his dad through lost jobs and two heart attacks, and you never heard her complain. Yeah, his mom was from another time, *and* she was from the Bronx. You couldn't knock her down with a lead pipe. That's what he wished for his son. He hoped he would find a throwback. What Jake needed was one tough cookie.

Jake

"If we're going to continue this relationship, you're going to have to answer some questions."

It turned Jake on, how businesslike Vivian could be, how she didn't even sound like the person who'd been telling him what a great kisser he was only seconds before she broke away from him and began her interrogation. *Pushed* him away was more like it. And the fierce look on her face let him know that she was determined to have it out.

There seemed to be an affection switch inside of Viv that she could flick on and off with ease. If she was feeling as out of control over him as he was over her, she hid it well. She made him work for every piece of encouragement she gave him, and he was enjoying the challenge of holding her interest, even though it did leave him feeling pretty crazed most of the time. Touching her made him crazy. Not touching her made him crazy. He was a mess, but not in his usual way. Being a happy screw-up was quite different from being a completely joyless lawbreaker. Even though he was itching to wreak some havoc on the Dairy Queen on Twelfth Avenue, he was itching for Vivian more.

"Fine," was all he said, trying to mirror her calm control. "I'll tell you as much as I can."

She arched an eyebrow at him and gave him a smile that unsettled him with its warmth and wickedness. "You'll tell me everything," she said.

"So, do I get to ask you questions too?" Because he did have a few of his own. Nothing that pressing, but they had gone on for weeks like this, two strangers making out. For the most part, this suited him fine, but he was starting to want to know a bit more about her than what he got from Google.

"Not this time," she said. "This time, it's my questions, my rules. Another day, it can be your game. Today, I really do want to learn everything."

"I don't know *everything*," he said, regretting that he sounded like a smartass right out of the gate and wondering if he scored a 100 percent on this pop quiz, could they get back to making out again? It was annoying, how girls always wanted you to reveal stuff, imagining that you thought things through as much as they did. He'd had a few girlfriends through the years, but none of them lasted long because he found all the talking that was required exhausting. Viv was the first girl who seemed worth the effort. He tried to sound more respectful and interested, more like the Boy Scout he had once been, many years ago, when Wendy was still around to drive him to the meetings. "I'll do my best."

Vivian wasted no time, shooting off questions as quickly as she fired her BB gun during the boardwalk games.

"How old are you?"

"Eighteen."

"How long have you been a diabetic?"

"Five years."

"Do you follow doctor's orders? Take care of yourself?'

"That's a weird question. Do I look like I don't take care of myself?"

"You will not attempt to answer my questions with questions of your own. You will not critique the questions!" Despite her harsh tone, Jake noticed that a smile still played at the corners of her mouth. Clearly, Vivian was enjoying herself.

"Yes, Your Majesty!" Jake said, with a flourish of his hand, and Vivian's eyes flashed at him menacingly, but still with a hint of humor. "OK, yes, I follow doctor's orders, use the glucose monitor, take my insulin, watch what I eat. And I'm in really good shape, if you haven't noticed."

"Oh, I've noticed. I've *really* noticed, but don't let that make your head get any bigger than it already is, Jersey Boy."

This game wasn't nearly as bad as he thought it was going to be.

Vivian drummed her fingers on the bench they were sitting on. They were looking out at the ocean, like two retirees with nowhere they needed to be, nothing in particular to do. "So you're eighteen," she mused. "Does that make you a senior, a high-school graduate, or a dropout?"

"High-school graduate, ma'am."

"Why aren't you in college?"

"I'm weighing my options."

"It's a money thing, isn't it? That's why you robbed me. Didn't you ever hear of a scholarship application? A student loan?"

"I'm coming into plenty of money shortly."

"Really?"

"Is that your question?"

"Yes."

"Yes, *really*."

"Then why the life of crime, Joker?"

"It passes the time."

"Unacceptable."

"Why?"

"Clearly, you've given more thought to your crime spree than that. There's a pattern to your madness. The paper calls you the 'serial robber with the sweet tooth.' You're a diabetic ripping off stores that sell stuff you can't have. It doesn't take a rocket scientist, but I'm just wondering if there's more. If it's not the money, then what else?"

"Then nothing else!" Jake felt agitated now. He felt like Viv was holding a scalpel to his brain, peeling back the layers, poking around inside where she really didn't have any business to be. He was now, officially, sick of the game. He decided to give her what she wanted, just to make it stop. "I'm really not all that deep, Viv. I just hate those places, the junk they sell, the way they're ruining Belmar, slowly killing the people who live here, quickly killing the wildlife, making it ordinary, uninteresting, nothing special. We done now?"

"So it's about the beach?"

"Everything's about the beach for me."

"You're more complex than you give yourself credit for."

"Is that a compliment?"

Vivian smiled at him. It was a close-mouthed, thoughtful smile. "I'm not sure yet."

"So that's it?"

"Of course not," Vivian scoffed. "I haven't asked the most important question."

"Which is?"

"Did you point a loaded gun at me?"

Jake felt the temper that had flared up when Viv demanded an explanation for the behavior that he didn't like to think about slowly subside. It was a compulsion to be a robber, a thrill, a comfort. Analyzing it? Well, it kind of robbed *him*, in a way. But this question? Of course she had a right to know the answer to "Could this guy I'm messing around with have caused me real harm?"

"Of course not," he said.

Vivian exhaled, and he realized she'd been holding her breath, waiting for him to answer. "I didn't think so. Even then, before I knew you at all. I didn't think you had that in you."

"No," he said. "Not that."

"What was it then?"

"A squirt gun my dad got for me when I was eight."

Vivian started to laugh. "I was robbed by an eighteen-year-old with a squirt gun? I knew I should have called your bluff. I *knew* it."

"It's a very realistic-looking squirt gun."

"Was it loaded?"

"With sugar-free Kool-Aid."

"Of course!" laughed Vivian. "You really are just a little boy inside," she said, and she drew him back into her, putting the game on hold for a while.

Jake gladly accepted the kiss, but he whispered, "Don't be so sure," into her ear, before he forgot himself in her, and in the sound of the waves, crashing to the shore.

Wendy

It was the summer of 2000, and Jake's boyhood obsessions were superheroes and reptiles. This combination of passions amused and delighted Wendy, so she took her six-year-old to the library weekly to check out books on snakes and turtles, X-Men and The Fantastic Four.

One morning while nursing her standard dull headache and drinking black coffee, she read in the *Asbury Park Press* that diamondback terrapins were in need of some local champions. It turned out that every nesting season, hundreds of egg-laying females got run over by beachgoers. Coastal development had destroyed many of the sand dunes where they used to lay their eggs, and getting to the embankments they had to utilize instead was often a fatal journey. The turtles moved about two miles per hour versus the car going an average of fifty, making their chances grim. The article said that volunteers were needed at the Wetlands Institute to help gather up the pregnant turtles and to put up fences to keep them off the major roadways. Wendy smacked her newspaper down on the table as the inspiration for the best summer she'd ever shared with her son took hold.

"Well, sign us up!" she yelled, even as she winced from the pain in her head and silently cursed last night's bottle of pinot grigio. She grabbed the phone and dialed the volunteer hotline's number that the newspaper had printed in bold at the end of the article.

"Sign us up for what, Mommy?" Jake asked.

"You'll see soon, Jakey," she said. "It's going to be awesome!"

And it was, for both of them. Volunteering at the Wetlands Institute gave them the opportunity to live out fabulous fantasy versions of themselves. For Jake, that meant being on equal footing with his comic-book heroes. He was in a stage where he wanted to wear a Superman cape everywhere. This drove Sonny nuts, not only because he deemed it "loopy" to run around in a cape all day, but also because Jake often got it caught in the car door. For her part, Wendy found this habit endearing and indulged it. She'd always had a feel for the brevity of life's stages, especially when those stages concerned her son.

"Next summer at this time, he won't be wearing a cape," she told Sonny. "He'll be on to something else, who knows what, and we'll look back at pictures of him and say, 'I miss when he wore that cape. Why does he have to grow up so fast?'"

Sonny smiled, shook his head, and kissed her cheek. "Well, when you put it *that* way, I guess I can put up with it for one summer."

"If it even lasts that long."

So Wendy draped Jake's cape over the chair in his room every morning, along with his T-shirt and shorts, and she let him wear it on what she dubbed Operation Diamondback Rescue. Two days a week, and sometimes more when the terrapins were heavily on the move, she and Jake would take off for whatever part of the coast the institute targeted as having the greatest need. Some days they drove all the way to Wildwood, exit 4B; some days found them getting off at exit 10B, Stone Harbor. Once they even took the trek to Cape May, where Wendy had vacationed with her parents and a nanny as a child, staying in a sprawling Victorian bed-and-breakfast. She smiled sadly at the memories that day awakened in her, because she couldn't recall any adventures in the idyllic beach city with her parents. All the photos of her from that trip were of her and that summer's au pair, but none of her laughing in the surf with her mom or her dad.

Regardless of their location, for most of June and July, mother and son could be found gently scooping up terrapins and carrying them to safety, or unrolling yards of chicken wire that would be used to keep the diamondbacks from going on their dangerous journeys in the first place.

The group of volunteers they joined referred to themselves as "Team Turtle." When Jake woke up on rescue mornings, Wendy would hand him his clothes and his cape and say, "Let's go, Jacob Sonny Donnely. Team Turtle needs their captain!"

"Let's go, Mommy!" Jake would yell back. "Let's go, let's go, let's go! It's Super Jake to the rescue!"

Energized by their good deeds and Jake's enthusiasm, Wendy cut back her nightly wine to just two glasses and was able to get up earlier in the morning, without the throbbing headache. There were times during that summer when she felt that perhaps Jake wasn't the only one deserving of a cape. In the evenings, she packed lunches for Sonny to take to work and for her and Jake too, to eat on the beach or in the car on the way home after their busy mornings. For breakfast, she scrambled eggs and buttered bagels for her family, gave them juice, and even made sure everyone took a multivitamin before they all headed out to do their work on the beach. She loved thinking of the three of them at the shore, separate yet together. Sonny flying somewhere high above them, and the two of them on the ground with their terrapins.

It fascinated Wendy, the science behind locating all the turtles. Local environmentalists tracked their movements with radio and sonic transmitters epoxied to their hard shells. Each turtle received a three-number code, so the workers at the institute could always tell where each one was at any given time. During nesting season, they would send five road patrols out in twenty-four-hour cycles to keep the turtles out of harm's way, and being a part of those patrols gave both Wendy and her little boy a feeling of pride and purpose.

Quite often, the terrapins would panic when they were picked up, flailing their hind legs wildly. The diamondbacks weren't aggressive, but they were pregnant, strong, and easily spooked. Although volunteers were required to wear gloves, once Wendy found herself carrying a very agitated one, and the claws of one of its thrashing legs caught her in the exposed skin between her gloves and T-shirt. Although the gash didn't require stiches, it was fairly deep, and Wendy had a moment of shock when she realized that a creature she found adorable had just drawn blood. She had it treated back at one of the institute's first-aid stations. They assured her that the turtle scratch wouldn't give her any diseases, but Wendy wasn't worried. She was actually pretty proud of the scratch, and part of her hoped it would leave a scar, a battle wound as proof that she had once done something important with her time.

But the protective mom in her realized that she'd been lucky it wasn't Jake who'd gotten the gash, and she rethought their volunteerism a bit. Instead of trying to pick up the turtles on the move, she and Jake switched to carrying large orange buckets and picking up the dead ones. Yes, it was sadder, but it was safer too. Every year, the Wildlife Institute was able to salvage hundreds of eggs from the road-killed terrapins.

"So we're saving the little guys today?" Jake asked her.

"Yep. That's what we're doing, Super Jake."

"I liked the other job better. But it *was* scary when you got scratched."

"Well, Jake, this is supposed to be fun. Are you still having a good time, or do you want to take a break from Team Turtle?"

"Aw, no way, Mom!" said Jake, his already large eyes opening even wider in disbelief. "The Donnelys aren't quitters!"

Wendy smiled. That was one of Sonny's catchphrases. That sentiment wasn't in her bloodline. She'd been taught that when things went south, you cut your losses and moved on. She didn't think of it as quitting per se, more like making a necessary change.

"But this is summer, sweetie, and it's important that you enjoy it. No need to torture ourselves."

Jake put down the bucket he was carrying that contained three expired turtles and threw his arms around Wendy's waist.

"You are the *best* mommy ever, and this is the best summer ever. Anything I do with you is fun, and I'm learning so much, Mommy! So, so much!"

Wendy shook her head and smiled at her sweet boy.

"So what's the biggest thing you've learned this summer so far?"

Jake looked down at his bucket of somber cargo with a thoughtful expression.

"I guess I've learned that even when you're dead, it's not over."

Wendy threw back her head and laughed, and the laugh came from her belly, from deep inside of her. She couldn't remember the last time she'd felt a joy so genuine.

"Jake, that's not the answer I was expecting."

"But it's a good one, Mom?" he asked her, grinning back and exposing two rows of sparkling white baby teeth.

"Yes, Jake," said Wendy, wiping her eyes. "It's a *very* good one. Now, I think it's time we take these back to the institute and call it a day."

As they walked side by side with their buckets of deceased terrapins and their hopefully still vital eggs, Wendy realized that she had never felt more in synch with another human being than her own son in all her life, and that she never wanted this summer to end.

Vivian

She stood in front of the high-school orchestra with her back to the audience and played a single note. There was a microphone attached to the collar of her velvet dress, and the plaintive sound of her clarinet rose into the air. Soon, all the other instruments joined her, doing their best to blend their notes with hers. As first-chair clarinetist, it was her job to tune up the band at the start of a performance. Some people referred to this moment before everyone was in synch as "the cacophony." How she loved that word, *cacophony*, loved that she was the one who had the privilege of taming everyone's wildness, all those different sounds, coming into synch with the purest note she played, the middle C. Mr. Rainey, the conductor, nodded at Vivian when he felt his charges sounded well tuned. Vivian sat down in her chair at the front of the stage, ready to perform.

It was a chair she'd practiced many hours to get, and she'd fought hard to keep it throughout her high-school career. It was customary for students to "challenge" each other during the school year to a musical duel of sorts. After one student issued the challenge, Mr. Rainey got to pick the song and the date, and the two bandmates would have to play for him. He would then choose the most flawless performance as the winner of the chair in question.

As a freshman, Vivian had started out strong. Her initial audition placed her in the fifth chair in a group of seventeen clarinetists. She then threw down her gauntlet and challenged her way up the ranks. She was first chair by tenth grade, defeating one junior and three seniors to get there. She had been challenged many times since, but never defeated. Yet she never felt smug when she was in the spotlight to tune up the orchestra or when she sat in that coveted chair. She was flooded with fierce pride and joy, yes, but she didn't derive pleasure from beating other people. She simply loved to be her best. Truly, all she wanted to do was shine.

Her mother was in the audience, and Hailey, and Jake said he was going to come too. She hadn't been sure she wanted him there, but he kept saying it was important to him to hear her play, and he promised to sit in the back. Her mom still didn't know about Jake, and the secret was starting to be less delicious. It was starting to bear weight, all the lies and the sneaking around. But she couldn't think about that now. It was time to play.

She'd chosen the clarinet all those years ago when her father offered to give her music lessons, because her fourth-grade music teacher had said it was the instrument that most closely mimicked the human voice. She liked that idea. From the moment she put the clarinet to her lips, she felt as if she was telling a story with each breath she blew into it, with every key she pressed. She felt as if it was doing the talking, and all she had to do was keep up. Thankfully, she was a quick study. Next to Hailey, that clarinet was her best friend. Next to Jake, it was her lover. It was also her ticket out of Belmar and into Princeton. She was shooting for a full music scholarship. Vivian knew she had a real shot at a big life. She could feel its rhythm, the pulse of her future, in every note she played.

Jake

Sitting in the last row, in the shadows, Jake watched his girlfriend on stage. It wasn't his type of music, but he felt it grabbing at him with an immediacy that knocked him out. Yeah, he thought it was *that* good. Not even his beloved Bon Jovi made him feel this way, and that was really saying something.

He wasn't even sure what this shit *was*, because he hadn't bothered to pick up a program. He'd arrived early and watched as all the families filed in, trying to guess which woman was Viv's mom, just to pass the time. She ended up being pretty easy to spot, because Vivian had told him that her mom usually wore red to all her concerts in tribute to Viv's dad. Red had been his favorite color, she said. It didn't take long for Jake to locate a woman in a dark dress that made him think of Chianti. That had been Wendy's drink of choice to get through the rough Jersey winters, and he'd watched his dad pour her many a glass once the blizzards started hitting. Wendy. Jake smiled ruefully when he realized he hadn't thought of her as "Mom" in years. Even when he wrote her a rare letter or two, he addressed her as "Wendy." She'd lost the title of "Mom" the second she'd walked out their door.

He had to admit that Viv's mom was kind of smokin'. Same eye and hair color, and she wore it long like her daughter too. But that was where the resemblance stopped. Viv's mom was shorter than she was, and her face was a different shape, more square and serious, where Viv's was rounder and a whole lot sweeter. To Jake, this jawline gave her mom a strong look, like a woman not to be messed with. He watched as she hugged a lot of people while she was making her way to her seat in the center of the second row, but Jake noticed that the seats on either side of her were empty. Although she seemed to know a lot of people, she sat alone.

He hadn't realized that classical music could be so loud. It was no rock concert, but it was powerful anyway. He could feel the drums in his chest, like the pounding of his heart, and when he watched Viv standing alone and playing that one note in front of the entire auditorium, he realized that he was holding his breath. What hit him the hardest was that even though she was performing, he felt almost like he was spying on her. He could tell that when she stood up there, she wasn't thinking of anything or anyone else. For a second, he felt crazy jealous of that clarinet.

It was weird for him, that moment. It was just one note that she played, but you could hear all of her talent in it. That one note contained the promise of all she could do, of all she could be. He glanced at Viv's mom while she held the note, and saw fierce pride in how straight she sat, all her attention focused on her not-so-little girl. In the thirty seconds it took for Vivian to warm up the band, Jake knew two things. First, Vivian's mom was a protector. Sonny used to take him camping in the Pine Barrens and had taught him all about wild animals and their babies, and he sensed that kind of fierceness in the air as he watched Viv's mom watching Viv.

The second thing Jake knew was that Vivian did need protecting from him. She was something truly special. And Jake? He was just bad news.

Ivy Caroline

She sat lost in thought as she pulled into the gas station, waiting for her turn at the pump. Lately, whenever she had a moment to think, she found herself toying with the idea of moving back to New Orleans. It had been Will's job as a mechanical engineer that brought them to the industrial state of New Jersey all those years ago. It had been his work that gave them the security she craved for her young family, but it was also his career that made her a displaced Southern belle, a perpetual fish out of water. Even after living in the Garden State for fourteen years, it still didn't feel like home.

Her middle name was Caroline, and in the South, everyone used it. "You sure do look pretty today, Ivy Caroline," her first boyfriend used to tell her on the bus to school. "Ivy Caroline! Get yourself in here and clean up this mess, before I tell your daddy to whoop your backside!" was a common refrain of her mother's. (Ivy hated to admit it, but she knew full well that Vivian's lack of organizational skills came from her end of the gene pool.)

In the North, she quickly discovered that most people dropped her middle name as if the three seconds it took them to say it was something rude and foreign she was imposing on them, instead of her rightful identity. The lilt of her Louisiana accent had all but disappeared too, usually only resurfacing when she visited New Orleans, and she always welcomed it back like a wayward daughter. Here in Belmar, her Southern roots had been so neglected that she didn't often think of herself as "Ivy Caroline" anymore either, and she had stopped introducing herself as such to new acquaintances many years ago.

But on late September days like this one, when she could no longer smell the scent of the tourists' coconut oil in the air, only the crispness of fall, she felt the impending threat of snow and ice bearing down on her, and she wanted to be her Southern self once more. She longed for the land where she'd gotten to Christmas shop in a sleeveless tank, a sheer skirt, and even sandals, in lieu of the heavy coat and clunky snow boots she knew she'd have to pull out of the attic soon. *Hang in there, Ivy Caroline,* she'd whisper to herself on those days. *Hang in there, girl. The shore is where summer lives. You can make it till it comes back around.*

No, Ivy Caroline wasn't one who needed four seasons. She craved sunshine and lots of it, and the fleeting beauty of a New Jersey summer was nothing but a tease. For most of the year, the skies in her adopted home were gray and cold. Will had always been the one who'd worked the snowblower, who had scraped the sidewalk with the shovel she would have to pick up for the first time in her life this year. He'd also lovingly deiced her windshield each day and driven Vivian to school, all so his wife didn't have to venture out into the bitterness of winter mornings. Thinking of that brutal season without his love and help made her want to run screaming back to her preferred side of the Mason-Dixon Line.

It was finally her turn at the pump. She pushed the button that made her window glide down and handed her credit card to the young attendant. "Fill it up. Regular, please."

The young man took her card and smiled at her. "Will do," he said.

Now if she ever really did vacate the premises, *this* was something she'd miss about New Jersey. The best part about living here in her opinion was never having to pump her own gas. She watched as the attendants inserted nozzles into everyone's tanks, going from one car to the next, leaving the hoses dangling from the sides of the cars like so many IVs. This sight gave Ivy Caroline some serious satisfaction due to the feeling of being well cared for that came with it.

Yes, she was deeply appreciative that it was against state law to do a job she hated anyway. On a trip to visit a friend in Delaware a few years ago, she'd needed to fill up and had sat for over ten minutes waiting for someone to come and help her before realizing that outside of Jersey, she was on her own. It had been winter then too, and she cursed standing out in the cold and hated the smell of gas that clung to her gloves for the rest of the trip.

She heard the loud click that meant her tank was full and opened her window again. The attendant took out the nozzle, gave the gas cap a quick twist, and closed the latch. He handed her the receipt and told her to have a good one.

Ivy Caroline thanked him and flashed a smile that quickly faded as she pulled away from the pump and drove toward the exit. She was on her way to the donut shop. Vivian wasn't supposed to be there, having claimed to have quit before the school year started. What was puzzling was that she was still getting home late most nights. When questioned, she said she was at the library working on her college entrance essays.

At first, Ivy Caroline bought that story, but one night when she gave Vivian a hug good night, she smelled the distinct scent of strong coffee clinging to her hair. She was always the coffee brewer at work, and she had often come home with its unmistakable scent all over her hair and clothes after each shift. She was obviously changing out of her uniform at work now, so it no longer smelled as if she'd bathed in java, but there was little she could do to mask its scent in her hair.

She felt the softer Ivy Caroline part of her slip away again as she pressed her foot down hard on the gas pedal, on her way to Ocean Avenue, on her way to discover the truth. She hoped she wouldn't find what she was looking for but was resigned to the fact that she was probably right.

"Oh, shit," said Vivian, when Ivy placed her order for a cup of coffee with two sugars and a shot of half-and-half. "Oh, *shit.*"

CHAPTER FOUR

Vivian

Unemployment was turning out to be highly satisfying. This came as a bit of a shock to the always industrious Vivian. She had more time for her music, for her college essays, and for whiling away the last of the sunny fall afternoons on the beach with Jake. In truth, she was spending more time whiling than working, and the break felt pretty great, *too* great sometimes.

"I'm getting lazy and dim-witted, always strolling the beach, kissing you instead of talking, lounging instead of working."

She and Jake were walking down the quiet boardwalk, hand in hand.

"We're talking *now*, Viv. I mean, this is a discussion, right? Why not focus on the now?"

"I'm talking about *usually*. What we do *usually* rather than what we are doing *now*, and usually we goof around, make out on the beach, ride your bike. I'm having fun, but I'm no longer evolving."

"You're seventeen, Viv. You really need to chill."

She smiled. "But that's my point. All I do anymore is chill, and I like it, and it worries me how much I like it."

They were now walking up the hill over Shark River Bridge that led to Avon-by-the-Sea, Belmar's neighboring beach. The day was unseasonably warm, and as they reached Avon's wooden boardwalk, Vivian noticed a tan, shirtless, forty-something man lying on one of the many benches, on his back, his arms splayed out to the side as if he'd been shot. So still that he appeared deeply asleep, he startled both Vivian and Jake when he suddenly sat upright and started screaming.

"But it's already October sixth!" he bellowed, and it was then that Vivian noticed the small headset he was wearing and the tiny mouthpiece he spat into. "There's no *fucking* way I can do that! The month's already shot!"

Vivian felt her eyes widen in amazement, and Jake squeezed her hand. He chuckled into her ear and whispered, "Yeah, there's so little you can accomplish in twenty-five days." Then he drew Vivian toward him, so she was looking directly into his eyes. They reflected the sky and the fall sunshine, and were no longer golden, green, or brown but a stunning combination of all three.

"Vivian," he said, "swear to me that you'll calm down, that you'll never grow up to be *that*."

"Define 'that.'"

"Blind," he said simply.

Feeling intoxicated by the unexpected warmth of the day, by those eyes that always got to her when they looked into her own, and by the urgency of his words, she nuzzled his neck, breathed in his scent, and whispered, "I swear it, Jake," into his ear.

And at once, she felt like the wisest girl who'd ever lived and a world-class idiot.

Hailey

If she were honest with herself, she'd admit that she was mad jealous of Vivian right now. And she hated herself for it, because wasn't a true friend supposed to be thrilled when something awesome happened to her bestie?

But Hailey wasn't thrilled, and she also wasn't completely sure that what was going on with her closest friend since the first grade was, in fact, awesome. Right before Vivian's mom made her quit her D & D duties, Hailey had finally met this guy that Vivian was ditching all of her responsibilities for, and he was this great-looking bad boy on a bike. But that wasn't all he was. Behind all his bravado, Hailey sensed a lot of sadness in Jake. She watched in amazement when he showed up at the end of Viv's shift one evening, took the mop out of her hand, and finished the floors for her, whistling all the while. Hailey saw the sadness in the tender way he looked at Vivian when he gently took the mop from her hand. It was as if she was a treasure he couldn't bear to lose but that he was pretty sure wouldn't be his for long. Every movement of his body cried out, "I don't deserve her!" But he soldiered on, mopped the floor, whistled a happy tune. Oh, and he wiped all the tables and the counter down for her too.

So it didn't take a genius to see why Vivian was losing her normally brilliant head. At first, she was more annoyed than worried, because Viv was the type of brain who could ace tests without studying. She had this hyperfocus during classes, and great test scores seemed to come effortlessly for her as a result. But lately, she knew that Vivian had been blowing off not just her studying, but her clarinet practices too. For years, they used to meet for stupidly big Slurpees at the 7-Eleven across the street from the music school where Viv took her lessons every Thursday, but she had been canceling both the lessons and her Slurpee time with Hailey for weeks.

"I do pretty well practicing on my own," she'd told Hailey. "Not to sound too arrogant, but I've been better than my teacher for about a year now."

"It's not arrogant if it's true," said Hailey. "I mean, as long as you don't say it to *everyone*, Squidward."

"Hey!" Vivian protested at the hated SpongeBob reference. "I'm no Squidward. I'm the clarinet *master!*" she yelled. "I am the *queen* of the Belmar Bulldog Band!"

"Viv?" Hailey said. "That doesn't sound arrogant. That sounds *in*sane."

"How insane?"

"Dr. Seuss on crack insane. Ease up on the alliteration, oh queen of the band geeks."

And Vivian had laughed hard at that, with that deep, infectious laugh of hers. Then she flashed Hailey the smile that drove all the boys crazy. Hailey felt lucky to be Vivian's friend, because some of her light seemed always to spill onto Hailey, making her feel less invisible. People liked her better for being Vivian's friend. She wasn't sure who she'd be without her.

Hailey sighed and scowled down at the poem she was working on. She was hoping to be accepted into Princeton's creative-writing program, and she valued her talent, but she often wished she wasn't a writer. Vivian was artistic too, but she could channel it and control it. Yet another thing to envy her for. She chose when to pick up her clarinet, pouring all of her feelings into it, and then the notes she played allowed them to escape, and she was free. But not Hailey. She was a recording instrument, a raw nerve. Always feeling, feeling, feeling. Her own feelings and everyone else's too. She could tell what the gestures of others really meant, like how Jake was saying, "Don't leave me, Vivian!" while he mopped the floor. It was too much, seeing how lonely and sad and insecure most people were, so she stuffed her feelings with food. She hated that she was a textbook bulimia case. For someone who could see the uniqueness in everyone, she felt that she appeared maddeningly ordinary to others.

Yes, Hailey was sick of being the person who people asked things like, "Do you have a pen?" and she always did have a pen, and they didn't ask because they knew she was a writer, but because she looked like the dependable person who always had the fucking pen, who always knew what time it was and when everyone had to be there. She was seventeen, but people talked to her as if she was forty.

Vivian never treated her that way. Vivian brought out the fun in her. She binged less and barfed less when Viv was around, and now that stupid-but-awesome boy had appeared out of nowhere and stolen her best friend. That fucking thief! She had to figure out a way to steal Viv back.

Wendy

She collapsed into bed around three in the morning after a helluva shift. The night wouldn't have been as hard had she not started it off in such an emotional state of mind. After a yearlong silence, Jake had started writing to her again on postcards that said things like "Greetings from Belmar Beach!" on the front and "Sunshine at the Shore!"

The backs of the postcards were very to the point:

Dear Wendy,
I met a girl. She's great.
Sincerely,
Jake

Dear Wendy,
Funds are low. Please send cash if possible.
Thank you,
Jake

Dear Wendy,
Thanks for the money.
I still don't understand why you do what you do.
But anyway, thanks again.
Jake

His silence used to kill her, but after so long she'd gotten used to it, and the unexpected contact from her son seemed worse somehow. She'd never thought she'd appreciate him not talking to her, but the last time he'd written, he'd still addressed her as "Mom." Wendy, huh? Of course she knew that she deserved that, but it didn't lessen the sting.

She'd dropped a tray of drinks shortly after she'd received that last postcard, and she snapped at a rude customer who complained to the manager who really chewed her out.

"If you weren't normally one of my best girls, I'd totally fire you," Steve said. Her boss was twenty-three, fresh out of business school. Freckles dotted his nose, and he still hadn't learned how to speak like an adult in staff meetings, occasionally muttering phrases such as "yeah, right," and "whatever" when things weren't going his way. She wasn't sure if she was insulted to be seen as a girl at age forty-four by a kid like Steve, or delighted. She guessed she was both, and that was a disconcerting feeling, to be sure.

Like an automaton, she finished her shift that night. Taking orders, making change, bringing the drinks, collecting the dirty glasses. Her eight hours passed by in a smudge of faces, flashing lights, and foamy beers.

When her torture was finally done, she bought a bottle of Chianti and took it to her room on the tenth floor. She uncorked it, got into bed, and sipped it right out of the bottle.

That night, she dreamed that she opened the window of her suite and stepped out barefoot onto the ledge. Then she stared down at the bright sadness that was Atlantic City and let herself fall into the cold, autumn sky. It was one of those dreams that felt real, so real she could feel the crisp air on her face and through her thin nightgown as she fell like a skydiver without a parachute toward the concrete below. She had good form, like all those skydivers she saw on TV had, her body compact, her hands in front of her chest, her legs bent at the knee, her feet pointing up to the sky, but in an instant, she became even more than that. She felt suddenly weightless, and just as she was about to hit the pavement, she stretched her arms out to the side, sprouted wings, and flew.

CHAPTER FIVE

Sonny

He had to admit that there were still a couple of pretty good things about his life. Jake was one for sure; he loved that crazy kid. And his piloting gig was the other. It was his final flight of the season today, a fall festival along the coast, and he was both elated and more than a little down. He hated being grounded until the gray of winter cleared and the beaches came alive again.

It didn't feel good to be only Mr. Sonny, the janitor. Even though no one at Saint Catherine's knew about his flying skills, that wasn't what mattered. He liked having another identity to hold onto while he sprayed Pledge all over the pews, the first step in what he thought of as one of his dullest duties. As he buffed row after row of sturdy red oak until everything gleamed, he thought of how he would soon be soaring five hundred feet above the shore, the waves below glistening, the seagulls in a panic of impatience beneath him, wanting someone to drop a half-chewed hot dog, a piece of greasy funnel cake, anything, anything.

Wendy had once told him that a group of seagulls was called a *flurry*, and while Sonny wasn't normally a person fascinated by words, this was an image he grew to appreciate. A flurry of snow that made it impossible to fly, a flurry of crazy birds trying to snatch that soft pretzel you stood in line twenty minutes for right out of your hand. A flurry of events that made it difficult to put one foot in front of the other. Yeah, Wendy's drinking problem, Jake's diabetes, and the end of his marriage were life flurries, just like greedy seagulls and blinding snow.

The only area of his life where flurries didn't exist was in the romance department. There had been only two women since Wendy left, and both of them had been brief encounters, desperate and embarrassingly seedy. Young women from the banner crew, legal, but just barely. One was a college junior, the other a senior, earning some extra cash and working on their tans while neatly arranging the two-hundred-foot banners in the Allaire Executive Airport field for the pilots to pick up. Sonny used the grappling hooks attached to his plane to snag the enormous sky ads from the ground. He was ashamed that he'd picked up those coeds as well. One of them had told him that "fifty was the new forty," and compared him to some celebrity who was "aging really, really well." He neglected to tell the girl that he was actually fifty-two, and later he wondered if twenty was really the new ten, and he shuddered with self-loathing and vowed to keep his eyes and hands off of the banner girls. Sure, he had his needs, but he was usually a better man than that.

Sonny planned to savor every moment of his flight today, to do his best to snag each banner off the posts on the first try, which was harder to do than it looked, and to enjoy the fact that it was going to be an unseasonable seventy-five degrees. He usually didn't opt to hang out once his work was done, but he decided to make an exception today, to kick back at the hangar and have a beer or two from the cooler with the other guys.

He was going to spend the afternoon flying "low and slow," the banner pilot's mantra. It wasn't that he gave a damn if his flybys made anyone change their wireless plans, or if they were tempted to shoot those Jell-O shots as Fat Harry's. It was the prospect of another winter coming that made his brain race. He was about to be grounded once again, and he had been asleep too long, and he was done with letting his life pass him by.

The Man in the Black Hoodie
She knew his cell-phone number, but not a call or a text came from her on November 1. She sent him pitiful, oh-please-forgive-me handwritten letters on a monthly basis, proving that she was still able to stumble to the post office to buy stamps. And although she wasn't very comfortable with computers, he had, on occasion, received an e-mail or two from troplady@gmail.com. But on his nineteenth birthday, did she use any of these forms of communication to reach out to him? No, she did not.

He hadn't even told Vivian that his birthday was coming up. She always made him feel better, and he didn't want to feel better. He was pissed, and he wanted to feel *that*.

Sonny had just texted him, asking him to pick up some milk to go with "the HUGE red velvet cake I picked up at Buddy's Bakery." Red velvet was his favorite, and Wendy used to make his cakes from scratch from a recipe she'd gotten out of a diabetic cookbook, but Buddy's sugar-free cakes were pretty awesome too. He rode his bike to the Walgreens around the corner to grab the milk. He was standing in the frozen-food aisle, contemplating the two Splenda-sweetened ice-cream flavors they had, when he started to shake. At first, he thought it was the cold—he had the freezer door open—or that his blood sugar was off, but then he realized that he didn't feel at all cold or dizzy. No, he was shaking with rage. He'd gone from deeply annoyed to furious in a matter of moments. He slammed the freezer door, threw the gallon of milk back into the cooler, and charged over to the card section. Why he was torturing himself, he didn't know, but he stopped in front of the area marked "Son" and started to read:

Hope you know how much you're loved, and how great it is having a son like you.
Happy Birthday To My Not-So-Little Dude! I Love You!

And the smarmiest one that put him over the edge:

You are loved for:
The little boy you were,
The special man you now are,
And the precious son you will always be.

He took a few breaths to steady himself until he was calm enough to go get the milk again, grabbed a pint of sugar-free chocolate ice cream, purchased both, and sped home. Once there, he moved quickly. He put away the groceries, pocketed a book of matches from the desk drawer, and then headed to the garage. Grabbing the thermos Sonny kept on his worktable, he filled it with gasoline from the container they kept to fill the lawnmower. Then he drove back to Walgreens, parking in the back, so no one would notice his bike. He walked to the card aisle. It was empty.

Surrounded once again by all the cards for wonderful sons, he unscrewed his dad's thermos and poured a full cup of gasoline into its lid. Then, he held it over the top row of cards and tipped it, watching as the gas flowed down over all the sickeningly sweet sentiments that he would have been grateful to receive from Wendy. Sure, he would have torn anything she'd sent in half and thrown it in the trash, but he would have been silently thankful for it anyway. It would have mattered. Quickly, he screwed the cap back on, struck his match and dropped it. Then he ran.

Behind him, he heard the whooshing sound of that first, wonderful flame, and an employee screaming, "Fire!" He was on his bike in a flash, laughing and crying at the same time. Arson was a new thing to add to his resume. Happy birthday to him.

Long after he'd blown out his candles and endured his dad's singing, and when Sonny was finally snoring on the couch, he turned on the evening news and watched himself on the store's surveillance tape. The words "Arsonist at Walgreens" popped up on the screen, and then the local news station rolled his tape. Luckily, he'd thought to put the hood of his sweatshirt up, and his features were hard to see on the fuzzy film. He was relieved to learn that no one had been hurt and that they were able to put out the blaze quickly. He hadn't thought about the fact that he could have hurt people until long after he was home. In the moment, he hadn't been thinking at all.

"Police have been looking for the man in the black hoodie, to no avail," said the pretty newscaster. Then she dropped her serious monotone, turned to her partner, and laughed.

"What? He couldn't find a card he liked?" she giggled.

Her coanchor started to laugh too. "Yeah, that *is* pretty random," he agreed.

From the comfort of his tiny beachside bungalow, Jake cracked a smile as well. He could see how the whole thing *could* look pretty ridiculous. He was glad he'd amused these people with his criminal antics, but he quickly stopped laughing and talked back to the screen.

"Nothing's random," he whispered. Then he snapped off the television and covered Sonny with the blanket on the back of the couch. Removing the Miller Lite from his dad's fist, he discovered it was still half full. He put it to his lips, tipped back his head, and drained the can.

That night while he was falling asleep, he realized that the channel 8 newscaster had called him "the man in the black hoodie." Not the boy, but the *man*. It was the first time he'd been placed in that category. He was a man. What kind of man he was going to be, he had no idea. He just knew that he hadn't made a very great start of it so far.

Lower-Than-Whale-Shit Wendy

She realized that she hadn't acknowledged Jake's birthday three days after the fact and was standing at a Hallmark, scanning the "belated" birthday cards. Does anyone ever really appreciate one of those? An apology after the celebration, a kind of ho-hum moment in an envelope? She doubted that anyone ever put one of those up on the mantle. You either remembered and acknowledged a person's big day, or you didn't. For Wendy, there was no in between. Besides, wasn't that all she ever really did anymore? Apologize? She'd missed her opportunity to say happy birthday to her son, her opportunity to say something other than "Sorry I messed up. Again." She doubted she could find a card worth sending.

Unbidden, a memory of a card Jake had made for her when he was little resurfaced. She had hit it hard one night without even realizing it, opening a bottle of chardonnay after she'd already polished off a bottle of merlot. Sonny had been drinking the wine with her, but he must have had very little, and she often lost track. Yes, that was the morning she learned that red and white not only do not mix, they kind of explode inside of a person. Not only was her head pounding and the morning sunshine terribly, maddeningly bright, but she also had to puke about every ten minutes.

The absolute worst thing was that the family was expected to show up at Saint Catherine's for ten o'clock Mass. Sonny thought church was a waste of an hour and that he spent enough time there cleaning the place, but Wendy had been raised a Catholic, going to services every weekend with whoever was that year's au pair, and she felt compelled to offer Jake a spiritual life, to give him a belief in something larger than himself. That morning after the night of wine, his religious education class was taking part in the mass. They were to present the communion gifts at the altar. Jake was one of the children chosen to carry up a sacramental item to give to the priest. It was a big deal, and they couldn't be late.

Wendy did her best to conceal her hangover from her boys. After retching at least a half dozen times, she felt somewhat better, as if she had a chance to get through the morning. She didn't even remember doing it, but she had laid out Jake's suit, shirt, and tie the night before. Not being able to bear the sight of food, she asked Sonny if he could take care of breakfast for himself and Jake while she "made herself beautiful." She squeezed Sonny's ass then and said, "That gym membership is really working for you, babe," and he gave her *such* a smile. She knew then that her flirting had left him clueless to her truly wretched state, just as she'd intended. Leaving him to tend to Jake, she took a cool shower, shakily put on a black pencil skirt, a fitted blouse, some heels, and a crucial pair of sunglasses. OK, so considering her bloodshot eyes, she guessed she should appreciate the sunny day. Looking in the glass, she felt both proud of the way she'd pulled herself together and deeply ashamed of her need to do so.

In the car, her stomach lurched, but she was able to keep the nausea at bay. During the service she broke out into a sweat, and her hands shook a bit, and Sonny gave her a quizzical look. During the homily she closed her eyes behind the glasses, to keep the church from spinning. When it was finally time for the presentation of the gifts, she turned to beam at Jake. He was carrying the ornate silver plate filled with communion wafers. Wendy glanced over and gave Sonny a smile too, realizing that he had probably been the one to polish that gleaming silver. Then she looked back at her son. He was seven, earnest and small in his gray suit and red tie. She took off her sunglasses, caught his eye, and gave him a quick wink as he walked by. He gave her a sideways glance, a proud smile. After he'd successfully delivered the tray to the priest and sat back down with his teacher and the other members of his class, the long ritual of forgiveness began.

When the usher tapped the pew in the back of the church where she and Sonny were sitting, they stood up and made the slow journey down the aisle for their shot at redemption. Although Sonny dismissed the whole thing as meaningless ritual, he never said so in front of Jake. He respected Wendy's desire to give him faith. He once told her that she was the most amazing mom in the world and that he'd always defer to her in matters of the heart or spirit. He said that he didn't believe in anything but her and their family, and that it was enough. She watched as the man who truly loved her took the paper-thin wafer in his open palm, looked the priest in the eye, and said, "Amen." He crossed himself respectfully as he walked back to the pew. Then, it was Wendy's turn.

Wendy was old school about communion. She didn't take it in her hand. She had been taught to open her mouth, allowing only the hands of the priest who'd blessed the host to touch it. He placed it on her tongue. Wendy closed her mouth and let it melt. She swallowed, with difficulty, and returned to her seat, almost running to avoid the line with the common cup filled with wine. The rest of the service lasted only ten minutes, enough time for that small wafer to hit her already troubled belly. It gurgled loudly, and she was embarrassed. Sonny looked at her again and whispered, "Are you OK?" She nodded and made it to the end of the service. Then she and Sonny waited in the back of the church for Jake to be dismissed by his teacher, so they could finally walk out.

It was pure relief to be in the car and on their way home. Sonny still didn't realize she had a hangover, and she was thinking up an excuse to break away and take a nice, long nap, despite the mountains of laundry they usually tackled together on Sunday afternoons, when she started to feel very sick again.

"Jake, you did such a great job today," Sonny was saying. "We're proud of you, buddy. You didn't seem nervous at all, standing up in front of the whole church."

Wendy's stomach was lurching. She couldn't take the motion of the car. Alarmed, she clapped a hand over her mouth.

"Thanks, Dad!" Jake said brightly. "What do you think, Mommy? How'd I do?"

Wendy wanted to answer, but she was trying with all her energy not to vomit in Sonny's car. Sonny finally noticed.

"Wendy! What's wrong?"

"Pull over!" she managed to say.

Sonny screeched to a stop on the shoulder of the road, and Wendy threw open the door. In her head, she heard the priest's voice again: "The body of Christ," he said.

Then she puked up her communion wafer in the grass.

"What's wrong with Mommy?" Jake asked from the backseat.

"*Nothing,*" said Sonny, with an angry edge to his voice. "She'll be *fine.*"

They drove home in silence. Wendy caught Jake's worried look in the mirror and gave him a weak smile.

Without a word, Wendy hurried upstairs to lie down. At least she didn't have to come up with some fake reason for bailing on Sonny and the laundry. When she awoke two hours later, she found a piece of computer paper shoved under the bedroom door. It was folded in half, a homemade card from her Jake.

A Band-Aid was drawn on the cover. Inside it read, "I hope you get well SOON, Mommy!" Inside, he'd drawn a big, smiling sun. It was signed, "I love you! From Jake."

It was a low point, to be sure. Perhaps her lowest thus far. Yeah, it was whale-shit low, what she'd done, getting so drunk the night before Jake was to participate in the Mass. No, it was lower. What she'd done was *lower* than whale shit, if that was even possible. In the restless sleep she'd had after Mass, she'd tossed and turned and wondered if a person was still forgiven if she couldn't keep her communion wafer down. If you barfed up the body of Christ, were you returned to the state of gracelessness you were in before the wafer was digested? Was the washing away of sin now null and void?

Holding Jake's get-well card for her self-inflicted state, she decided that the answer was definitely in the affirmative. She, Wendy, was a lousy parent to the best kid in the world, a terrible spouse to the most fabulous of husbands, and most definitely and completely, unforgiven.

She shook the memory from her head and walked out of the store without the apologetic card for Jake. What *would* be her rock bottom anyway? That's why she'd left them all those years ago, because she didn't want them to be around to see her hit it. Even after all this time, she still didn't know the answer to that question, and it made her want to scream in frustration. The only thing she was certain of was that she couldn't keep going on like this.

CHAPTER SIX

Ivy

In disbelief, she reread the letter she'd received from the music school where she paid dearly for Vivian's weekly lessons:

Dear Mrs. Ellis,

It is with concern that we need to inform you that your daughter has missed five consecutive lessons. As per our attendance policy, and the contract that you signed, in order to hold her spot in our school, she will need to make up all absences prior to winter break, which begins on December 15.

Please contact the front desk to schedule these makeup sessions. If we do not hear from you by Friday, November 15, we will assume Vivian is no longer an active student and will terminate her contract. As we have many applicants to our program and a long wait list, we will be forced to give her slot to a new student if we do

not hear from you by the aforementioned deadline. We thank you in advance for your attention to this urgent matter.
Sincerely yours,
Ms. Elaina Buchanan, Dean [signed]
Ms. Elaina Buchanan, Dean of Music

She wasn't really sure why she kept rereading the letter, why it wouldn't sink in, but in denial or not, she knew she had to do damage control. Frantically, she dialed the school's number and found herself rambling to the receptionist about Vivian's dad passing away only a few months ago and the pressures her daughter was under as she applied to colleges and dealt with the aftereffects of being a robbery victim. She realized that in her distress, she was instinctively dropping her *g*'s, saying things in her native drawl. "To sum up," she said, "it's really been a very tryin' time." She drawled out the word *time*, making it two syllables, like a sigh, *tie-uhm*. When she was in trouble, Ivy Caroline usually came to her rescue. Very few Yankees, even no-nonsense Jersey ones, could resist her honeysuckle-soaked lilt, and she knew it. When she was forced to stop talking to take a breath, the receptionist said, "Of course, Mrs. Ellis, I'll connect you to Dean Buchanan's office immediately."

By the time Ivy Caroline was finished with the dean, not only had she secured Vivian's spot, but she also got Ms. Buchanan to reduce the mandatory makeup sessions from five to three, and to give her an apology for such a cold note after all the years that Vivian had taken lessons under her school's tutelage.

"Oh, that's all right, Dean B.," Ivy Caroline said. "Now, I assure you there won't be a next time, but just pretendin' there was another little slipup, if you have any future concerns, a friendly phone call would clear things up so much nicer, don't you think?"

Ivy Caroline knew all was forgiven when the dean started to chuckle, predictably taken with the novelty of her slow-talking charm in fast-paced Belmar, and she felt a pang of guilt. Was it wrong to be this self-aware? To use every ounce of charisma she had to manipulate someone? She'd never been this, well, this *creepy* before. Or this crazy. She'd have to think about that later. For now, she had a daughter in danger of losing everything she'd worked for years to build, and Ivy just couldn't stop herself from using each and every one of her formidable skills to keep that from happening.

"Of course, of course, Mrs. Ellis," the dean continued once she was done expressing her delight over having a conversation with a real Southern belle. "And on a more serious note, my sincere condolences on your husband. We had no idea about your family's loss, or the robbery. It's surprising how much Vivian's been keeping to herself."

Shocking. Disturbing. Maddening. Ivy could think of many adjectives to apply to her daughter's newfound secretiveness. As she felt her anger resurfacing about the mess Viv had left for her to tend to, she could feel her Southern manners slipping away, and she knew she needed to terminate the phone call.

"She's a strong girl, my Vivian," said Ivy, her lilt withering faster than a magnolia at the end of June. "And she won't disappoint you again, Dean B. I'll see to that."

Vivian

Looking down at her goldfish, she sprinkled some food into the bowl, which she kept sparkling clean. It was decorated with dark blue gravel, a few favorite shells that she'd collected during all those romantic Belmar Beach walks, a small aquatic plant for her pet to nibble on, and a ceramic figure she couldn't resist when she'd seen it at the pet store, a tiny motorcycle. She kept the bowl in a place of honor on her dresser next to all of her music trophies.

"You're a pretty boy, Jake," she said, and then she smiled and sat down on the edge of her bed, still watching her fish swim, its see-through fins rippling gently in the water. It was a calming scene to focus on, and she needed to quiet her mind, so she could think. The smile that both her pet and the thoughts of its namesake had brought to her lips faded as her mind started running over the events of the past few weeks. She took a deep breath and then let it out, focusing on the main issue at hand. As her dad had taught her to do long ago, she was going to sit there and "work the problem," a phrase she had heard many times in her life as the daughter of an engineer.

Well, to sum up said problem, her mom was driving her *nuts*. She wondered how often she and her dad had agonized over the obstacle to happiness that Ivy could often be. How many times had they shared this worry and puzzled through it all alone? Not for the first time, Vivian felt robbed that she would never have a grown-up relationship with her dad. She also thought about the fact that having only one parent to turn to when that parent herself was the dilemma was a very lonely place indeed. In fact, at least where her home life was concerned, Vivian felt that she just might be the most desolate high-school senior on the planet. If she still had her dad to confide in and said these words to him, he would have pointed out that she was being a bit melodramatic, but he would have also admitted to being impressed by her use of the word *desolate*. Still staring at her fish, she smiled again and said, "Yeah, that was a good one, huh, Dad?" to the empty space in front of her. Then, she decided to stop complaining and get to the serious work of thinking, of simplifying what seemed the most complex.

First, she realized that she'd justifiably lost her mom's trust by saying she'd quit her job when she hadn't, but Ivy's behavior toward her had been over-the-top long before Vivian felt that she deserved it. The very fact that her mom demanded she quit a job where she had good hours, decent tips, and her best friend to keep her company was crazy-making enough. Her mother needed to face the fact that places got robbed from time to time. Sometimes by her own boyfriend, yes, but that was beside the point. The world wasn't always safe, and Ivy couldn't keep her locked up like some princess in a tower. And the way she'd harassed Hailey on the phone when Vivian had used her to cover up her first date with Jake was pretty bad too. Checking up on Vivian was one thing, but threatening her closest friend, saying that she might just call Hailey's mom? Inexcusable.

But what was absolutely unforgivable was the fact that Ivy had read Vivian's journal. It was the ultimate betrayal. Worst of all, her always-right-in-her-own-eyes mother hadn't even tried to hide it.

"So tell me, Viv. Who's Jake?"

That's how she was greeted when she came home from her date last night. She was outside, shaking the sand out of her sneakers, when she heard her mother's voice through the screen door. No, her dear mom couldn't even give her a chance to come inside. God knew how long she'd been sitting there waiting for her to arrive, and she just *had* to start the interrogation before Vivian could even cross the threshold.

But Vivian's recovery was swift. "If I'd wanted you to know, I would have told you," she said, letting her voice drift through the screen door that she kept her back pressed firmly against. With the sand out of her right shoe, she moved onto the left. Then she slipped both shoes back on, because she was determined not to stay long. She pushed open the door and stepped inside but went no farther than the mat in front of the door. Einstein was dozing between them on the living-room floor. Vivian met her mother's gaze and did her best to match its intensity. "You had no right to read my journal."

"I had *every* right," Ivy said. "After I cleaned up your mess with the music school, I decided it was time to know what other disasters might be on the horizon. Your behavior's been secretive, erratic, and so out of character lately that I'm scared, and I decided I needed a tracking chart for Hurricane Viv."

Vivian winced at the way her mom used her childhood nickname, always said affectionately in the past, as an insult.

"But reading my journal is the *lowest* you can go. It's like snooping around in my brain! I'll never be able to trust you again!"

"The feeling is more than mutual," said Ivy. "So I repeat, who is Jake?"

Vivian said a silent prayer of thanks that she'd never written anything about his crimes. Protecting Jake had been instinctual to her from the start. She wasn't stupid enough to create evidence that could condemn him. She used the journal to talk about the way he looked at her, the way time seemed to have more weight, to move differently when he was around. None of it was bad in any way, but not a word of it was written for her mother.

"He's my boyfriend, and he's great. But you already know all that now, don't you?" She spat out the words, and although she felt herself shaking with anger, she willed herself not to start screaming at Ivy. Vivian always found people's anger more impressive when they stayed in control of themselves, and she wanted to be very frightening to her mom in that moment.

"I want to meet him."

"What you want no longer matters to me."

Her mom inhaled sharply then, and Vivian saw the vein on her neck begin to pulse. She relished the sight, knowing that she'd scored big with those cold words. *Good*, she thought. *Good. You need to feel how angry I am, because you completely screwed up this mother-daughter thing we had going.* Then she almost laughed as a phrase she'd learned in French class popped into her head: *Je t'aime, mais je craque.* It was the final line of a poem about a relationship gone wrong that the class took turns reading aloud. It meant "I love you, but I've had it." Vivian was the one who got to say that last line in front of everybody, and she'd felt a world of passion and hopelessness in those few words. Yes, she could relate.

"You're crying," said Ivy. Furiously, Vivian wiped her cheek with the back of her hand. She hadn't even noticed when the tears started. "I don't really think this is cry worthy," her mother continued, in a falsely calm voice that rivaled Vivian's own. "You broke my trust. I broke yours. We're on equal footing, so I think we should simply move on and start again from here."

Again, something Vivian had learned in school started running through her thoughts. It was always this way with her. In moments of confusion, her brain jumped to some concrete idea that she had a clear understanding of. Facts and phrases comforted her. She had loved seventh-grade algebra, because its rules were clean and their application pure. She could still hear Mrs. McNight's voice and her squeaky whiteboard marker as it tried to keep up with her words: *The most important thing to remember when working with equations is to always do the same thing to both sides of the equation.* With that rule in mind, the "equal footing" idea her mom just described was quite logical at first glance:

$$x = betrayal$$
$$x + \text{Ivy} = betrayal + \text{Vivian}$$

So while the constant was betrayal on both sides, the error in her mother's thinking became glaringly obvious to Vivian when she reduced it all into the simplest of algebraic terms. Adding a teenager's dishonest act to a mother's universe was simply not the same as adding a mother's dishonest act to a teenager's. Clearly, the biggest difference was that:

$$betrayal + \text{Ivy} = completely\ let\text{-}down\ \text{Vivian}$$

It wasn't even; therefore, it wasn't the least bit logical or justifiable! With her thoughts worked out, Vivian proceeded to win her argument.

"No, Mom, *no*. We aren't on equal footing. We never have been, and we shouldn't be. I'm a teenager, and that means I'll screw up sometimes. Yeah, there will be times when I'll lie to you to get what I want, and when I think you don't trust me, I'll lie to you even more, because I'm a *kid*. But you? Why should you get to act the same way I do? Shouldn't you be above me? When did we become twin sisters? When, huh? When? If you look at the difference in our ages, what you did was so much worse!"

"You're yelling at me," said Ivy. "Stop yelling at me."

Vivian hadn't realized that she'd lost her battle to stay calm until Ivy pointed it out, but she didn't care anymore. It felt good to get her anger outside of her head. She had one more thing to add, and she said it in a low growl:

"Never. Read. My Journal. Again."

Ivy sighed heavily then. "If only your father were here—"

Those words infuriated Vivian so much that she refused to let Ivy finish: "He's not. Get over it."

Silence fell between them then, broken only by an occasional meow from Einstein, whom they'd woken up with their arguing. He kept pacing back and forth between them, trying to get someone to pet his out-of-control fur, but both Vivian and Ivy ignored him, neither one seeming willing to break the fierceness of her gaze. Vivian had used those words to wound Ivy, but it looked as if she'd failed. Amazingly, although the look Ivy was giving her was intense, it was also deeply sympathetic, and Vivian didn't want that. In fact, she hated it.

"I think you're the one who's the most not over it," Ivy began. "The only thing that adds up, that explains why you're risking your future, is that you're not dealing with your dad's death." She paused for a moment, nodded. "Yes, mourning a loss can make a person act out. I'm going to look into grief counseling, maybe we can go together—"

Vivian started laughing at Ivy's words, and she knew that she sounded like a crazy person, but she was past caring.

"Stop trying to pin all this on Dad dying! You read my journal. You went where you had no business to be, and I'll never forgive you for that. And I'm not going to grief counseling, or anywhere else with you. That's stupid!"

With that, Vivian ran back outside, letting the screen door bang shut behind her. She caught a bus back to the beach and sat in the sand for over an hour, bundled up in her winter coat to block the ocean's breeze, and stared up at the fat, full moon above her, until she was spent enough to go home and get some sleep. It occurred to her that she should probably be impressed that Ivy hadn't followed her and demanded that she come home. But still, it was too little trust too late.

With all the night's events replayed, Vivian's thoughts came back to the present moment, and she reached for her journal out of habit. It had been a birthday gift from Hailey, who had always told Vivian that if you don't keep a journal, you "don't really know yourself." Well, she was done pouring her heart out in ink for the world (Ivy) to see. She realized that the more time she spent with Jake, the less she'd been seeing Hailey, and she'd been using the gift of the journal as a replacement for her best friend. She hadn't needed a diary when she had Hailey to talk with and confide in, and now that the journal could no longer be her haven, she felt as if she was about to explode with secrets.

With her eyes still fixed on the soothing sight of Jake the Fish, she decided that she was done. She couldn't take it anymore. She was going to tell Hailey everything.

Hailey

How could the smartest person she'd ever known also be such a dumb ass? It was a thrill, at first, when Vivian showed up a complete wreck at the end of Hailey's shift at the drive-through window. It was usually Vivian who was giving advice and encouragement to her, and Hailey liked the role change. Oh, yes, she liked it tremendously. It wasn't that she wanted Vivian to be in distress. Of course she didn't like to see the best friend she'd ever had troubled. It was simply that, for *once*, she got to be the wise one in the relationship, the one with every answer. The only times she'd bailed Vivian out in the past were when her scattered friend lost her bus fare or misplaced one of her brilliant assignments or, lately, when she needed to use her as a cover with Mrs. Ellis. Yes, the always well-organized Hailey was a great finder of lost items and an excellent spinner of respectable excuses, but she was introverted, a social disaster. To have popular, accomplished Vivian Ellis wailing to her, "Oh my God! What should I do?" was a real confidence booster, a real shot of Red Bull to the self-esteem.

And she'd really missed how Viv could completely crack her up. Instead of coming inside Dunkin' Donuts, Viv had just ridden the bus to the beach, walked up to the drive-through speaker, and said, "Hailey, it's me. And yes, you absolutely may. I mean, I really, truly hope you can." This was her response to Hailey's "Hello and welcome to Dunkin' Donuts. May I help you?"

She quickly clocked out and met Vivian outside. Gripping an extralarge pumpkin-spice latte in each fist, she handed one to her friend and then followed Viv across Ocean Avenue, across the boards, and then down the stairs to the wild beauty of the beach in late fall. The wind raged and the cold waves broke loudly on the shore. Hailey thought the ocean looked as pissed off as she was that summer was long over. Like everyone else in town, she was missing the warm months. The sky was typical November, stark and gray. But she had to admit that it was still a breathtaking, if desolate, sight.

"Pretty cold day for the beach," she said, stating the obvious just to break the silence.

"It's the only place where I can think straight," said Vivian, and Hailey was struck by how pale her friend looked, the dark circles under her usually mischievously bright eyes saying more than her words ever could. She looked as if a good night's sleep hadn't come her way in days.

"Then something must really be wrong, because the Vivian I know can think straight anytime, anywhere," Hailey said, shivering as the cold wind blew tiny particles of sand in their faces. She wiped the grit from her cheeks with one of her gloved hands.

"Oh, Hailey, I think I've made a huge mess out of everything. And I don't know how to stop. I'm not sure things are fixable."

"Ha!" said Hailey, shaking her head, still filled with the rush of being the friend Vivian chose in a crisis. "Who doesn't make a mess? I don't know anyone who isn't secretly making all kinds of messes, if they're being really honest with themselves."

"Well, there's I-haven't-dusted-anything-in-two-weeks messy, and there's I-have-rooms-people-can't-even-go-into-without-getting-hurt messy. You know the kind of messy you see on that show *Hoarders*? Just all kinds of crap stuffed into every nook and cranny? That's the kind of mess I've been making, Hailey. I'm a hoarder of secrets. And it's killing my relationship with my mom, and I've been a bad friend to you lately, I know. I'm sorry, and—"

"It's OK," Hailey broke in, and despite how lonely she was and how angry she'd been at Vivian, she discovered that she meant it.

"And it's killing me."

"Why?" Hailey was truly bewildered, unsure of how anything could have gotten this bad in the short time she and Vivian had been apart. And that's when Vivian grabbed Hailey's mitten-covered hand and led them as close to the ocean as they could be without getting wet as the tide rolled in and out, as regular and powerful as a heartbeat. Then she sat down in the sand, pulling Hailey into a kneeling position beside her.

They hadn't held hands since they claimed each other as best friends in the first grade, and Hailey felt a fierce rush of love for Vivian at the memory of them swinging their joined hands in a smooth rhythm and skipping across the blacktop during countless elementary-school recesses. She felt a pang of sentimental sadness when Vivian let go, cupped her hand to her mouth, and leaned into Hailey, so close that Hailey could smell the vanilla sweetness of her friend's lip gloss. Then Vivian let all of her secrets tumble out into the sliver of harsh November air between her mouth and Hailey's left ear. Vivian had to compete with the waves and the howling wind, but still, Hailey was able to hear every astonishing word. And the more she spoke, the more Hailey's feelings of self-importance drained away.

What was Vivian saying to her? As much as she'd craved answers for why her best friend had ditched her and stopped confiding in her, she realized that being in the dark had been better. No, she didn't want to know this. She didn't want to know *any* of this.

Hailey wanted to be more supportive. She did, but what Vivian was telling her...It was too much. As soon as Vivian paused for breath, Hailey jumped in and, in a blind rage, began tearing her into jagged pieces. "I can't believe your boyfriend is the one who robbed us! And you didn't report it! How couldn't you tell those cops that questioned you? You worked there for almost two years! And you ditched me for months! For some criminal loser? Where's your loyalty?"

Vivian gave Hailey a look of disbelief that briefly silenced her. She put her hand to her lips and rubbed them hard for a few seconds, as if Hailey had punched her in the mouth and she was trying to soothe the pain of it away. Although Hailey felt terrible for every word that was pouring out of her, she just couldn't stop talking.

"You're going to screw everything up if you keep dating this guy. All of our plans! You know that, right?"

Vivian gave Hailey a hard stare then. She had been hunched over since Hailey first started yelling, but she straightened up, squared her shoulders, and walked over to one of the huge metal barrels the township used for trash. Still looking directly at Hailey, she threw her coffee away, untouched.

"I guess I'm really alone in this. Telling you, confiding in you— it was a mistake."

Hailey pressed her hands into her face, felt the wool of her gloves scratching her closed eyelids.

"I just want you back, Viv. I felt like I was losing you before you told me the score, and now, if you're going to keep dating this guy? You're going down a path I can't follow."

"I didn't ask you to. I just wanted you to listen. Not to judge. I'm out of hiding places for my thoughts, and I need you, Hailey. I thought it would help to hide my secrets with you, to have someone to share all of this with."

Hailey felt all the anger that had been subsiding after her initial outburst flair up again at Vivian's words, and she made the most of it.

"I'm not just a trash bin where you can dump all of your problems! And I'm not a priest to confess to either! Tell Hailey. Expect her to absolve you, keep your secrets, so you can just tra-la-la and skip away? Just keep doing what you're doing with my blessing? Did you expect me to make you feel good about all of this? I don't think so."

"I thought you'd be on my side, no matter how much I messed up, because I thought that's what a good friend did." She stopped for a moment, sighed. "At least I know you won't tell, Hailey. I know you well enough to know that." Then Vivian turned away from her, started the walk back to the boardwalk alone.

Hailey, frozen with anger and cold, chose not to follow.

"I won't bother you with this again," said Vivian over her shoulder, yelling to be heard over the wind and the distance that was now between them.

"Yeah. Good. I'd appreciate that," said Hailey, but inside she was screaming. *Don't leave me, Viv!* was what she really wanted to yell, but she had too much pride for that, and she was hurt and betrayed and freezing, and there were so many walls inside of her, keeping her from following her friend and doing her best to make things right.

So she watched Vivian walk away, saw her catch the green light and cross the street to the bus shelter. Just as she got over the shock of learning about the company her best friend was choosing to keep over her own, she heard the rumble of the bus, and she started to run. She *was* a good friend! She was! She would prove it to Viv, and she would do her best to really listen this time, to try to understand, to give it another shot. They would sort through this mess together. Hailey had never run so fast in all her life, and the sand that was pulling at her feet made the exertion even harder, and the cold air was burning her lungs.

When she finally made it to the boardwalk, she was just in time to see the bus pull up to the shelter with a loud burst of exhaust. It was rush hour, and traffic was heavy. She flew down the stairs, but there were too many cars, and she couldn't cross. The light wouldn't turn for her. She couldn't catch a break.

"Vivian! Wait!" she yelled, as her friend climbed the steps and flashed her well-worn pass at the driver. "Vivian!" Other people filed onto the bus, and Hailey watched helplessly from across Ocean Avenue as the driver closed the door and carried her dearest friend away.

CHAPTER SEVEN

Wendy

She and eleven other waitresses walked single-file into the dingy office where Steve, their freckle-faced manager, had told them to convene at ten o'clock in the morning. Earlier, as they waited outside the closed office door, the women had been talking nervously about the mystery meeting and what its topic might be. The casino had recently been bought out, and the rumor was that the new owners wanted to attract a younger clientele.

"And none of us are young," cracked Isabelle, one of the few waitresses that Wendy socialized with when she felt up for some company and was craving a few laughs.

"So you think we're getting canned, Izzy?" asked another woman who had worked at the resort for over a year, but whom Wendy hadn't bothered to get to know. Outside of Isabelle, she kept to herself.

"All the Botox in the world couldn't save us now, sweetie," was her friend's blunt response.

"Well, I think we all look *fabulous*," said Wendy, in an attempt to defuse the nervousness that filled the hallway. "And not just for our age, for any age."

"Speak for yourself, pretty lady," said Lilly, who at fifty was the oldest one of the group in the musty corridor and the de facto mother figure. "A meeting right at the start of Steve's shift? New owners? All of us in about the same age bracket? It doesn't look good."

"Or *legal*," Wendy added. "I'm not worried."

Isabelle, who knew a bit of her back story and the privilege from whence she came, gave her a look, not mean, but very direct, and said, "Of course you're not. But some of us actually need our jobs, Wendy."

This silenced her, because she did know just what to do if she lost her job: *Hello, Mom. Hello, Dad. It's Wendy-in-Need-of-Rescue...* The thought sickened her, and although she made no further comment, she thought, Isabelle, you're wrong. I need this job more than you could ever know.

Steve came bounding down the hall then, keys jangling in his fist, his iPhone clipped to his leather belt, earbuds in, talking too loudly in order to hear himself over the songs on his playlist.

"Good morning, ladies!" he yelled, as he unlocked his door. "We have a special treat for you! Come on inside!"

Lilly, who was first in line, squared her shoulders and walked through the open door. Wendy and the rest of the waitresses followed slowly, as if no one really wanted to see what awaited them inside that room. Wendy felt her heart start to pound, and she was annoyed with herself for being nervous. Who really cared what was about to happen? Wasn't that why she'd taken this crummy job? Because she just didn't care anymore? And wasn't it a classic (if overdone) Jersey native's move to head to Atlantic City to lick one's self-inflicted wounds and sob over spilled milk in a comfortably gaudy atmosphere? Ah, with that thought, she suddenly understood her feelings of panic. What if Atlantic City was done with her? What would she do then? She didn't know, but she needed to calm down. She inhaled, exhaled, entered Steve's office, and looked around.

Their boss's digs looked like the inside of a bordello, circa the Roaring Twenties. Skimpy flapper costumes were strewn all over Steve's chairs and couches, and when he ran out of room to display them on his furniture, he just dumped the rest out onto the floor. Once everyone was inside, Steve closed his office door and cleared his throat, rather nervously, Wendy thought.

"As you know," he began, "the Trop is under new ownership, and we've all been very lucky to keep our jobs, myself included. With that feeling of gratitude in mind, the new bigwigs want to make a few changes, and they need all of you to be on board."

"What's with the tacky outfits?" Isabelle asked.

"Yes, yes, I'm getting to that," Steve said cheerfully, ignoring Isabelle's criticism. "These are your new uniforms, ladies! We think you'll be pleased."

It didn't escape Wendy's attention that Steve used the pronoun *we* any way he liked. Sometimes he threw in his lot with the waitresses; sometimes, with the new owners. Steve did what suited Steve. Wendy had always pegged him as an opportunistic snake.

All the women began picking up the barely there "uniforms" and talking at once. It got loud quickly in the small room.

"Now, we know this is very exciting," Steve said, yelling to make himself heard over the increasingly agitated group. "As you can see, we are embracing a flapper theme. Yes, these are more revealing than your current uniforms, but we think the historic nod to one of the most exciting eras in America, and especially in Atlantic City, makes them sophisticated as well."

"Yeah, *right!*" yelled Isabelle. Again, Steve ignored her and continued droning. Wendy couldn't stand how rehearsed he sounded, as if reading from a teleprompter.

"I'll be leaving the room shortly to let you try these on."

"Do you have one picked out for each of us?" asked Wendy, also speaking loudly to be heard over all the angry voices. "How do we know which one to try on?"

"Oh, yeah," said Steve, "just grab one and try it. Any of them will do."

"But," said Lilly, "I've been going through them, and there isn't anything here bigger than a size four."

The room that had been buzzing with nervousness and confusion fell silent. All eyes were on Steve.

"Yes, about that," he said, "it's important to the new owners that everyone have a certain…" His voice trailed off. He cleared his throat again. "A certain look," he continued. "All they want is to see how each of you carries the costume, and then decisions will be made from there."

The room erupted again.

"What do you mean, *decisions* will be made? What kind of decisions?" shouted a waitress in the back of the room.

"I'm a size eight, there is no *way* I can cram myself into any of these!" yelled another woman, who was holding one of the tiny outfits against her hips.

"*How* are the new owners going to see how we look in these? Are they going to come to this meeting too?" asked Lilly. Wendy marveled at how calm the elder waitress was keeping her voice. She thought she might like to be a person like Lilly, whenever she finally decided to grow up.

"Oh, no no no," said Steve, "they're far too busy. I'm to snap a photo of each one of you in the new look and put it in your file for their review."

"You've got to be *kidding*," said Isabelle. "Stuff like this isn't supposed to happen to women in this day and age. It just *isn't*, Steve!"

Steve straightened his shoulders and began speaking in his rehearsed-sounding voice again, as if from a pamphlet on how to deal with disgruntled cocktail waitresses of a certain age.

"When you ladies applied for these jobs, it was in your contract that there were certain expectations concerning appearances. Obviously, you all met the criteria of the original owners at that time, or you wouldn't be here. As the new management has different expectations, they have every legal right to review the current staff in order to see if said expectations are being met by the people in their employ."

"Aw, Steve, say it once more with *feeling*," said Isabelle, and Wendy couldn't help but laugh at her friend's always insubordinate attitude.

This time, Steve chose not to ignore her. "Isabelle, no one is making any of you stay. If you don't want to try on the costume or have your photo taken, then you can walk out the door. It's that simple."

"It's not simple at all, Steve," said Lilly quietly. "If it were, we'd have all walked out already."

"What*ever*," Steve said, losing his practiced speech and turning into the petulant man-child Wendy was used to dealing with. "Try them on, or don't. I'll be back in twenty minutes with the camera." As he walked out the door, he turned around and said, "You know, this new-boss stuff isn't easy for me either. I'm just following orders!" Then he was gone, and the room went quiet, but only for a moment.

"Well, it's been fun, guys," said the size 8 waitress. "But there aren't enough tips in the world to put up with this kind of humiliation. Thank God my husband has a decent job. I'm outta here. Good luck, everyone." And with that, she was gone. Another woman shook her head in disgust and silently followed. That left nine of them standing in the middle of the room.

"I still have my youngest in college," said Lilly. "I've got to at least try to keep my job." Wendy looked away from her then, as she was starting to undress in order to try on the flapper costume. Steve hadn't bothered to bring in a screen or even to hang up a sheet to give them a little privacy, and there wasn't a public restroom anywhere close enough for them to get to and back again in the allotted twenty minutes. So all of the women who remained followed Lilly's example and did their best to fit into the 0s, 2s, and 4s strewn at their feet.

It was snug, but Wendy did manage to squeeze into a 2. The 4 would have fit her just right, but she wanted to leave the next size up for the women who were bigger than that. Hah! What a cruel and twisted joke *that* was, making all of these perfectly in-shape middle-aged women feel huge for not being the size of a high-school cheerleader. Wendy knew the only reason she was so tiny at her age was because she was on a pretty much all-liquid diet, not something she would recommend to anyone—that was for sure. Her breakfast that morning had been a Bloody Mary, her only protein the two olives that were pierced through their middles with a decorative toothpick that said *Tropicana* in bright yellow script. She had yet to show up for work plastered, but she did find it harder and harder to even function if she didn't have at least one drink before each shift to take the edge off.

"You look good, girl," said Isabelle, breaking into her thoughts, and as there were no mirrors in the room, Wendy had to take her word for it. Her old uniform was a black bustier with black slacks, formfitting, but also forgiving, hugging the waitstaff in all the right places, accenting cleavage, not tiny thighs. Wendy and Isabelle went around pulling at all the women's seams to make the outfits yield a bit more. Many of the waitresses were still ranting, and one who couldn't get her zipper to close was in a corner crying. Wendy walked over to her.

"What's your shoe size?" she asked the sobbing woman.

"I really need a steady paycheck, steady hours, my benefits. I can't just start from scratch."

"Your shoe size?" Wendy asked again.

"Seven," she said. "Why?"

Wendy had come to the meeting wearing her favorite thigh-high boots with five-inch heels. "Look, your uniform looks fine from the front, and it holds together well enough since you can zip it halfway. Borrow my boots; they'll make you look taller, which will make you look thinner, and they'll accentuate your long legs. Then just keep your back to the wall when Steve comes to take the photo. You'll look so great he won't even notice the back. Honestly, you're so pretty you could pull this off without the boots. I just think they'll help you with your confidence."

"What if he makes us all turn around?"

"Well, then we'll deal with it. But it doesn't hurt to distract him, does it?" Wendy said, taking a seat on the couch and deliberately smashing the size 0s that were still on it because nobody could get into them. She tugged off her boots. "Your feet are a lot smaller. I'm an eight, but you can make it work with all the more time this will take."

"OK," said the woman, who was becoming calmer as Wendy talked, "so, say I keep my job today, and they give me a tiny uniform to wear all the time. What then?"

"As sick as it sounds, I guess you diet to fit into it. I mean, only if you really want to stay. You're a lovely woman. You don't need to lose an ounce."

"It's incredibly sick," said the woman. "But I do need this."

"It's a sick, sick world sometimes," agreed Wendy. "And I'm sick of it," she said, feeling rage bubbling up inside of her like lava, burning her belly, rising into her throat, flushing her cheeks.

"Are you OK?" asked the newly booted woman who now towered above Wendy.

"Oh, sure," said Wendy. "Just great. You look awesome in the boots, by the way."

"Thanks," she said, "so much. You're Wendy, right?"

"Yeah. I'm Wendy."

"Carly," she said, extending a French-manicured hand. "Really, thank you for helping me get a grip."

"Not a problem."

From Wendy's right, came a sigh of relief from Lilly as Isabelle zipped up her uniform for her with ease.

"Junior gets to stay at Rutgers," she said with a laugh. Then she stopped. "This is the most degrading day of my life."

"Mine too," said Wendy, "and that's really saying something."

Isabelle laughed. "Wendy, you're a riot. I'll miss you."

"Don't say that. Why would you say that?"

"Try to zip me up." Wendy turned to her friend then, whom she hadn't even glanced at in the flurry of helping the more panicked waitresses. Of course she should have realized and worried about beautiful, voluptuous Isabelle immediately. The uniform not only didn't zip up halfway; it didn't zip at all, and it squeezed her thighs, leaving bright red marks where it cut into them. Isabelle was a favorite of the high rollers for her saucy attitude, her wit, and her legendary shapeliness. To let her go because she couldn't squeeze into a stupidly small size was utter madness.

"I'm taking this damned thing off and letting Steve snap a shot of me in my underwear. I look *good*, girl, and they're gonna see it, one way or the other."

"You show 'em, Izzy," said Wendy brightly, but inside, the rage that had awakened in her was getting harder and crystalizing, waking her up, helping her to forge a plan.

There was a knock on the door.

Wendy squared her shoulders and stood up tall in her distasteful new costume. "Come on in, Steve," she called. "We're ready for you."

Jake

Lately, it felt as if he couldn't do anything right by Vivian. She was uncharacteristically moody. He was used to being the brooding one. Girls always dug that. He didn't wallow in sadness for that reason; it just seemed to be one of the big perks of being a young and melancholy person with excellent hair and a motorcycle. His past girlfriends had done everything short of handsprings to keep him interested and smiling. This was a new thing for him, trying to cheer someone else up.

They were doing the usual, walking side by side on the boardwalk in Belmar, but Jake missed having Vivian's hand in his. As soon as they'd started walking, she stuffed both of her hands deep inside the pockets of her winter coat.

"We could go to Avon today," he suggested. "When I drove by, there were lots of surfers out." It was one of Vivian's favorite pastimes, watching winter surfers in their full bodysuits, braving the icy Atlantic. She always told Jake that one day she'd join them:

"In my heart, I'm a girl born in the Deep South, and Southern girls don't swim when it gets below eighty degrees. They simply don't. So for me to do that? Well, that would take some serious guts, a real blasting away of something I believe about myself, and to me, that's bravery."

But today she showed no interest, not even bothering to answer, and this concerned him, so he pushed harder.

"Really, Viv, I'm not a fan of the cold either, but I'd rent the suits and the surfboards. Everything. You can show me what you're made of."

"Not into it," was Vivian's curt reply.

"Well, we could hang at the library. I like to watch you work." And he honestly did. When he wasn't dragging Vivian away from the last of her college application essays, she was dragging him to the library while she worked on them. Sometimes he'd flip through a magazine. Sometimes he'd just doze in the chair beside her. He didn't care. Being next to her, anywhere, anytime, was the closest he ever came to feeling content. "Don't you have a few essays left to pound out?"

"Those are just my backup schools. The only place I care about is Princeton, and I had that application done—the essay, everything—before I even met you. I spent my entire summer polishing each word until it shone. Everything I am, I condensed into a thousand words. It's all I want. I should know any day now if I scored an interview."

"So that's why you're crabby? You're worried they won't call?"

"Oh, they'll let me know, one way or the other. I'm just worried I won't like the answer."

"Don't worry. You're brilliant."

"I wouldn't go that far. I'm smart and good at what I do, but so is everyone else who's applying to Princeton."

"So why don't I take you there today?"

At that suggestion, Jake was happy to see Vivian stop walking. She turned and looked at him, and he felt the thrill of victory when he scored a smile. She was shaking her head at him, but still, he'd finally erased the scowl from her face.

"To Princeton? It's a long, cold drive. At least on a motorcycle in December."

"Aw, come on," he tempted. "I've never set foot on an Ivy League campus. It might be fun. I'd like to picture where you're going be, to know the roads to take to get to you next year.

"Next year?"

Jake was hurt by the surprise in her voice. Why wouldn't there be a next year with him in it? Now it was his turn to be out of sorts, and he fell into his own silence.

As if sensing the pain she'd caused him, Vivian slipped her hand into his, pressing her cold fingers into his palm. "OK. You win. Let's go."

And as quickly as her words had wounded him, Vivian's sudden willingness to let him take a good look at where she imagined her future self living for the next four years lifted his spirits. He must have misunderstood the surprise in her voice. Maybe it didn't have anything to do with him. Maybe her bad mood really was linked to the fact that she was going to start hearing from colleges soon, all of her biggest goals attached to one hard-to-get-into university. Maybe he'd understand her feelings more if he'd had any real dreams of his own. Sometimes Jake knew that he really should try to think beyond the present moment. In his most conceited state, he convinced himself that his reckless approach to life was a big part of his charm. In his lonelier moments, he was just as certain that this attitude would be his downfall. Pushing these thoughts to the back of his brain, he met Vivian's gaze, brought her hand to his lips, and kissed the back of her freezing hand.

"So you're ready to go," he said. "Now? Just like that?"

"Yes," Vivian answered with a self-assured nod. "Just like that." She glanced at her watch. "Unless you need to eat lunch first? It's almost noon."

"No," Jake said, not wanting to risk giving her time to sink back into her gloom or to back out of the trip. "I'm good if you are. Had a late breakfast. We can grab something when we get closer to those sacred Ivy League grounds of yours."

"Then prepare to be dazzled by the most beautiful place on earth." She paused, laughed. "Well, at least the most beautiful place in Jersey."

"Really? You think Princeton's better than the beach?"

"Oh, you'll see," she said, as she climbed onto the back of his bike. "There's nothing more awe inspiring than seeing the gargoyles on the rooftops glaring down at you." Jake noticed her voice had changed. It sounded quieter, but full of emotion, the way he noticed some people sounded in church after they'd said their private prayers, tucked the kneelers away, and were waiting for the service to begin. "And you'll like the ivy—it's the darkest shade of green, and I love how it climbs up the brick walls to meet those

creepy, cool stone monsters. I like to think the gargoyles are protecting the whole campus, keeping guard over all those people,
pushing so hard to reach their goals. Really, you can just feel the
energy in the air. Prepare to be amazed."

"I already am," said Jake. "At least, I find *you* amazing." He
flashed a smile at her then. "That, and kind of crazy too."

She laughed again, and he loved it when she punched him playfully in the arm.

"All right then," she said. "Excellent. Let's go."

Vivian

She was aware that she'd hurt him. She hadn't meant to, but that was beside the point. She was usually more thoughtful than that, more in tune with the gift of perception she'd gotten from a childhood of watching her dad dance around on the eggshells her easily agitated mother had strewn at his feet. She usually knew when a person's mood was delicate and when to tread carefully. But she just kept screwing up with people lately. She hadn't read Hailey right last month, had revealed too much too soon, and now they were barely speaking to each other. Or, more accurately, Hailey had tried to mend things with her, and she had shut her former best friend down. Right in the middle of a heartfelt invitation to Vivian to get together and talk things out, she had allowed herself the thrilling immaturity of hanging up on Hailey—*click*. And with that simple action, she effectively screwed up eleven years of friendship. Nice work, Viv. Way to go.

She shook her head in an attempt to clear it of thoughts of Hailey, but this did little to calm her as she felt trapped inside the helmet that Jake had bought for her to wear whenever she rode with him, a touching purchase to be sure. He'd even bought it in green, her favorite color. But, really, she would have loved to have felt the wind in her hair right now, safety be damned.

Why had she acted so surprised when he brought up visiting her at college next year? It wasn't as if she hadn't been daydreaming about them being together, being something greater than they were right now. But things...well...Things were moving much too fast. Jake had started out as her beautiful secret. The naughty diversion of a very good girl. To be honest, he was a throwaway adventure to her, at first. She'd *never* meant to care for him so deeply. Having a boyfriend visit her at college? That meant something. That implied a real future.

Before she met Jake, she'd imagined she'd date a few fellow musicians during her college years. She really dug guys who played the saxophone…mmmm…the saxophone. She gripped Jake's waist tightly, a bit guiltily, as she imagined the future encounters that might come her way as a young person pursuing her passion, surrounded by like-minded people at one of the most important universities in the country. Maybe she'd even date some tortured but brilliant writer. Someone who wanted to attend Princeton because he idolized Fitzgerald and who was young enough and romantic enough to want to walk along the same paths as his hero. As if his spirit would rub off on him somehow, inspiring a great work of fiction. Maybe she would even become one of his muses, a Zelda to his Scott. Oh, yes, she'd enjoy a guy like that.

Perhaps she'd even give someone scientific a whirl, maybe a brainy physicist who felt ready to crack open the secrets of the universe.

"Hey, Viv!" Jake called over his shoulder to her, turning slightly, so she could see his profile. "Are you all right? Too cold?"

After assuring him that she was fine, she closed her eyes and rested her head for a moment on his back, disgusted with herself for daydreaming about imaginary Princeton guys when he was taking this absolutely freezing trip down there just for her. But at the same time she was beating herself up for her callousness, she knew that no matter how much she wanted her thief of a boyfriend, she also wanted more than he seemed capable of being at this point in his life. Why didn't he have any dreams for himself? Why did it seem as if he was pursuing nothing in life but her?

It was all so confusing, and for the first time ever, she had absolutely no one to talk to, no safe haven, no place to ease her conflicted mind. As she and Jake drove down Highway 33, a bumper sticker on the back of a Honda caught her eye: "New Jersey: Where Only The Strong Survive." Ha! She couldn't agree more.

They had been racing through the frigid air toward her dreams for over a half an hour when Vivian felt Jake's body start to shake. At first, she thought the cold was finally getting to him. Even with his body to shield her, she'd been shivering for a while, but then she noticed with alarm that he was beginning to drift out of the lane he was supposed to be in.

"What's wrong?" she yelled.

Jake didn't answer. Alarmed, she screamed, "Pull over!"

She took a deep breath of relief when he did as she asked, still driving erratically, but managing to turn safely into the parking lot of the first gas station they came to, a huge Wawa with its cheerful red sign, twenty gas pumps, and lots of attendants on the clock to keep the motorists' pit stops as quick and efficient as possible.

As soon as they were safely parked, Jake slumped over his handlebars.

"Jake! What's wrong?" Vivian tore off her helmet and ran to the front of the bike. She got Jake's helmet off too, and with just one look at him, she knew immediately what to do. She'd seen the same thing happen to her dad more times than she liked to remember.

"Oh, we should have eaten lunch. Your blood sugar's too low. Can you sit here without falling?"

He was terribly pale, slick with sweat and shaking, but he nodded, and Vivian chose to believe him. She ran into the convenience store, grabbed an orange juice and a banana, and cut to the front of a very long line, enduring a series of curses from people holding bags of beef jerky, Slurpees, and subs.

"My boyfriend's diabetic. He's about to pass out. He needs this stuff, and he needs it now. OK?"

The disgruntled woman, who was supposed to be next before Vivian had pushed her way in, nodded. "OK, honey. Do what you need to do."

"Thank you," Vivian said, throwing down ten bucks and not waiting for the change. She was relieved to find Jake slumped but still on the bike, still conscious. "Here. Drink this. You'll feel better."

She'd been smart enough to grab a straw, to make it easier for him as he was shaking uncontrollably now. Although her heart was racing, she stood as still as one of her beloved Princeton gargoyles and feigned calm while she waited for him to slowly drain the bottle.

When it was half gone, he shook his head violently and pushed the juice away with such force that Vivian almost dropped it.

"I don't want anymore. *No* more."

She remembered this with her dad. The way he seemed almost childlike in the middle of a hypoglycemic attack, often on the verge of a temper tantrum. Jake was still slumped and looking down at his handlebars. Vivian bent her head down to his, got him to make eye contact with her.

"Finish it up, Jake. You know you need every drop." She brought the straw to his lips again and was flooded with relief when he finished the rest of the bottle.

When the shaking had subsided, she helped him off the bike and led him to the curb. She put her arm around him, let him lean on her. The cashier came out with her change. "Is he going to be OK? Should I call an ambulance?"

Vivian looked into Jake's eyes. The sun had made a rare winter appearance while she was inside the store, changing his eye color to the more golden side of hazel, and she was struck, as always, by their beauty.

"Should we call?" Vivian asked him. "You might need the paramedics to give you a shot of glucagon."

"I'll make it," he said in a raspy whisper she had to lean in to catch. "I'm sorry I screwed up. I lost track of time…should've eaten something a long time ago."

She took the change from the cashier and handed Jake the banana. "No, thank you. We're OK out here." The color was slowly returning to his face. His hands still trembled while he was eating the banana, but she'd seen far worse than this. They'd caught the dip in his blood sugar before it got too severe, but she did need to get him home.

"I don't know how we're going to get back. I can't drive," Jake said.

Vivian smiled. Her dad, the engineer...Well, he was a real straight arrow most of the time, but he had taken her up on that stage all those years ago to bang those pots and pans for a reason. She knew he'd always encouraged her to embrace her wilder side, because he had a pronounced one of his own. It was the part of him that had been born and raised in New Orleans that was rebellious. That city was a hedonist's playground. He'd always drank and eaten and smoked whatever he pleased, his illness be damned.

What was the point of living, he'd say, if you didn't enjoy life? Of course a guy like that knew how to drive a motorcycle, and of course he'd taught his Little Miss Chaos how to drive one too. She'd cruised down Royal Street, one of the prettiest sections of the French Quarter, on the back of his bike as a kid. When she was a teenager, he'd let her take the lead on many of the streets she and Jake now traveled in Jersey. Her dad always knew how to show her a great time. Whenever he thought Ivy was pushing her too hard with the music lessons and the studying, he'd usually whisk her away for a bike ride.

She handed Jake his helmet and put hers back on as well.

"I've got it covered," she said as she took the front seat, turned the key, and made the engine growl. Jake gave her a look of wonder but was clearly too weak to ask any questions. With a humble bow of his head, he shared his address with her for the first time. Then he took the backseat, wrapped his arms around Vivian's waist, and rested his head on her shoulder. Vivian could feel his exhaustion in the way he leaned his body so heavily into hers, and she felt a tenderness toward him that made her ache. Letting go of the clutch, she made the bike roar to life and drove back onto Highway 33. Knowing he couldn't hear her over the bike and the winter wind, she said, "I love you, Jake," just to see if it was true. Of course she discovered that it was, and with fierce determination, she found their way back to Belmar.

Sonny

He hadn't seen Jake in such bad shape in a long time. Usually, his kid was pretty self-regulating, at least about the diabetes. Jake got that he had to be careful, knew the risks of seizures, shock, and even comas if he let his blood sugar slip too low. He'd had one really bad incident that led to a hospital stay, but that was how they'd discovered he was a diabetic. Once they were given the knowledge, he and Wendy had spoken to Jake about how crucial it was for him to do a few basic things to keep it from ever getting that bad again. The kid knew what to do, but when Sonny got his first look at his son's girlfriend, he could see exactly why Jake had lost his head.

Wow—that was really all he could think when he came home from Saint Catherine's and saw her sitting on the arm of his couch. Her hair was a dark jumble of curls that fell down her back, and she was gently stroking the head of his son, who was sleeping on the sofa. *Wow.* He'd been pretty sure there was a girl responsible for all of the positive changes he'd seen in Jake lately, and finally, here she was, a real beauty—that was for sure. Then he felt a gut-twisting sensation of guilt when he realized she didn't look that much younger than his banner girls. He silently renewed his vow to keep his hands off of them next season.

She smiled at Sonny, but her expression quickly faded as she stood up and extended her hand.

"Mr. Donnely, I'm Jake's...I'm Vivian. He didn't want to go to the ER, but he was pretty sick today."

Sonny took her hand and shook it warmly. Then he walked over to Jake.

"Pretty pale still, but his breathing sounds normal. How bad was it?"

"Scary, because I never saw that happen to him before, but as soon as he had some juice, he stopped shaking pretty quickly. I asked him if he needed a glucagon shot, but he didn't want an ambulance. He just wanted to come home."

Sonny shook his head, amazed that someone as young as Vivian had been so knowledgeable and capable in what he knew all too well to be a white-knuckle situation.

"So are you premed or something? How did you know to give him juice? About glucagon? And he couldn't have possibly driven home. How'd you get him back here?"

"I can drive a bike."

Sonny was in awe. Jake had hit the girlfriend jackpot. Despite the concern he felt for his son, he was elated for him too. Finally, something for Jake to be happy about again.

"He was lucky you were there."

At that, he saw Vivian wince.

"If I hadn't been there, he would have been fine, Mr. Donnely."

"Sonny."

"OK...Sonny," she said, and she looked grateful at his attempt to put her at ease at the same time she seemed determined to stay uncomfortable. "But if we hadn't been together, this wouldn't have happened. He waited too late to eat because he wanted to do something nice for me, and I let him. I should have known better. My dad was a diabetic."

"Was?"

"He passed recently."

Sonny shook his head. "I'm very sorry," he said.

Sonny and Vivian looked at each other then, and a world of conversation occurred between them in that moment. Sonny saw, even in eyes so much younger than his own, the knowledge of what it was like to love someone with a chronic illness. For him, it was like piloting an airplane that had reached its weight capacity ten suitcases ago. It was dangerous, and he felt as if he might crash at any moment. He was sorry someone as young as her had to feel the heavy burden of worry like that. He knew there were no words for what Vivian had been through with her father, or for what she'd just gone through with Jake. But there was recognition.

"Vivian," he said, "you know that it's not your fault. Jake's a grown man. You're not responsible for him."

"Yeah, OK. Thanks."

Seeing that she wasn't ready to let go of her guilt just yet, Sonny decided to distract her from it.

"So you're the mystery girl, huh?"

Vivian's already large eyes widened, and Sonny felt almost ashamed of himself for poking around in the romance department when her face flushed. Almost. This was a rare opportunity to get information about the secret life of Jake.

"I guess that would be an accurate description of me. He's never mentioned me, huh?"

"Not in words, but I had no doubt that he was seeing someone pretty special."

Vivian stared down at the floor at that, but a smile played at the corners of her mouth.

"I suppose you know that Jake's mom left us when he was thirteen."

Vivian looked up again with an expression of shock. "No, he never mentioned it. He doesn't talk much about personal things."

"Well, then he'll just have to be mad at me for cluing you in on his situation. To sum up the last six years of my kid's life, he's been really miserable, but in the last few months, that's changed. He whistles all the time, and he smiles, and I worry about him a whole lot less. Maybe you'll even inspire him to get a job or go to school or at least *think* about his future. Vivian, this is my long way of saying, I'm really glad to meet you, and thank you for being a good influence on Jake."

Sonny saw Vivian relax as he spoke, but she still wore a troubled expression.

"Thank you for that, Mr. Donn—Sonny," she said. "I don't know if I deserve it, but thanks. But I was wondering…You said

Jake's mom left at thirteen and that you would clue me in on the last *six* years of his life. That would make Jake nineteen?"

"Yeah," said Sonny. "Jake's nineteen."

"When did he have a birthday?"

"November first. All Saints' Day. And, no, the irony of his birth-date isn't lost on me. I guess he didn't tell you?"

Vivian looked incredulous as she stared down at the still sleeping Jake with a look of loving exasperation.

"No. He did *not* tell me."

"Welcome to my world, Vivian," Sonny said with a sigh and a bemused smile as he too stared down at his impossible son. "Welcome to my world."

CHAPTER EIGHT

Wendy

The flapper costume hurt. It squeezed her breasts tightly together, and the underwire that was cutting into her flesh pushed them up so very high that they felt as if they were right under her chin. When she caught a glimpse of her reflection in Steve's office window, she thought she looked like a superhero cartoon drawn by a twelve-year-old boy in a prepubescent frenzy.

But she took it. Her plan to fight back depended upon her taking it. So she stood in line with the other women and waited for her turn to pose for Steve the Snake.

"So, Wendy," said Isabelle, who was still standing around unabashedly in her dark purple bra and underwear, "you think they make a middle-aged version of *Playboy* we could pose for after this, or what?"

"Sure, they do. I think it's called *Hot Flash*."

Isabelle, who wasn't easily amused, dissolved into a fit of laughter, and Wendy felt a thrill of victory at being witty enough to defuse the tension in the room for a minute. But as her turn in front of Steve's lens came closer, she stopped joking around and took a moment to really look at the other women in the room. No, they were no longer young, but she found her comrades in disgrace to be some of the loveliest women she had ever seen. There was a quiet dignity about them, an ability to carry much on their shoulders, and Wendy wondered if the photos would show that depth, despite the degrading costumes. Lilly had been the first to pose, and she set the tone. She didn't smile at the camera, but she didn't look ashamed either. She stood tall and stared the damned thing down, somehow managing to be both composed and powerful, despite the casino owners' attack on her self-respect.

"What is this? Some kind of joke?" Steve asked when Isabelle stood saucily before him, one hand on her bare waist. "Put on your new outfit and stop wasting my time!"

"It doesn't fit, Boss Man," she said. "But I still want my turn with your camera."

Steve blinked at her for a moment with a vacant expression on his face. "Well, that's a shame," he finally said. "You're a customer favorite—that's for sure."

"Are you going to take my picture, or what?"

"That's pointless, Isabelle. Go collect your things and come back here in half an hour. I'll have some paperwork for you to sign. We might be able to find you another job in the casino that's a little less...visible."

"Less visible means no tips! I *depend* on those tips from my high rollers!"

"This is out of my hands, you know," said Steve, shifting nervously from foot to foot.

"That's because you don't care enough about any of us to fight. You're a real rat bastard, Steve."

"Hey! I won't have you acting unprofessionally in *my* office. This is *my* office, and I want you out of it. I'll see you in half an hour when you've put on some clothes and gotten some control over yourself!" Steve yelled, and Wendy had to stifle a laugh when she noticed that his face was almost as purple as Isabelle's bra.

"You'll be sorry. My customers *ask* for me. At least *they're* loyal."

"Out!" Steve repeated, opening the door for Isabelle's not-so-hasty retreat.

Wendy watched in amazement as Isabelle picked up her clothes without putting them on, slung her purse over her shoulder, and sauntered out the door.

"Later, ladies!" she said over her shoulder, giving a regal wave. Although part of Wendy's plan was to fly under the radar for a bit, she couldn't keep herself from applauding the fabulous performance of the only friend she'd made in the past six years. The others joined her, hooting and yelling their approval. As soon as Isabelle crossed the threshold, Steve slammed the door on her.

"What*ever*," he said. "That's enough with the clapping. That's *enough*! Who's next in line anyway?"

Wendy gave one final clap and said, "That would be me, Steve."

"Finally," he said. "Someone who actually looks good in this damned thing."

It was weird for Wendy, realizing that whether the outfit flattered her or didn't, the moment was equally demeaning. Looking bad in it, looking good in it, were oddly similar things when put into a context like this one. And as Steve took his shots, something else that was disconcerting struck her, the realization that for the first time in more years than she could remember, she wasn't craving a drink. This was a hugely stressful situation, but she wasn't fantasizing about what drink she would have to soothe her after it was over. Amazingly, she didn't want the numbness. She wanted to be—no, she *needed* to be awake, and a voice inside of her head said strongly, Wendy, this is *not* it for you. There's now so much you need to do.

Jake
He was sitting on his favorite bench on the boardwalk, the one that had a metal plaque with the inscription "Enjoy the view—on us. From the Carino Family," when his cell phone went off. Again. He hit delete repeatedly. Text after text from Viv:

Hey, handsome! What's up?
What r we doing 2day?
OK…what r U doing 2day?
Hello? Anyone there?
K. Let me know when u want 2 hang.
C u later.

Why couldn't she get that he didn't want to see her right now? She'd had to be his nurse the other day, and he'd acted like a stupid little kid when she tried to give him that juice, so he'd made her act like a mom too, when she had to coax him into drinking it. So what that he couldn't help it? That didn't make it any less humiliating. No girl had ever seen him like that, and now the only one who'd ever mattered knew what a wreck he could turn into if he didn't have a snack? God, he wanted to die. She had seen him at his weakest moment, and he hated feeling weak. Hated it. Hated everything about his stupid disease. He knew he needed to wreak some serious havoc in order to feel better, to feel powerful again. He was working it out in his mind. His next hit. It was going to be *good*. Confidence-restoring good. He deleted the last of Viv's messages and shoved his phone into his pocket with a shiver. It was the coldest day of winter so far.

Vivian. Really, was there *anything* she couldn't do? She had brains, talent, and she was so beautiful that his hand involuntarily squeezed hers more tightly whenever they were on the boardwalk and a single guy walked by. And every time that he reflexively tightened his hold on Vivian, he realized how terrified he was to lose her. The college countdown clock was ticking, and for the first time in his life, he was aware that his charms were more limited than he'd once thought and that he wasn't remotely in her league. Dear God, Viv could even drive a bike, and she could do it *well*. What other gifts did she keep secret inside of her, just waiting to be opened? And what made him think he had any right to receive them?

Jake turned up the collar of his jacket and shoved his freezing hands deep inside his pockets. He hadn't owned a pair of gloves since Wendy left for AC. Gloves were something he and Sonny just never thought to pick up. They were beach people. Winter always took them by surprise.

It was snowing now, the beach deserted, which suited Jake just fine. He had a lot to work through, because the way he saw it, he had three choices: (1) Do nothing. Just keep bumming around on the beach with Viv and hope for the best. (2) Make a commitment to her and hope she'd be willing to make one back. (3) Push the fast-forward button on the whole thing and break up, saving them both from dragging out the pain of...whatever this was...any longer.

His cell phone went off again. Another text. Damn it, Viv! Can't you give me a minute to think? I don't do it that often, you know! He tried to ignore it, but his curiosity got the best of him:

I love you, Jake. U know that, right?

In disbelief, he shoved the phone back into his pocket, only to have it go off again.

Right?

He stared at the words, unblinking, for how long he didn't know. The snow continued to fall. Really? She loved him? Really? She *loved* him. He had it in writing. Vivian Ellis loved *him*. So he was actually a lucky diabetic/abandoned son/thief. Pride be damned, it was time to break the silence. He began to write a response to her as fast as his frozen pointer finger would allow:

R u free now, Viv? There's so much 2 say.

Vivian

She didn't bother to ask him where he'd be. She knew. It was snowing, and only a crazy person would be on the beach. *Her* beautiful, crazy person. How long had he been out here anyway?

She found him on his favorite bench, his face to the ocean. There was snow on the collar of his leather jacket, in his hair, and when she was finally standing in front of him, she noticed a dusting of white in his long eyelashes too. He stood up and brushed off the bench, making a place for her next to him. But instead, she slipped into his arms before he could sit back down.

"I'm listening," she whispered in his ear.

"And now that you're here, in all your..." He pulled away for a moment, still holding onto her hands, looking her up and down. "In all your *Viv*ness," he continued, "I'm speechless. That was some text."

Vivian was glad. She didn't need words for the big things. She wanted the moment, the realization. She pulled him back into her.

"So, you too?"

"God, yes. From the first second I saw you."

She tasted the salt of the Atlantic Ocean on his lips, and although the kiss was very, very tender, she felt its weight. Vivian realized that everything was decided for them in that moment, and it turned her inside out. They were a couple. There was no going back.

Hailey

It was bound to happen at some point. When a person puts all of her eggs into one friendship basket, she's going to get burned. High school had been pretty sucky before, but without being on good terms with Vivian, the experience was now at medieval-torture levels for Hailey. Really, if Grendel suddenly appeared in their school and targeted her as his next victim, tearing her limb from limb and feeding on her bloody corpse, she would probably only feel slightly less abused.

It would have been better if Vivian had cut her off completely, ignored her totally. At least then she'd get sympathy from others and maybe the chance to join another social group. No, what Viv had done to her, whether she realized it or not, was far worse.

Vivian still walked with Hailey in between the classes they shared, still sat with her at lunch, still said, "Hey," and, "How's it going?" when they passed in the halls, but there was one crucial change—it was all an act. Hailey didn't see warmth in Vivian's eyes anymore, heard no real interest in her voice when they talked, and was turned down so many times whenever she suggested hanging out after school that she finally quit asking. And whenever Hailey tried to revisit that day at the beach, Vivian shut her down completely.

The first time she called and tried to discuss the issue that was tearing them apart, Viv hung up on her, which pissed Hailey off so much that she waited a long time before bringing up that day again. Now, whenever she did, Vivian would just hold up her hand and say, "No. There's nothing to talk about. We're good. We're good."

Except they obviously weren't. Being anywhere near the now oh-so-distant Vivian was lonelier than being without her. Finally, Hailey couldn't take it anymore. After another solitary weekend, one Monday at lunch, she exploded.

"Viv, we either matter to each other, or we don't!"

Vivian tipped her head to one side and looked at Hailey quiz-zically. Some of the other seniors who were sitting at nearby tables turned their way too. Hailey had spoken more loudly than she'd intended, but at last, she had Viv's attention.

"I'm not sure what you're talking about," said Vivian. "You matter to me. You've *always* mattered to me." It didn't escape Hailey that Vivian spoke in a hushed tone, the way someone would to a hysterical child or a crazy person, as if hoping to show her what an appropriate manner of speaking was and that she would mirror this calmer approach.

Well, screw *that*. They were going to have this out.

"But I don't mean that much to you anymore, no matter what you say!" Hailey was yelling now. On purpose. "You don't pick up when I call! You don't answer my texts! And remember how you promised to read that essay I wrote for Columbia's writing program? Huh? Do you? I e-mailed you that *four* weeks ago. I've proofread *every one* of your college applications. Every grandiose fucking word!"

At the sight of a small smile forming at the corners of Vivian's mouth, Hailey paused for a moment, feeling even more enraged. "I don't see how anything I'm saying is worth smiling about!"

Vivian's face became serious again, and she stayed silent for a moment, as if struggling to decide whether she should let Hailey in on the joke. Then she shrugged, and the mischievous flicker of her smile reappeared. But she spoke as slowly and cautiously as if Hailey were a wounded animal that she was being forced to play with, one that she had once loved, maybe even still did, but that she could no longer trust. Yes, a crazy, unpredictable, wounded animal. She guessed that's how her former BFF saw her these days.

"It's just that…If we're playing the who's-more-full-of-herself game," Vivian said, "*grandiose* is a pretty grandiose word to use, you know? It just struck me funny."

Hailey locked eyes with Vivian, and in spite of her best efforts, she laughed. She had to admit, it was a good hit. She could be just as insufferable about her brains and talent as Vivian, probably even more so, if she were being honest with herself. It was one of the reasons they were friends. Their ambition burned brightly, and not too many people were comfortable around their intensity, their almost constant striving, and their occasional flashes of outright arrogance. Yes, they'd been quite a pair.

Vivian looked relieved and began laughing with Hailey. It was as if the sun had burst through a storm cloud, but only for a moment. Hailey still had more to say, and as the joke's effect wore off, she realized the moment was making her sad. Their laughter was nothing more than a reminder of the long friendship they'd shared that was now so altered. As she began speaking, the sky turned back to gray.

"OK, enough of that. *Enough.* Yes, you can still make me laugh, but it changes nothing." Hailey's heart was racing. In the corner of her tray was a piece of chocolate cake with gooey vanilla icing. She used her fork to cut and spear a huge piece of it, closed her eyes, and put it in her mouth. Relief flooded her, giving her the strength to continue. When she opened her eyes, Vivian was looking at her, waiting patiently, with a look that resembled compassion. But Hailey wasn't about to accept any easy comfort. She didn't dare risk losing this spotlight, maybe her one chance to say it all to Viv.

"Speaking of grandiose plans," she continued, "I thought we were partners in world domination! We had so many dreams that intersected, but we never work on them together anymore. I thought we could disagree and still be friends. I didn't know that I had to approve of your boyfriend, or else!"

"I'm really sorry about the Columbia essay," Vivian said, reverting back to the calm voice that was so grating to Hailey. "A lot of big stuff's going on that you don't know about."

"Try me," said Hailey. "Give me another chance to listen."

Vivian looked at Hailey then. She really looked at her, and it was a true moment. The huge wall that Hailey felt between them finally had a hole in it, and they could see each other at last. She was flooded with relief again, but it was as short-lived as the laughter.

Vivian looked as if she was turning things over in her mind as she held her friend's gaze. Then she broke eye contact, shook her head gently, and softly said, "No."

"You have to be fucking kidding me!" Hailey screamed.

Mr. Gellis, the teacher on lunch duty, started to walk over to them then, but the bell rang, saving them all from the discomfort of working through the situation with a teacher involved.

Vivian stood up to go, but before picking up her tray, she put her hand on Hailey's wrist.

"That day on the beach. You showed me how you really felt. I'd been keeping so much to myself, and I wasn't fair to you, shocking you with it all and expecting you to just act like anything I do is OK." Vivian paused, and Hailey found her expression grim. It was clear that whatever she was about to say, her mind was made up.

"How's this, Hailey?" she continued. "I'm still in a relationship that you can't stand, and I even found out that I love the guy. And I'm seriously screwing some stuff up, but I don't want to stop, and I can't risk pouring my heart out to you again, just to have you still not approve. I mean, it's obvious that's not going to change."

"So what does that mean for us?" Hailey asked, but even as she said it, she realized that she already knew the answer, had known it from the second Vivian's bus had pulled away, all those weeks ago.

"It means that Jake isn't going to be something I share with you, OK?"

"If you don't share the big things with someone you call your best friend, the term *best* no longer really applies, you know?"

Vivian gave Hailey a sad look then, but at least, thought Hailey, it was an honest look. "I do know, Hailey. And I love you, but I've had it with all of this. I want to stop talking about it and do our best to go on."

"But it's even worse to pretend things are the same, when they aren't even remotely close." Hailey's voice cracked, and she fought back tears.

"I wanted to keep hanging out," said Vivian. "I wanted to try to still be your best friend."

"It doesn't work that way. If you won't let me be yours, you can't be mine. And by the way, you weren't trying all that hard."

The cafeteria was almost empty. They were about to be late for their next class.

"Are you saying you want me to leave you alone?"

Hailey stood up now too, put her tray on one of the stands, and came back to face Vivian.

"I'll miss you terribly, but being left alone is way better than this friendship purgatory you've stuck us both in."

"Wow, all those years of religious ed really messed you up," cracked Vivian, but she didn't smile this time, and there was a note of desperation in her voice, in this last-ditch attempt at humor, and then her shoulders slumped, as if she realized she didn't have the tools to fix what was broken between them.

Hailey walked over to Vivian and gave her a quick hug.

"I'll see you around then, Viv," she said, and this time, she was the one who got to experience what it felt like to leave a friend behind. She realized that this moment of walking away was supposed to feel powerful, maybe even thrilling, but in reality, it just sucked.

She stared at her face, reflected in the still water of the toilet in the girls' bathroom. Was she really going to do this now? *Here*? Really? She was usually able to hold it together at school, but the huge piece of chocolate cake in her belly felt like a solid brick of sugar, and it would be such a relief to be rid of it, to purge herself of all those despicable calories, along with the memory of her confrontation with Vivian. *Confrontation* wasn't even the right word. *Game-ender* was more accurate. To be rid of the memory of the look on Vivian's face when Hailey refused to laugh at her joke, even if it only made the moment fade into the background for the five minutes it took her to puke, would be an intense relief.

So, yeah, she thought, as she noted the anxious look in the eyes of the watery girl beneath her, the deep crease between her brows, I am most definitely doing this now. As the bell to begin classes had rung ages ago, she was blissfully alone. Conditions were too temptingly right.

She discovered that she didn't need to stick her finger down her throat today. She was upset enough that she was able to use the power of her emotions alone to get her body to do as she willed. Soon the offending dessert, along with her entire lunch, disappeared with one satisfying flush. Feeling dizzy, she stood up, put a hand on the stall wall to steady herself, and closed her eyes. She savored the rush of relief and the odd sense of calm that always came over her in moments like these. Moments that were becoming increasingly, alarmingly common.

But her relief was soon replaced by panic because she couldn't clean the bowl here. It wasn't as if the flush didn't take care of the evidence, but she couldn't pretend it had never happened if she wasn't able to scrub everything to a sparkling white. She hated not being able to complete the ritual. She vowed never to do this again at school.

Hailey dug her toothbrush and paste out of her backpack and walked to the sink. After brushing her teeth and using one of the school's rough paper towels to wash her face, she met her reflection in the mirror. Damn it, she'd burst a blood vessel in her left eye, and her skin was splotchy, but she would have to do. She tucked her things back into her bag and walked quickly out of the bathroom. Her fight with Vivian had driven her over the edge this time. Maybe she really was better off alone.

CHAPTER NINE

Ivy

Ivy hugged Will's pillow to her chest. She breathed in, making her lungs expand like a balloon, and out again, slowly, watching the balloon in her mind gently deflate, as she'd been taught to do in yoga class. In and out, in and out, trying to quiet her mind and soothe herself into the sanity of sleep.

It was hopeless. She was a mere five feet tall, and she felt ridiculous and lost in the vastness of the king-sized bed she now occupied alone. She needed to make it a priority to get rid of this marriage bed, to find something more suitable to her present situation. A full-sized mattress would probably do. A single would feel wrong too and almost as lonely as rattling around in this huge one. Yes, a full would be the more optimistic choice. Cozy enough for one, but still keeping the door open to the possibility of entertaining an occasional guest in the very, very distant future.

Ivy's eyes flew open in a panic at the thought of this nameless, faceless lover.

"I'm sorry," she said into the air, directing her words to the empty space next to her. "Will, I'm sorry for even thinking about that already. It's just…I miss you, and thinking about maybe having someone here with me again, some…some *distraction*…Well, I need that. I need something to keep my mind off Vivian. Oh, Will, I don't know what to do!" Her voice broke, forcing her to stop talking to her late husband's ghost.

Ivy hated to cry. The lack of control and the total loss of rational thought that came with it were both highly irritating. Mourning Will was normally something she did without tears. She even hated the word *mourn*, because it sounded too much like *moan*, which also reminded her of crying, of giving in to the chaos of emotion.

What Ivy preferred was to remember. She remembered the careless way she used to throw her arm over Will's waist in the middle of the night. The way she could press her lips into the back of his neck for the briefest of moments, inhale the scent of her mate, take note of his warmth, and then drift back off to sleep. Having someone to reassure her that there was connection in this lonely world, even at three in the morning, was one of those things she suspected most married couples took for granted until the first time one of them reached out in the night to find the other one gone. In sleep, she kept forgetting she was a widow, reaching out again and again.

She'd thought she and Vivian would be a comfort to each other, but Will's death was the first of many things that had led to their current, fractured state. When she'd first started to put up old photos of the best times of her marriage to Will, Vivian cried hypocrisy.

"You couldn't wait for him to die!" she'd screamed, with tears that seemed to come more from rage than sadness flowing freely down her cheeks. "You blamed him for getting sick, and yeah, OK, he *should* have stopped smoking, but still, you cut him no slack! You're never satisfied unless everyone is as perfect as you *think* you are!"

Ivy's dignity wouldn't allow her to stand there and be attacked. But she realized now that she'd made a huge mistake. She should have let Vivian get everything out. Maybe after she'd calmed down, they could have had a real conversation about Will's last days. Maybe Ivy could have gotten Vivian to understand that there were always many ways to look at the same story, and that each version, even when vastly different, could be true. Instead, Ivy had chosen to turn her back on her newly fatherless daughter, walking into her bedroom and closing the door in Vivian's face.

Revisiting the awfulness of that moment, Ivy's tears stopped as she turned Vivian's accusations over again in her mind. She felt ready to speak to Will again, wherever he was. She stopped clutching his pillow and stared up at the ceiling through the dark.

"So, by now you know that Vivian doesn't think much of the wife I was to you at the end. Blames me for making your last days unhappy. And I admit I wasn't a sympathetic nurse, and I did think you were weak. Good God, you really did smoke until your heart stopped beating." A humorless laugh escaped her. "You know, what our daughter has yet to understand is that a spirit can actually be *too* free." She sat up, now as wide awake as if she'd captured the eight hours of uninterrupted sleep that had been eluding her for months.

"But just because we ended up a mess, doesn't make the good things about us not count. And I have a *right* to hang onto those memories. For a long time, you and I were good together, but Vivian can only see the screwed-up ending of things. I mean, even though I have photographic proof that we once made each other happy, she sees even that as a bunch of pretty lies."

Ivy turned on the lamp on her nightstand. She picked up a picture of Will on his college graduation day that she'd taken. Her fingertips traced the contours of his image, caressed the memory of his twenty-two-year-old cheek. She loved the photo because it captured the way he'd looked at her when they were most in love. Their opposites had indeed attracted, and for many years, it had been good.

But things shifted once Vivian came. They could never agree on how to best parent her. Will always felt that Ivy put Vivian in a cage of routine. Ivy quickly recognized that Vivian was gifted and feared she wouldn't live up to her potential if she gave into Will's desires to ease up on all the music lessons and to "leave her free time free." He argued that he had been chasing a good time and new experiences his entire life, but he still became an engineer with a great job, still met all his responsibilities. "I just don't have to kill my soul to do it," he said.

"But Vivian has the chance to be extraordinary, Will," she'd said. "I'm not killing her soul. I'm helping her soar."

It was a constant battle between them, and Ivy was surprised when she found it even harder to be Vivian's mother once the game of tug-of-war they'd been playing abruptly ended and she was left holding up her end of things alone, the rope now slack and ineffectual in her hands.

"I think Vivian's throwing her future away to stick it to me," she said into the empty air.

She sighed heavily then, resigning herself to the fact that she was in for yet another sleepless night. Gently, she returned Will's picture to her nightstand and looked deeply into his smiling eyes, his gaze directed at her past and future selves simultaneously.

"Who knew that the fight we were always having over Vivian was keeping this family together, rather than pulling it apart? It's funny, isn't it, Will? A real laugh riot, if you think about it, right?"

No longer able to bear the sight of his fun-loving blue eyes, Ivy turned off her lamp, buried her face in Will's pillow, and indulged in a fresh round of distasteful tears.

Wendy

She knew she was in the minority, but she really loved lawyers. Good, stick-it-to-'em lawyers who actually gave a damn. Yes, she was aware that the boatload of money she'd convinced her parents to put behind a lawsuit toward the new owners of the Trop certainly helped the litigators in her employ to give a great, big damn, but that was beside the point. These people really knew their stuff, and she thought that as long as she could convince some of the other wronged waitresses to stand with her, they had a true chance of winning more than just a lawsuit. What victory in the court-room would really restore was their dignity, and maybe her own improved self-image would be her bonus prize. If all went well, she, Wendy Donnely, might end up being not only a winner, but a leader. Imagine that.

But for now, she was keeping it all a secret, playing the duti-ful employee until she and the law firm of Dunlap, McNab, and Pezzano were ready to act. Her current goal was to gather testimo-nials and evidence, and she planned to do everything in her power to make an airtight case against the casino before they formally filed suit.

What Wendy needed most were some allies. Unfortunately, she was going to have to search for them in the midst of a group of women desperate to keep either their jobs or, for those who left, their references. She was also battling the fact that she'd had a fortress around her for years and was thought of as something of an ice queen among the others. Now she was going to have to spin herself not only as a player on a team she'd never wanted to be a part of before, but as its captain as well. Isabelle was the only one she'd ever let in, and for the first time in her life, she was regret-ting her antisocial ways. And of course, the alcohol withdrawal she was on the cusp of was a huge issue. A terrifying one.

One of the partners at the firm had poked around and discov-ered that her indulgences hadn't gone unnoticed. She was seen as a functional alcoholic around the Trop, and the only reason she'd kept her job all these years was because she was able to hold it together on the floor and was, as Isabelle had been, a favorite of the high rollers. But if she didn't dry out soon? Her bosses would be able to paint her as a pathetic drunk telling desperate tales. A melodramatic exaggerator, grabbing at straws to give her wasted life some meaning.

"So, you mean, they'll destroy me with the truth?" she'd asked the very grim-looking attorney, McNab, as he went through all she could expect in the courtroom.

"Of course they will try, Ms. Donnely." He smiled at her then and arched an adversarial eyebrow. "And we'll do the same to them, I assure you." Then he lowered the impressive brow and continued. "If you have the strength to get sober and the courage to show them your fortitude on the stand, it will greatly add to your credibility."

Wendy took his words to heart, and now here she was, in her hotel bed, slick with sweat. Her head pounded with pain that no amount of aspirin could soothe. But the worst part? The symptom that made her almost give up and run to the bar, begging for mercy and vodka? That would be the endless shaking. It was frightening, uncontrollable, and it wracked her entire body for days. She'd accrued some sick leave throughout the years, and she was using it, calling off for the entire week, claiming the flu.

With one, trembling finger she traced the faint scar on the back of her arm many times during that long week. Maybe she might be good for something again. She only hoped the body she'd abused for so long would do what her mind was asking of it.

Vivian

The same afternoon that things fell apart with Hailey, Vivian was greeted by her mother shaking a copy of the *APP* at her and reading from an article that named New Jersey and Illinois as "the two most left states in the union." New Jersey in particular was cited as having ridiculously high property taxes that had risen "twice the rate of inflation" in just one year, and apparently this was one of the main reasons for the mass exodus.

Ivy kept quoting from the anti-Jersey article, and Vivian tried to tune her out. It really agitated her, the way that Ivy was acting as if nothing major had passed between them. Vivian could barely look at her after the journal incident, but Ivy just forged ahead every day anyway, chattering about nothing, pretending that Vivian wasn't shooting daggers at her with her eyes. Most of the time, Vivian just ignored whatever Ivy was rambling on about, refusing to take part in a conversation if she could help it, but today, Ivy actually seemed serious, as if her words were more than a ploy to get Vivian to speak to her.

"A lot of people simply can't afford to live here anymore, Vivian. *We* can't afford to live here," she said.

While Vivian was aware that protecting the money her father had left them was one of Ivy's biggest concerns, she was also sure her mother's newfound loathing of the state they'd called home for fourteen years was based on more than their current money woes. No matter what her mom said, she knew that her anti-Jersey stance had everything to do with what she saw as Vivian's "downward spiral into aimlessness," as she'd put it during their last argument, and it was obvious that Ivy blamed her daughter's descent on Jake. Vivian had yet to introduce them, and she'd be damned if she ever would.

"So," she said saucily, in an attempt at distraction, "we all know Jersey gets no respect, but what the heck's wrong with Illinois?"

Ivy gave Vivian an exasperated look. "Please focus, Vivian. Just because this is the only place you've ever lived long term doesn't mean it's the only good place to go to school," Ivy continued. "You know, there *are* other colleges to apply to than Princeton."

"Hmm...let's see," Vivian said, quickly losing her composure. "Gee, I think I'm aware that I might not get into Princeton, so I applied to Rutgers, as well as Juilliard and Columbia, two more long shots, *and* NYU—*all* East Coast schools, Mom! There's absolutely nowhere in the South that I want to go!"

Ivy fell silent, and Vivian forced herself to summon a good memory of the mom she seemed to be constantly at odds with these days. Whenever she wanted to scream, "I *hate* you!" at Ivy, she played a time-travel trick instead. One of the last coherent things her father had said to her was that she should never lose her temper to the point where she felt the need to tell Ivy she couldn't stand her. "Trust me, my baby," he'd mumbled. "Those are words you'll live to regret."

Oh, how Vivian longed to say those words now as her mom suggested they abandon her beloved Garden State, her long-cherished dream of Princeton, and her newly cherished boyfriend. Why, oh why, couldn't Ivy be normal and show less interest in her? Why couldn't she be distracted enough by the drama of her own life to give Vivian some space to breathe?

But this wasn't to be, and she knew it. Ivy had lived vicariously through her from the moment she'd drawn her first breath. She'd married her high-school sweetheart, had Vivian at the age of twenty-three, and set up housekeeping. Had Ivy ever had any other visions for herself? Vivian thought being a homemaker was noble as long as said homemaker wasn't sitting atop a mountain of unfulfilled dreams. Ivy pushed her so hard that Vivian often thought there had to be some buried talent inside of her mother, something major that Ivy didn't express, for Vivian to be under such scrutiny. For as long as she could remember, she'd felt like an ant under a child's magnifying glass on a ninety-degree day. She felt ready to burst into flames at any moment. And although she longed to unleash her rage, her father's deathbed advice haunted her, and in times like these, she focused on better days.

When she was very small, Vivian loved it when Ivy would tuck her in at night, whispering, "You, my amazing Vivian, are the best girl in the world, and I'll love you every day and every night, forever and ever." Ivy's breath felt warm and sweet against Vivian's cheek, and Vivian remembered how her heart felt as if it would burst open with joy whenever she heard those comforting words.

Ivy said this phrase each night, without variation, until Vivian turned eleven. This was when she told Ivy that she felt too old to be tucked in anymore. So, for eleven years, she'd heard that she was Ivy's "best girl in the world." And she'd believed it. And those simple words, that one little ritual, had given her the self-confidence that came with the knowledge that she wasn't only loved by her mother—she was cherished.

So now, as Vivian met the withering stare Ivy was shooting her way, she did the math. For 4,015 consecutive nights, her mother had professed her undying love for her. Yes, that was something to hang on to in times like these.

"I never thought I'd raise a Yankee *snob*," Ivy said, finally breaking the silence, and those words pushed the sweeter memories of her mother right out of Vivian's head. How dare Ivy accuse her of turning her back on her Southern heritage?

Yes, Vivian loved New Jersey, but she was also a New Orleanian. Her father had played Louis Armstrong and Dr. John for her in the cradle. She'd been to Jazz Fest and Tipitina's in the Quarter countless times to hear the most gifted of artists play. She had listened to the blues in the heat of Preservation Hall, so close to the musicians that when they released the spit valves on their trombones and trumpets, she got splattered. She didn't find it gross. On the contrary, she felt as if she was home. When it hit her bare knee, she thought of holy water, and that was the moment she knew she had to be a musician. As her dad wiped it off of her with the back of his hand, he laughed and told her it was "trumpet blood." That was when Vivian accepted that being good at anything meant sweat and exertion, meant pouring everything you had into your work. Yes, she also saw herself as an ocean child, linked to the seasons and the shore, but those moments in the French Quarter showed her who she wanted to be. No matter where she lived, she was a Louisiana native to her core.

And therefore, she was no Yankee snob. She'd always known where she came from, and that blow from Ivy was inexcusably low. To hell with it, she thought. Sorry, Dad.

"I hate you, Ivy," Vivian said.

"I know," Ivy answered. "But I love you, so I'm taking you back to New Orleans to clear our heads, and we'll make our decision from there. I've already spoken to all of your teachers, and I have your work. We leave in two days. It's time to go home."

CHAPTER TEN

Jake

Asweet ride idled in the parking lot of the 7-Eleven, a yellow Camaro convertible that reminded him of Bumblebee from the Transformers. He'd loved that cartoon as a kid, and he still went to see the movies they kept churning out, even though he knew he was too old for that kind of stuff now. His arm was draped across Vivian's shoulders, and he tightened his grip, pulling her in close to warm her.

They'd just finished a long jog on the boards that he'd urged her to take. The winter wind was intense, and Vivian blamed it for the tears Jake noticed streaming down her face as they ran, but he didn't buy it. She'd been on edge and quiet about her looming trip to New Orleans, and she wasn't acting at all like the girl he loved. He missed her confidence, her joking around, her entire spirit, really, and he kept wondering what it was that she wasn't telling him. Sure, it sucked that she was going to be gone for Christmas, but she'd be back, and he really didn't see what the big deal was. Absence makes the heart grow fonder and whatever, right? But if he were honest with himself, he'd admit that her tears unnerved him. He worried that there was more to this trip than he understood.

So while he didn't get why Viv was just a shell of herself, he did recognize the desperate look on her face. She wore the expression of a person who needed a serious distraction from whatever thoughts were tormenting her. Yeah, what Viv needed was a thrill. Jake was certain of it. He leaned into her, nuzzled her neck, and pointed at the Camaro, whose motor sounded like a low growl.

"Wanna take a spin?"

He knew it was a long shot, but it was an impressive car, and he hoped she'd lose her mind and say yes. His hands itched to hold the steering wheel, and his foot wanted to press down hard on that pedal. When he pulled his attention away from the car and back to meet Vivian's gaze, he was flooded with excitement when he realized she was giving him her thoughtful look, rather than saying no right away as he'd expected. She was obviously turning the adventure over in her mind, and he couldn't afford to waste a second.

"Picture it, Viv," he said, with one arm still around her shoulders. He stretched his free arm in the direction of the open road that lay before them. "We'll fly down the coast, music blasting. It'll clear your head or numb it. Whatever you need. Then we'll ditch it. Catch a bus back. And the best part? That comes after. When we can laugh our asses off at what we got away with." He stopped. Vivian had her lips pressed together. There was a crease in her brow. Was he about to get that no?

"The car will get back to its owner. I promise," he added. "No harm done. And, Viv, you'll have the ride of your life."

Appealing to her sense of decency (of *course* the car will be returned!) and to her thirst for adventure, to the allure of having some stupid teenaged fun (oh, how we'll laugh!), turned out to be exactly the right approach.

Vivian's eyes flashed, and Jake knew it. The game was on.

"What the hell," she said.

He knew he had to move before she regained her sanity, but he still managed to display the art of calmness he'd perfected since his first hit. Over the years he'd learned to act as if there wasn't any urgency. As if he had a right to whatever it was he was doing, no matter how wrong.

Casually, he walked over to the Camaro to try the passenger door's handle. Who in his right mind would leave the motor running in a car like this? An *idiot*, that's who, he thought, finding it unlocked. As he held the door open for Vivian and motioned for her to get inside, he started to laugh. Of course it was unlocked. While most of his life was a directionless mess, whenever he felt the urge to do something devious, the whole thing seemed to come together effortlessly. Maybe his darker impulses were the ones to follow after all.

And his prediction about one other thing was correct too—never had a steering wheel felt so warm or so right in his all-too-willing hands.

"Ready?" Jake asked Vivian. Although she was breathing as heavily as if they were still jogging, he didn't think his heart rate had gone up at all. Just another day at the office for him. She gave him a curt nod.

"You'd better do this fast, before I come to my senses," she said.

He put the car in reverse and roared out of the parking lot, thinking, whoever the bonehead is who owns this car, he doesn't deserve a *sick* ride like this. No, he felt zero guilt. This was going to be *fun*. He put a hand on Viv's knee and found himself wondering if the moment they were having would make tomorrow's paper.

As they grew more numerous, Jake was becoming prouder of his anonymous write-ups in the *Asbury Park Press* and the mentions of him during the nightly news reports. He had all the clippings in an envelope stashed in his nightstand. If this amusingly short car theft made it to press, he was thinking of starting a scrapbook.

The story of his secret life. A chronicle of his dumb-ass rebellion. Because he never fooled himself into thinking his actions weren't stupid. He knew that everything he'd done in the heat of anger or confusion or while feeling helpless was wholly brainless, but it was necessary for his survival too, in some twisted sort of way.

He glanced over at Vivian and felt a second's remorse for tempting her, for showing her the really crazy way he dealt with his emotions, and for trying to pass it off as an acceptable coping mechanism for life's hard knocks. But she looked more than OK. She looked delighted. Thrilled. *Alive.* Maybe his remedy wasn't that bad after all.

He saw her reach out and turn up the song that had been playing since he'd turned the key. The volume had been low, and he hadn't been able to make it out, but now he recognized "Heaven," by the Walkmen, blasting from what he noticed was the car's CD player rather than its radio.

"At least this moron has decent taste in music," he said.

Vivian started to laugh. Soon, she was shaking with it. Jake was both amused and perplexed.

"I know what I said wasn't *that* funny. Wanna let me in on the joke?"

"Little Miss Chaos returns," she answered, in between fits of laughter. "And it feels great."

"I have *no idea* what you're talking about; you know that, right?"

So she turned the song down again and filled him in on her toddler triumph, her amazing stage debut, and how proud she was, to this day, of her wacky title.

"I get it now," he said. "I *finally* get why you're with me. You used to be just like me. A part of you is *still* like me."

He glanced at her again and saw her smile waver. She leaned into him, put her head on his shoulder, and said gently, "Jake, everybody has a part of them that's just like you. Lots of us steal a pack of Hubba Bubba from the candy counter when we're little.

But most of us end up putting it back. We say we're sorry. We grow up and acquire a moral code."

Jake had to put some effort into ignoring the criticism.

"Viv, I know you've got a lot on your mind and all, but enough with the lecture. Have a joy ride, for God's sake. Leave Vivian Ellis, honor student, on the curb. You aren't little anymore, so just be Miss Chaos. Live in my world for one afternoon."

He forced himself to push her words out of his mind. He hated that she was getting serious on him and decided to do all he could to keep her head in the game.

"Oh no, Vivian," he continued, "you are *not* bringing me down right now. Now that I know you have a reputation to uphold, I get the pressure you're constantly under. It must be a lot of responsibility, living up to that title." He wondered if she still had her sash, imagined her wearing it, a tiara, and nothing else.

She stopped lecturing him, and her wicked smile returned. "It's quite crushing, really."

"Well, then I'm glad I can help you relieve some of the tension. Brace yourself. It's about to get insanely cold."

Despite it being only thirty-five degrees outside, Jake hit the button to make the convertible's top glide down, and they both started to laugh and whoop. Then he felt Vivian's cold lips, slippery with cherry Chapstick, against his neck. It was going to be hard to ditch this car. He wanted to drive on and on and on. Vivian kept kissing him, and he wasn't sure if his urge to hang onto the car longer was a symptom of regaining his mind or losing it. He was already struggling to keep the Camaro on the road when a voice came from behind them.

"Mom! Could you put that up? It's freezing!"

Jake felt Vivian break away from him, saw her whirl around. Then she gasped and covered her mouth, looking as if she was about to scream. In the rearview mirror, he caught sight of movement, a boy pushing himself up from a reclining position in the backseat. "And did you remember my bag of Combos? I'm star—"

The voice cut off when its owner's eyes met Jake's. With his attention no longer on the road at all, the car swerved dangerously.

"Pull over, Jake! Pull over before we crash!" Vivian yelled. "We've got to take him back! Oh God, we screwed up bad!"

Jake felt heat rise to his face, despite the freezing cold, his heart racing at last. His attention kept darting back and forth between the road and the rearview mirror that reflected the alarmed blue eyes of a preteen boy, clutching an iPad, earbuds firmly in place. It took everything Jake had not to lose control and to pull onto the shoulder. He put the Camaro in park and turned around to look at the kid who was already shaking and crying.

"Are you guys going to kill me?" the kid asked, tears streaming down his face. Then he yanked out his earbuds, dropped his iPad, and flung himself over the side of the open convertible.

Shit! Jake said, as he too, jumped out of the Camaro, at first planning to chase the boy down the shoulder of the road. Out of the corner of his eye, he saw that Vivian had her cell phone out, punching in some numbers.

"Kid! Stop, and I'll drive you back to your mom!" he yelled, but the boy kept running, and Jake thought the better of the chase, realizing that no one would believe the story that he and Viv hadn't meant to steal the kid if he was seen tackling him on one of the most well-traveled streets in Belmar. Oh God...Vivian! How could he let her get infected with his madness? He was such a brainless jackass. With his heart really pounding now, he got into the car again.

"I called the police and told them where to find the boy," she said, her voice devoid of emotion, her eyes still fixed on the child's retreating figure. Jake wondered vaguely if she was in shock.

"Then we should stick with our original plan and ditch the car now," he said. "You don't need this kind of trouble."

"No, Jake. It's too late. They'll trace the call back to me, and it's wrong not to face this."

"Viv, damn it, why'd you do that? I could've let you get out. Driven back to the 7-Eleven! Told the mom and whatever cops are waiting where to find the kid! No one would've ever known you were involved!"

Still in the emotionless voice that unnerved him, Vivian said, "I did it because I didn't trust you, I guess. I didn't trust you to do the right thing."

It was a verbal punch in the gut, but what could he say? What could he possibly say? They were screwed, and it was his fault.

Jake noticed that Vivian was shaking and put the top back up. Robotically, she stopped watching the boy's escape, turned around, and put her seatbelt on for the first time. Then she sank deeply into the Camaro's luxurious black leather, a look of exhaustion on her face. In silence, they headed back to the 7-Eleven, and Jake watched as the frantically running boy grew smaller and smaller in the driver's side mirror. This time, he drove his dream car the speed limit. He was in no hurry to meet what awaited them now.

⚏⚏

The parking lot was filled with police cars, sirens flashing. A forty-something woman, clutching a bag of nacho-cheese-flavored Combos in one hand and a fistful of lottery tickets in the other was standing on the sidewalk and gesturing wildly with her arms as she spoke to the police officers. She had the deeply orange sheen of a person who frequents tanning beds. Jake saw her eyes widen in alarm and confusion as he pulled in. He pushed the button to make the driver's side window glide down.

"Your kid's about a fifteen-minute drive south, still on Ocean Ave.," he called out. "I'm sorry. I didn't know he was in the car when I took it. My girlfriend called nine one one, so another cop might have already picked him up."

"You son of a bitch!" the boy's mom screamed.

Dropping her tickets and her son's snacks on the sidewalk, she ran to her car and lunged at Jake through the open window. She raked red fingernails, like talons, across his face, drawing blood. Vivian came to life then, trying to shield him, and received a bloody scratch of her own.

"Leave her alone!" Jake yelled at the boy's mother, horrified at the gash on Vivian's arm. "She had *nothing* to do with this!"

Finally, a police officer pulled the boy's mom off of them. Then he stepped between her and her Camaro. As the officer opened the door, telling them both to get out, something inside of Jake broke open. Despite the fact that he knew this mother had every right to want him dead, he completely lost his head.

"You know, you're one shitty mom!" he yelled. "I just wanted to see what it felt like to drive such an awesome car, but *you're* the one who left your kid inside, with it *running!*" He felt Vivian's hand on his arm, squeezing. She was silently begging him to stop, and he knew it, but once he lost control, there was no gaining it back.

"What kind of mother *does* that? What kind of awful mom are you, anyway, leaving your kid all alone? Somebody should arrest *you*, Wendy!"

Jake realized what he'd said immediately, and his face flushed with embarrassment. He saw a look of confusion pass over the mom's face at being addressed by a name that wasn't hers. She also looked frightened of him for the first time, and Jake got it. He sounded nuts. She turned away from him and grabbed the arm of the closest officer. "I want to press as many charges against this filthy punk as possible. Anything you can pin on him—*do it.*"

As Jake felt the steel cuffs encircle his wrists, his rage erupted again, words pouring out of him in a tirade.

"You don't deserve a car like this!" he screamed. "And you know what else you don't deserve? You don't deserve a *son*! Some people shouldn't be moms. Maybe you'll do better by your car *and* your kid from now on. Yeah, maybe you should thank me!"

Almost delirious with fury, he felt Vivian's fingers slip from the arm that was now bent behind his back, felt himself being dragged toward a police car. On his way, he kicked the door of the Camaro with all the rage in his body, denting it beautifully.

The mom started to scream obscenities at him, but another officer calmed her down, telling her he'd just gotten a call and that her son was fine. Another officer had picked him up and was driving him back to the 7-Eleven.

Jake was glad to hear the boy was all right, and his relief made all the fight drain out of him. He didn't struggle when a firm hand pressed down on his head and shoved him into the back of a police car. He was resigned to going to jail, knowing that's where he'd really been heading all along. He winced when the door next to him opened, and Vivian was pushed into the car just as forcefully. He hated seeing her treated like a criminal. Like a loser. Like him.

"Viv, I'm so sorry."

"It's OK," she said, pausing, before breaking him in two. "You never hid yourself from me. I knew what kind of a mess I was getting into from day one."

She turned away from him then to look out the window, and he wanted to reach out to her, to comfort her, but his arms were locked tightly behind his back. He imagined stroking her dark hair. He longed to feel its softness beneath his fingers. But no, even if he'd been able to do so, he could see that she wouldn't have wanted him to touch her. Everything about her seemed closed to him now. She didn't speak another word to him on their drive to the police station. Even when he asked her if her arm still hurt, she remained silent, making it painfully obvious to Jake that the first girl he'd ever loved was done with him.

CHAPTER ELEVEN

Jailbird Princess

She wouldn't have thought she could eat at a time like this, but she was starving. She and Jake had started the day with that three-mile run on the boards, and not wanting to work out on a full stomach, she'd skipped breakfast. They'd been planning to buy some food at the 7-Eleven when they saw the Camaro and the lure of doing something fun and wrong and crazy had overwhelmed them both. She had no idea how many additional calories one expended during a theft and accidental abduction, but from the way her stomach was growling, she was sure it was a pretty large sum. Her mind raced to Jake at that thought. In the back of the police car, she'd wanted to kill him, but as soon as they were apart, she realized she was really only angry at herself, at her own weakness in that moment, and her feelings of tenderness toward him returned. She hoped he'd spoken up and told the officer who led him away that he was a diabetic. She knew he'd started keeping some food in the pockets of his jacket, some dried fruit, a pack of crackers, enough to keep him from any more scary episodes, but who knew if they'd let him keep his coat?

They'd let her keep hers, which surprised her. She'd imagined herself patted down for weaponry and then ordered to change into one of the humiliating orange jumpsuits worn by criminals picking up garbage on the roadside, but that hadn't happened. While Jake had been led off to booking, she was told that as a minor, nothing could be done to her without a parent present: no fingerprinting, no mug shots, no questioning, nothing. She was led to a small, and thankfully empty, cell by a female officer, where she was asked if she wanted to call her mom.

"No thank you," she'd said.

"You're sure you want *us* to do it for you? Think it through, now. It's always an even nastier shock to parents when it's the voice of authority on the other side of the line," said the officer, as she held open the door to what Vivian immediately thought of as her cage. She, Vivian Ellis, potential valedictorian, first-chair clarinetist, Princeton applicant, was now a problem to be dealt with by authority, and she was about to be locked up like a zoo animal, only with a lot less space to roam.

"Yes, please," was all she said as she walked inside, hearing the loud click of the lock behind her.

"I get that," said the officer, not unkindly. "If I were in your place, I'd put off talking to my mom as long as I could. She's tough?" She took out a notepad and pen and looked at Vivian expectantly.

"You have no idea," Vivian said, meeting the officer's serious gaze with her own before mechanically reciting Ivy's cell-phone number.

"I'll go take care of that call then," she said. "Is there anything you need?"

"Food please," said Vivian. "For me, and for the boy I was..." her voice trailed off, and she sighed, knowing there was no other way to say it. "...*arrested* with, Jake. He's a diabetic. He really needs to eat something."

"It's not dinner for a few more hours, but I'll tell them to send you both something from the kitchen," said the officer as she walked away, leaving Vivian alone with her hunger and her racing thoughts.

She kept reliving the moment when Jake had called the boy's mom "Wendy." She couldn't stop hearing the anguish in his voice or seeing the manic look in his eyes when he'd kicked the Camaro. She regretted being too furious with him to show him any sympathy. Even though she knew Jake's mother was alive, after Vivian witnessed his slip of the tongue, she saw Wendy as ghostlike. Her boyfriend's mom had abandoned him, and it was as if she were now haunting him at every bend. And Vivian had refused to soothe him when just one word from her would have grounded him. She was certain she could have scared away that Wendy-ghost, and then he wouldn't have made everything worse by damaging the car. But she chose not to do it out of spite.

Nice.

Finally, a young officer came in, carrying a sandwich, some corn chips, and a drink she couldn't identify on a tray. As he shoved her meal through the slot in the bars that was designed for food delivery, he smirked at her.

"We don't get too many girls your age in here. What'd you do?"

Vivian turned her back on him, blindly grabbed her sandwich, took a bite, and gagged. Looking directly at her meal for the first time, she saw that the white bread was dotted with mold. She pulled it off and was greeted by the sight of two pieces of bologna. The first piece looked fine. She peeled it off the sandwich to look at the other one. It was slimy and green.

The officer who delivered it was still standing there, staring at her with a smug-looking smile.

"I know this isn't a five-star hotel," said Vivian. "But this isn't a meal fit for an animal."

"Oh, you're beneath an animal in here, sweetheart," he said, his smile widening into a grin, apparently enjoying the sport of taunting her. "You did what you did to get in here, and now you get what you get."

Vivian sighed. He was going to insist that she access the Jersey-girl aspect of her personality. So be it, she thought, squaring her shoulders, readying herself for the confrontation. She slammed her tray down and glared at her tormentor. "I have rights. My mother pays taxes that contribute to the food in here. I know it can't all be moldy. You *will* bring me something else, or I'll report you."

The young cop stopped smirking at her. "So Princess wants a new sandwich?"

"Yes," she said. "And don't spit in it." She picked up the glass with the liquid she couldn't identify and sniffed it. With a shudder, she realized it was water tinged with rust. Locking eyes with the detestable man-boy again, she turned the glass over, letting its contents pour out onto the cement floor.

"You'll bring me drinkable water too."

He looked at her with what Vivian correctly guessed was new respect.

"I thought my sister was the only girl I'd ever met with balls bigger than mine. Be back in a few, Queenie," he said, opening up the thin slot again, so she could shove the offending food out of her cell.

"Thank you," Vivian answered.

Within ten minutes, he presented her with a new meal. Still only bologna on white bread, but the bologna was the right color, the bread mold-free, and there was a packet of mustard, which she gratefully squeezed all over it. Her water was now in a bottle; her chips, in a bag. There was a banana that was ripe, but not in a horrifying, not-even-good-enough-for-banana-bread kind of a way. It wasn't great, but it was acceptable.

"Better, Your Highness?" asked her former persecutor.

"Much," she said. "I appreciate you making this right."

With an exaggerated flourish of his hand, the exasperating man finally left her alone.

Famished, her teeth ripped into the bread. She hardly chewed or tasted anything, just gulped it all down to fill the hole in her stomach. She closed her eyes, flooded with relief to have nourishment at last. By the time she hit the banana, she was full enough to slow down, and she chewed it thoughtfully. Although the exchange with the officer with the food had been unpleasant, it had reminded her that she was strong. Knowing how to stand up for yourself was crucial everywhere, she mused, but in no other place she'd ever been did she find she had to have more of a backbone than in her beloved New Jersey. Her adopted state wasn't a place for the weak. It was where you had to prove yourself again and again, where respect wasn't given unless it was commanded. Earned.

As Vivian tipped her head back, draining the water bottle, delighting in the fact that it wasn't only clean, but chilled, she realized that despite her desperate circumstances there was one thing she knew.

She was going to be just fine.

Ivy

She learned it was no joke when people said they aged five years in the course of one terrible day. She believed that she aged ten in the three minutes it took to talk with the officer who told her that Vivian was in jail, awaiting booking. She placed a call to a lawyer who said he'd meet her at the station and then decided that if ever she needed to see how fast her car could go, this was the moment. On her way out the door, she grabbed a red silk scarf, quickly wrapping it around her neck.

As soon as she hit the parkway, she pressed the pedal down, weaving in and out of lanes, passing anyone that got in her way. Horns were honked. Fists were shaken. F-bombs were hurled. None of it mattered. She noted when the needle of her speedometer was shaking and when it stuck at one hundred miles per hour. She sped on until she heard the sirens, saw the lights flashing behind her. The absurdity and deadly seriousness of her situation hit her as she pulled over to the side of the road.

In her rush to grab her license and registration, her hands got caught up in her red scarf, absurdly tangled. She was like a cat befuddled by too much string. Her hands felt as useless as paws, and she batted the scarf around in a frenzy. When she finally broke free and was able to hand her information to the patiently waiting police officer, she was embarrassed to see a small smile beginning to lift the corners of his mouth.

"Please, could you write the ticket fast? My daughter is in real trouble."

She knew better than to say, *My daughter is in jail.* Not only did those words stick in her throat, but she was sure he'd write her the worst ticket possible, thinking that the apple really didn't fall far from their proverbial family tree. Oddly, she discovered that she couldn't access Ivy Caroline. She simply didn't have the heart to pour honey on this situation. Peering inside of herself for a moment, she realized that her well of Southern charm was drained dry. Dear God, she had to get out of Jersey. If only she'd had the foresight to schedule their trip back to New Orleans a few days earlier! If only. She'd been full of "if onlys" ever since that awful call came. If only Vivian still had her dad. If only she hadn't read Vivian's journal and lost her trust. If only Vivian hadn't been working the day of the robbery. Everything seemed to have gone wrong from there. If only, if only...

She slumped down in her seat, realizing that any time she'd gained from her breakneck trip on the parkway was now being lost. Like so many of her endeavors to help Vivian lately, this one, while full of good intentions, was turning out to be messy and practically worthless.

When she looked up at the officer, she saw her face reflected in his kind brown eyes. He shook his head and put his pad of tickets back into the inside pocket of his jacket.

"I have kids too, ma'am," he said. "Teenagers. I shouldn't do this, but I'm going to let you go. Whatever is going on, wherever you're going, please, *slow down.*"

Ivy took a shaky breath. "Thank you *so* much," she said. "I promise I will." She pulled away, relieved that he was letting her go, but she knew it wasn't only because he identified with her worry over her child. When she'd caught sight of her miniature self in his eyes, her reflection in duplicate, she'd flinched at the desperation she saw there. Really, he probably shouldn't have let her go, because when she looked into the face of the harried mother he pitied, what she saw was her true reflection. What she saw was a woman completely unhinged.

Sonny
On his way to the police station, a memory resurfaced of a day he'd spent with Wendy at Great Adventure, New Jersey's fun-but-subpar answer to Disney World. He tried to push it away, turning up the radio, unrolling a window to let in the cold air, but it kept washing over him, so he gritted his teeth and squeezed the steering wheel more tightly, resigned to the fact that he'd have to let himself relive the experience in order to shove it to the back of his brain again. It was taking too much energy to fight it anyway, and he'd need all the strength he possessed to confront the image of Jake behind bars. He didn't want to lose control with his kid in front of the cops. To be a good dad in a moment like the one that was closing in on him now, he knew he needed to help and protect Jake first, resisting the impulse to unleash his rage until later. Only when they could grab a private moment would he scream himself hoarse, but for now, he was going to stand up for his son, no matter what crazy thing that kid had done.

The word *crazy* made him circle back to images of thrill-seeking Wendy. Jake had definitely gotten his reckless love of speed from her and his need for almost constant stimulation. No, although he didn't think of it often, May 21, 2005, was a date he'd never forget. Wendy had circled that day on the calendar and scheduled a sitter for Jake, who, predictably, loved coasters as much as she did but hadn't yet reached the height requirement for a ride that extreme. All of this excitement because she simply couldn't wait to drag Sonny to Great Adventure for the grand opening of Kingda Ka, its newest roller coaster. It was 456 feet high and accelerated up to 128 miles per hour in 3.5 seconds. At the time, it was the tallest and fastest coaster, not only in the United States, but in the world. Wendy kept pointing this out whenever he tried to get out of it.

"How can you not be excited to ride the fastest, highest coaster on the *planet*? I mean, I'd *travel* to do something like this, and here it is in our own backyard: 7A, baby! Everyone is on the turnpike today, heading to *our* exit. We are stupidly lucky."

"Or just stupid," Sonny had said. He was no chicken, but if he was going to take a risk, he wanted to be holding the controls. Giving the keys to someone else in a situation like the one he was about to find himself in, well, that was bonkers, in his opinion. The damned thing kept getting hit by lightning too; its opening had already been delayed twice for costly repairs. No, nothing he'd read about Great Adventure's newest thrill ride had inspired any confidence in him, and yet, Wendy was determined for them to experience it together. Unfortunately for him, May 21, 2005, came, the day was sunny, and the coaster was operational. The sitter was healthy, and Wendy was childlike in her excitement. It didn't matter that he flew planes. Sonny's heart was in his throat.

The crazy thing flew *up* the hill. There were signs posted all over the place not to be alarmed if it suddenly slid back down. Apparently, this happened from time to time if the combined weight of the passengers was "a bit too high." He didn't like the vagueness of these posts. Knowing the exact weight of cargo was crucial to safety. Yeah, let's just make a record-breaking ride and then be all willy-nilly about crucial numbers. Holy shit, was he really going to do this? That was his last coherent thought until his sickening descent was over.

Time both flew and stood still. He blinked, and it was done. He realized that if this had been his last moment on earth, there would have been no deep final thought. All he could do was scream. Next to him, he was vaguely aware of Wendy's joyful whooping. His scream? It was undiluted terror.

She rushed to the photo display at the end of the ride, wanting to buy their picture, and it *was* a great shot. Of her. Her green eyes were shining; her dark blond hair, in a ponytail, looked as if it was standing upright on the top of her head, which was both cute and hysterical. Even though she was obviously screaming, she was doing it with a smile. But next to her, Sonny looked pathetic. He was as pale as if he were suffering from a grave illness. His hands were in a white-knuckle grip on the bar in front of him. He was obviously screaming too, but not in delight. It looked as if he were pleading for his life. *Screaming* wasn't even the right word. It looked as if he were wailing. And worst of all? His eyes were squeezed tightly shut.

Wendy was kind enough not to push to buy the picture even though it was obvious that she had very much wanted photographic evidence of her bravery. And it really was an amazing shot of her in her thrill-seeking element. But when she saw the photo, all she said was, "Aw, too bad it's blurry." It wasn't, but Sonny appreciated the lie, pulled her into him, and squeezed her tightly.

Sonny ran his fingers through his hair with one hand and then returned it to the steering wheel, gripping it harder than ever. He was going to see Wendy for the first time in years in just a few minutes. Of course he'd had to call her to tell her that their kid was in jail. Of course she'd dropped whatever it was that she'd been doing in Atlantic City these days and rushed to Jake's jail cell. Of course. And suddenly it made sense why that memory of his ride on Kingda Ka with his ex-wife resurfaced after all this time. With a deep sigh, Sonny realized that the coaster was a lot like their union. He and Wendy had simply flown through all of their good years. They'd raced right up the hill of marriage—lots of laughs, great sex, Jake. And their descent was just as sudden—alcoholism, illness, abandonment, divorce. Up, down, over. Blink, and you'd miss it. And for all of his days in that marriage, whether things had been good or bad, he was in denial about the true state of affairs. Oblivious. Eyes shut. Well, not anymore. He was going into this situation with a full grip on reality. He was going to look at this trouble, at Jake, at Wendy, at all of it, squarely in the face.

"You look like shit," he told Wendy. He didn't say it to be cruel. Her appearance horrified him. She'd always been thin, but now she looked emaciated, her eyes too big, her skin stretched too tightly across her cheekbones.

"I know, but at least I'm sober. Finally."

"Everything about you is sober. Somber. Grim."

"Like the situation?"

"Exactly," he said, shocking himself by pulling her into him. Maybe it was that memory of their ride on the coaster. Her kindness to him. Her gentle lie. He wasn't sure if she'd let him hug her. He was relieved when she did.

He breathed in her scent, and it was like coming home. He didn't believe in God, but he'd always believed in Wendy. What was it about her that drew him in? As bitter as he was about her leaving, he was also equally lonely, and the emptiness inside him trumped the anger when his lips found hers.

The sound of a guard clearing his throat ended their reunion as abruptly as it had started.

"Jacob Donnely is out of questioning now. You can go on back."

Sonny and Wendy broke apart, exchanging a bewildered look, because, really, what the hell had just happened? Then they followed the guard down the hallway to see their son.

CHAPTER TWELVE

Wendy

As she met Jake's eyes, she was acutely aware of her heart thumping against her chest and feeling dizzy from its lack of any discernible pattern. It seemed as if it were skipping beats. Her son's steady gaze coupled with his refusal to break the silence unnerved her. Where would he be today had she not run away? Not fresh from his first mug shot. She was certain of that.

There were things she ached to tell him. She wanted to say that all of this mess was every bit as much her fault as his. She wanted to express that she'd recently had a lot of time to think and that, during those torturous days, the realization hit her that a good mother could act as a compass of sorts, the child leading the way, the mother guiding him toward the best paths to explore. She wanted to apologize that she'd left him behind with no true north. More than anything, she wanted to tell him that she was getting better and that she felt as if she might be ready to be his mom again soon. She longed to ask him if he thought he'd ever be ready to let her back into his life, just as much as she feared the answer.

She touched her fingers to her lips, still reeling from that kiss with Sonny. She felt too warm, as if she had a fever.

"Hi, Jake," she finally managed to choke out, still squirming with discomfort under the weight of his gaze. His eyes were as striking as ever, framed by those long lashes he'd inherited from his dad. She remembered how he used to complain when she insisted that he wear sunglasses to the beach. His eyelashes were such an astounding length that they pressed against the dark lenses, and he'd once yelled, "It feels like they're being smooshed every time I blink! I *hate* it!" At five, he'd had a temper tantrum about the offending shades, hurling a Buzz Lightyear pair into the frothy sea. Although she was against physical means of discipline, she'd had to resist an overwhelming urge to spank him.

"Wendy, it's *super* of you to come," he said at last, in a low voice she had to lean in to hear, "but I don't want you, and I don't need you." Despite how softly he spoke, his voice shook with emotion, and it sounded like a growl. The eyes she'd been getting reacquainted with looked through her with scorn. She deserved it. She knew that. But Sonny, God bless him, rose to her defense.

"Jake, *I* called her, and you won't be disrespectful to your mother."

"Then get her out of here, Dad! I don't know how else to be!"

Sonny grabbed her hand then and squeezed it. Jesus, Mary, and Joseph, was she getting sick, or did he really still affect her this way? Her heart continued to race along in an awkwardly bumpy way. She wondered if her face was flushed and longed for a damp washcloth to press against her forehead.

"Wendy, he needs me to be direct. Can you take it?"

She returned the pressure of his hand and then reluctantly let go. "Do what you need to do."

Of the many things she would forever adore about Sonny, how he acted in that moment displayed the character trait she'd always most admired in him. While so many people couldn't handle a noiseless moment, and filled it, whether they had anything worth-while to say or not, Sonny had no trouble living in the silent spac-es of life. Even in the worst times, he was quietly strong. He never seemed to feel the need to prove anything to anyone, because he was so obviously a man confident in his own skin. He was some-one who handled things. He met their son's piercing stare with his own frank one until Jake's face reddened, and he looked away.

"What, Dad? *What?*" he said, directing his attention to the floor of his cell.

"We do need your mother," Sonny said calmly. "Whether you like it or not, we need her parents' money. And we need her access to their lawyers. And if we wind up in court, I'd think the testi-mony of a mom who clearly cares for you—"

At those words, Sonny was interrupted by a humorless laugh from Jake. Wendy appreciated that he didn't acknowledge it.

"Testimony from a mom who loves her kid couldn't hurt," Sonny continued. "So if you want a shot at a future, it seems to me she's it."

"I don't think about the future," Jake said, still looking at Wendy, who squirmed under the weight of the contempt in his eyes. "Not. At. All."

"That's obvious," said Sonny, "but you're nineteen years old. It's time to start." Sonny's lecture abruptly ended, and he looked down into the plastic grocery bag that Wendy had noticed he'd been clutching since she first saw him. She watched as he reached into it and pulled out Jake's glucose monitor. He handed it to their son through the bars. Without a word, Jake pricked his finger and tested his blood sugar.

"It's a little low," he said quietly.

"Did they feed you?"

"Yeah, they got me food pretty fast, actually. Before I even asked. Bologna. It was gross. I didn't eat much." Sonny reached into the bag again and came out with a bottle of orange juice and a granola bar. Jake reached out for them.

"Thanks," he said.

Wendy had to look away from her ex-husband as he competently dealt with the reality of Jake's illness. Shame crashed over her then like high-tide waves, and she knew if she focused on the feeling for too long, it would knock her flat.

She comforted herself by imagining a Tanqueray and tonic in her hand, its perfume, intoxicatingly soothing, like pine needles on the floor of some deep, dark wood. She imagined raising her glass and feeling the tonic's bright fizz as it kissed her lips, savoring its promise of forgetfulness. But after working hard to detox, she knew she wasn't going to give in to her craving. She'd battled ones even more wicked during that week of hell in her suite at the Trop. At this early stage of her recovery, though, she had yet to figure out how to keep her mind from conjuring these images of herself indulging in that quick comfort. Even though it had been killing her, she missed the security of drinking herself into a nightly fog that settled over her guilt like a soft blanket, over her troubled thoughts, over her self-loathing, over everything. Yes, she still had a long way to go.

While Jake ate, Sonny fell silent again, only speaking after their son was nourished.

"When you have no regard for your own future, you mess up other people's too," Sonny began, and his words cut through Wendy's drinking daydreams. "The officer who briefed us on your arrest said that you were brought in with a girl. Vivian?"

"Yeah," said Jake, still in that quiet voice that vibrated with emotion. His head fell and his shoulders slumped. He ran a hand through the waves of his dark hair, the thick hair Wendy had once freely run her own fingers through when he was a little boy and needed to be soothed into sleep. She saw her moment and seized it.

"I do have good lawyers, Jake," she said, resisting an overwhelming urge to call him "honey" or "sweetie" or any other comforting mom-ism. "I placed a call to the firm, and one of the attorneys is on his way. I could solicit his help for your girlfriend too."

At these words, Jake met her eyes again, and she was relieved to find them looking at her with an expression that bordered on gratitude. He must have some strong feelings for this Vivian if he was willing to shelve his contempt in order to help her. At last, Wendy had offered him something he would take.

"I'd appreciate that. Really." Then he paused. She saw him swallow hard. "Thank you."

Although the words were barely audible, they flooded her with relief. It did not escape her notice that he'd simply said, "Thank you," and not, "Thank you, *Wendy*." It was a knife to the heart when he hurled her name at her that way. How she missed the days when that voice had called her "Mom," but even being referred to as nothing felt like a beginning, no matter how minor. *Mom.* She was determined to earn the right to that title back. She'd be damned if she screwed up what was beginning to look like her second chance.

She and Sonny were deeply shocked when an officer calmly looked over what he referred to as the "station-house bail schedule" and informed them that getting Jake out of jail that evening would cost them $135,000.

"One hundred thirty-five thousand dollars!" she echoed. "For a prank?"

"Your son kidnapped a minor, ma'am," said the officer very slowly, as if he was used to having to convey stunningly obvious information all the time. "We're adding two felonies together here. You take kidnapping plus a little grand-theft auto, and that's your sum. The formula we use to figure all this out has been around since before *I* was a cop. It couldn't be more clear."

"I'm not saying that what he did wasn't wrong. I mean, it was deeply, deeply wrong, but the kidnapping was an accident. And our son's only nineteen!"

"No longer a minor, Mom," he said, even more slowly, and it struck Wendy how very sick she was of people using the names she answered to in the worst, most condescending ways possible. "You'll just have to wait until tomorrow if you can't post that amount tonight. Your son's set to meet with the judge at ten a.m. That's where the official bail will be set, which might become more affordable after he tells his story. But to take him home tonight, that's what you have to pay. No exceptions."

"There are *always* exceptions!" she said, folding her arms across her chest.

The police officer shook his head. "No," he repeated, as if talking to a child, and even though she knew that's how she was acting, she resented it. "No exceptions."

"But he's diabetic!"

"And we give medical care here. He doesn't appear to be in distress, and he'll be monitored. Your husband already went over everything with the nurse on staff before you arrived."

She turned and looked at Sonny, who nodded.

"I know you didn't ask for my advice—"

"No, I did *not*," Wendy said through clenched teeth, but the police officer ignored this and continued.

"If he were my son, he'd spend the night, even if I could afford to post bail."

She turned her back on him.

"Sonny, I'm going to call the lawyer again...see what's taking him so long. And my parents...just to see."

She started to dig through her purse for her cell phone. She had silenced it, because it kept vibrating with text after text that she didn't have time to even glance at, and now she couldn't find the stupid thing. Sonny put his hand on her shoulder.

"No, Wendy," he said. "Asking for that kind of money is ridiculous, and I agree with you." Sonny was now directing his words at the police officer who'd so enraged Wendy. "Jake's staying here for the night until we can sort this all out."

⚊⚊⚌⚏ ⚏⚌⚊⚊

Sonny was kind enough to invite her back to their old home—to *his* home, Wendy had to remind herself—when Jake's allotted time for visitors ended. It was over an hour's trip back to Atlantic City, and it was late. She would stay in Jake's room for the night. Sonny headed straight for the fridge when they got in, and Wendy watched him grab his nightly can of beer. She turned away from him to look out the window, and in the reflection, she saw him glance at her just as he was about to open his cold Miller Lite. Instead of popping the tab, he put it back. She knew that he noticed her notice him passing on the beer, but neither one of them said a word. This night felt as if it was going to take awkwardness to its highest possible level. She needed to at least try to make things feel more normal.

"It's OK, Sonny. Have it."

"Are you sure?"

"I'm doing better. I won't say that I don't want it. I really, *really* want it. But I can handle it."

Wendy met the directness of Sonny's gaze with a blunt look of her own. There was certainly nothing left to hide.

"Good to know," said Sonny. He opened the fridge again, reclaimed his beer.

They sat side by side in their old places on the couch. Sonny picked up the remote. "Might as well see what they're saying." He flipped through the channels until he found the eleven o'clock news.

Jake's arrest was a top story, of course, and they stared in numb silence as the newscaster with the deep voice painted a picture of carefree youth on a joyride gone bad. Wendy's lawyer, in this case, the last in the trio of the Dunlap, McNab, Pezzano firm, had promised her on the phone that he would "make this go away," but she was still shocked when the newscast cut to him giving an interview to a reporter about Jake. So that's why he hadn't shown up at the jail. She'd assumed he would go there first, but, no, his top priority was to get in touch with the media. Amazing. Attorney Pezzano made a statement about "opportunistic theft" being a far lesser crime than a premeditated one, and then he began to rant with style.

"The keys were *in the car*! Despite the fact that nineteen is, for all intents and purposes, an adult age—come *on*! We need to think back to ourselves at nineteen! Isn't it a small miracle we're still alive, despite all of the dumb stunts we pulled? So Jacob Donnely screwed up! Haven't we all? He wanted a joyride and had no prior knowledge of the minor in the backseat for which he is incredibly remorseful and cannot be held accountable."

"It sounds as if you're ready to close this case," the reporter said.

Wendy stared, open-mouthed, into the piercing eyes of her lawyer as he stared into the camera. "I will prove that Jacob Donnely is a good kid who, as we all did in our youth, made a very poor decision. He shouldn't have to lose years of his life in jail to pay for it, though, and if his mother and I have anything to say about it, he won't."

Wendy and Sonny exchanged startled glances at the segue that they soon discovered couldn't have been any smoother.

"Yes," the reporter said, expertly picking up the ball that had been tossed to him. "Coincidentally, we'd been planning on airing a story on the woes of the Tropicana cocktail waitresses, featuring

Jacob Donnely's mother, Wendy. I understand you're the lawyer of that case as well?"

"Yes," he said, "and if ever there was a more noble character witness to have, it would be Jacob Donnely's own mother."

It was a perfect synergy of stories. A few weeks ago, Pezzano had set up an interview between a reporter, Wendy, and some of the other waitresses she'd been able to persuade to join her in the lawsuit. Wendy's mind could barely process seeing the mug shot of Jake, quickly replaced on the screen by the image of her dear Isabelle, wearing her old costume to make a point. Wendy felt a wide grin spread across her face at the sight of her friend's defiantly saucy expression on the screen.

Isabelle was undeniably the star of the piece that followed, detailing the humiliation they'd endured that day in Steve's office. She told of how the skimpy costumes had been strewn all over the floor, of how most of them had been unable to zip up their too-tight and too-trampy outfits.

"How did that make you feel?" the reporter asked.

"Degraded," shouted one of the women who had walked out that day.

"Dehumanized," said another who had chosen to stay.

Then the camera closed in on Isabelle, who was striking a pose in her still alluring older costume. Her hand was on her hip. "The only thing I felt was outrage. To say I'm only attractive as a size two or four, and then to fire all of this?" She spun around for the camera, clearly loving every second. "That's plain crazy. I want my job back, and I want it *now*."

The reporter then turned to Wendy. "You're the one who got the ball rolling on this lawsuit, yes?"

Wendy squirmed on the couch next to Sonny. Unlike Isabelle, she loathed the spotlight. Seeing herself on camera was one of the most uncomfortable sensations she'd ever experienced.

"Yes," she watched herself say. Her eyes looked almost alien to her in their hugeness. Wendy noticed that in her nervousness, she never blinked.

"Why? Weren't you one of the few who were able to wear the new uniform?"

"Yes," said Wendy, "but wrong is wrong. Good women were fired." Wendy watched this TV version of herself look over at Isabelle. "My best friend was punished just for being her wonderful self."

"To play devil's advocate, don't you all have an image to uphold?"

"We were *all* upholding the original, more reasonable image. It wasn't our fault that they changed it. Whether I, personally, can wear the costume or not is not the issue. None of us should have been put into such a humiliating situation." Unbeknownst to Wendy at the time, the camera was closing in on her. She was getting a close-up.

"As women, as human beings, we have to fight for what is right."

The story ended. The newscast continued in real time. Pezzano got the last word.

"And that is the mother that raised my other client, Jacob Donnely. I think the kid will turn out OK, don't you?"

Sonny

They made love that night. What led up to it was Sonny's suggestion that they take a walk on the shore.

"Come on. It'll be like old times," he said when he made the suggestion to his ex-wife, who looked both lovely and strange to him. When the news ended, he'd flicked off the TV. In the new dimness of the room, the haggardness of her too-thin features was softened, and she looked a little more like his Wendy of long ago. But only a little. He remained as alarmed by her frailness as he'd been when he first saw her back at the police station. When Jake's mug shot flashed across the screen, he instinctively put his arm around her, feeling the boniness of her shoulder pressing into his flesh. Since their divorce, whenever he'd had a dream with Wendy in it, she always appeared a bit ghostly to him, and it troubled him that she resembled that specter now, much more than the woman he remembered from their marriage.

Everything about this evening was too much for him. He felt as if his brain was going to explode while he watched that news report, staring bug-eyed at Jake's mug shot, followed by that interview of Wendy, of *his* Wendy, shining with purpose and conviction. But sitting next to her on the couch as if nothing had changed? As if all of that soul-sucking loneliness had been just a bad dream, one that lasted for five goddamned years? Well, the whole thing made him feel nuts, the truth be told. Funny-farm nuts.

The ocean always put things in perspective for him, which was why he'd suggested the beach walk in the first place. He felt a longing for summer and his plane, to fly away and get his head straight, so strong that it hurt like a fist in the gut. Well, if she wasn't up for coming with him, he was resolved to go anyway. And why couldn't he find a comfortable position on the fucking couch? He kept shifting, not knowing what to do with his hands, and then tap, tap, tapping his foot.

"Let me get my coat," said Wendy.

As they were walking out the door, she handed him gloves and a hat.

"Where did you find those?"

"Back hall closet, third drawer down, where they always were."

"Huh," said Sonny.

He did love how deserted the shore was in the winter, especially at night. It was as if they were the only two people alive.

"Are you warm enough?" he asked her as they strolled down the boardwalk, the Atlantic a faint roar in the background. It was cold to be sure, but the high winds from earlier in the day had calmed down, so they didn't have to yell to be heard.

"Fine," she said, but there was a tremor in her voice. Instinctively, he pulled her close, and, as if acting on instincts of her own, he felt her relax, felt her body molding into his. It shook him to his core, how natural this all felt, as if she'd never left.

"It's been years since I've walked on the shore. Years since I've really looked at the ocean," she said.

"What do you mean? You work in AC, and the Trop's on the beach, last time I checked."

"That doesn't mean I leave the casino to indulge in it."

"I don't get it," Sonny said, touching the arm with the scar on her wrist, obscured from his view by her heavy wool coat. "You love the shore. You and Jake pretty much lived there every summer."

He watched then, as Wendy closed her eyes and took a deep breath, clearly enjoying the ocean air. Usually, quiet suited him just fine, but he felt impatient, waiting for her to speak. After ten minutes or so of this silent walking—in which his brain felt as if it was going to collapse in on itself from the weight of his confusion over the fact that this morning he was scraping some kid's gum off of a pew at Saint Catherine's, and now Jake was in jail, and he was having a moonlit stroll with Wendy—she finally broke the silence.

"You have to have a true sense of self-worth to give yourself the ocean," she said in a low, thoughtful voice. "You have to love yourself enough to treat yourself to this feast of a view. My heart was full of love for Jake, so I wanted to give that gift to him, and I liked those days when we were down here, and I knew you were in your plane somewhere, enjoying it too. Once I didn't have that..."

She trailed off, clearly wanting to choose her words carefully. Sonny looked into her eyes. The only light they had was from the streetlights that lined the boardwalk, and Wendy's eyes, usually so light in the sunlight, looked dark, as green as moss in the dimness. They looked mysterious to him, filled with secrets, and it struck him how terrifying it could be to be bound to another person, by marriage, by a child, by love. Nobody ever truly knew anybody, really. You could live a lifetime with someone, and there would still be parts of that person that she kept hidden. Pieces of her that you could never know, never completely understand. When she spoke again, the emotion in her voice was almost too much for him to bear.

"I'm sorry, Sonny. For so many things. What I just said...It sounded as if I saw myself as the victim or something. Scratch that, please. Once I left the people I most liked to share the view with, *that's* when I stopped looking at it." She shrugged. "Just didn't think I deserved it on my own."

"So that's what all of this was about?" Sonny was incredulous. "You didn't like yourself?"

"You really didn't spend a lot of time with all those letters I wrote, did you?"

Sonny sighed. "They were really long. Too emotional. Too much."

Wendy started to laugh, in a humorless way. "That pretty much sums up my entire personality. What did you ever see in me anyway?"

Sonny fell silent. Wendy was a mystery. Love was a mystery. He cupped her cold face in his hands.

"Just you, Wendy. I only saw you."

He saw a look of gratitude in her eyes, but he also noticed that the weather was too much for her. He couldn't believe it was possible for her face to look any paler, and yet it did, despite her coat and her old knit hat that she must have found in that back hall closet, third drawer down.

"Let's head back," he said. "I think it's time to call it a night."

She didn't argue, and when they were home and she started to go down the hall to Jake's room, he stopped her, resting his hand on her shoulder. She turned to face him.

"You're welcome in your old room. I think you might be more comfortable there. I think you'll find that not much has changed."

His heart had been pounding as he spoke, but it started to race when she slipped her hand into his and followed him through their door.

CHAPTER THIRTEEN

Jake

Before Sonny and Wendy left him alone for the night in his eight-by-six-feet cell, his dad had a few parting words. Jake was making up his bed with the fitted sheet he'd been handed after his booking. It was faded and rough, but he felt relieved to have something to cover the grungy mattress.

"Don't do anything else stupid," Sonny said. "I heard you had to go and kick that Camaro you took." He paused, and Jake knew his dad was staring at him, waiting for him to be man enough to look him in the eye. He stopped making up his bottom bunk and faced his father.

"Yeah, I…I messed up. I know. Not sure what you think I could do that would make things any worse, though." He was glad that Wendy had stepped outside and given them a moment's privacy. But since they couldn't get him out of here, what he really wished was that they would *both* just leave. He'd lost Vivian tonight. He was sure of that. No matter what happened to him after he saw the judge at the bail hearing tomorrow, there would be no punishment worse than that and no shame deeper than looking into his hard-working dad's disappointed eyes.

"All I'm saying is, get a hold of yourself tonight. I knew you were an angry kid after your mom left. And you had a right to be. I just never knew it was this bad. That it was *still* this bad. You're a man now, Jake. A *man*."

He was relieved when Sonny finally looked away from him. He watched as his dad's eyes quickly darted over his cell, taking in the tiny bunk bed, the desk attached to the wall, the steel toilet and sink.

"I want to make sure you're all done for the night. Just don't trash the place or anything, OK?"

"Dad. Seriously, I don't think even I could make this place any worse."

Sonny closed his eyes and sighed then, slowly and deeply, and Jake realized that this wasn't the time to make light of his situation.

"Hey, Dad, I promise. I won't make this any worse."

"I have your word?"

"Yes."

Sonny grimaced, and to Jake he looked old for the first time, his eyes tired, the lines on his forehead very deep. "I just wish that meant as much to me as it did when I woke up this morning."

Jake's stomach, still comfortably full from the food that Sonny had remembered to bring him earlier, suddenly felt sick.

Although he'd never been more tired, his brain was too full to sleep. He wasn't used to feeling remorse. He was usually too busy blaming everyone else (Wendy) for his miserable life and for all of his miserable choices. He'd been living in a self-made fog he didn't even bother trying to see through; he just pushed haphazardly ahead, not caring who he smashed into or whose life he wrecked, doing whatever he wanted to do. And now he was a petty thief filled with petty grudges leading a petty life. Vivian and Sonny were the two good things he'd had, and he'd betrayed them both. And his dad was right. Like it or not, time hadn't stood still for him. It hadn't waited around until he got his shit together. He was a man. And he was a mess.

His cell was chilly. He closed his eyes and pulled the coarse blanket up under his chin. His exhausted yet frantic mind continued to race. He was only mildly surprised when his thoughts turned to the Jersey Devil, a mythical beast well known by residents of the Garden State, its story told to children over campfires or whispered by big kids to little ones on school buses. Images of the Jersey Devil were so deeply embedded in the state's consciousness that even its hockey team bore its name.

While Jake wasn't big on symbolism, it didn't take a literature professor to understand why he felt a kinship with a creature most often described by its believers as a "hideous monster." He'd first heard its story when he was ten years old on a camping trip with Sonny deep in the Pine Barrens, a heavily wooded area in South Jersey, beautifully unspoiled by the suburban sprawl Jake grew up to loathe. He and Sonny liked to go to a fire tower on Apple Pie Hill, the highest point in the Barrens, to take in the view of the miles of pines, oaks, cedars, sassafras, and dogwood trees. This natural sight, both spectacular and rare in Jersey, was also one of the few places where Jake felt true peace. He supposed it was a shame that it was haunted. Or so said the guy who was hiking up Apple Pie Hill as he and his dad were coming down. Jake shuddered at the memory, feeling like a little kid again, listening to ghost stories in the dark.

"You ought to be careful with your young son," called the fellow camper as he approached, a man who looked ancient to Jake back then, but who was probably only a few years older than Sonny was now. He leaned heavily on a walking stick as he made his way up the steep hill. "People've been saying they heard screaming in the night. Doesn't sound human, they say." He paused and wiped his brow with the back of his hand. "Lots of chickens on the farms around the campgrounds are turning up dead."

Jake felt the urge to grab Sonny's hand but felt far too old to do so. Instead, he moved closer, walking as near to him as his dignity would allow.

"Thanks for the tip," Sonny said with a cheerfulness that seemed forced. He kept walking, but Jake slowed down as they were about to pass the man. Despite how weird this guy was, he took the bait. He had to know.

"What does everybody think it was?" ten-year-old Jake asked. "That killed the chickens?"

The man stopped walking, and Jake saw his ice-blue eyes light up. Even at ten, it struck Jake as odd that someone would look happy telling a kid a scary story. Apparently Sonny agreed, because he started taking longer strides down the path and away from the strange man, who was pointing at the sky.

Jake turned his attention upward as well and saw about ten dark birds with enormous wingspans, soaring in a circle high above them. Their featherless heads were bright red as if someone had scalded them with boiling water; their beaks, hooked and sinister. Normally, Jake enjoyed birds. Seagulls were his favorite. Their squawking and the way they puffed out their chest feathers like body builders showing off their pecs at the beach always made him laugh. But these sharp-beaked birds unnerved him. There was nothing remotely comical about them.

"Yeah," the man said, nodding gravely, with the odd excitement Jake noticed in his eyes now coming through his voice. "You're seeing a kettle of turkey vultures up there. Know what that means, don't you?"

"No," Jake said.

"It means there's been more death."

"Jake, never mind about all that," Sonny said again. "Come *on*." This time, Sonny took no chances and grabbed Jake's hand as he used to do when they were about to cross Ocean Avenue when he was small.

But their abrupt departure didn't deter the man. He just kept on talking to the backs of their heads. "Some think it's just a bear," he called after them, "but the tracks people are finding aren't right. Cloven hooves. A scream that curdles your blood to hear. That, son, is the Jersey Devil."

"What's that, Dad?"

"Never mind about that, Jake," Sonny repeated. Jake's feet skidded down the hill as Sonny dragged him back to their campsite. "You never told your boy the story?" the man had to yell now to be heard.

"We're not big on fairy tales," Sonny called back, still not breaking his stride.

Before they were out of earshot, Jake heard him call, "It's not safe to keep your boy in the dark! Good luck to you, though!"

Sonny just shook his head while Jake continued the struggle to keep up with him.

"What's he talking about, Dad?"

When they were finally far enough away from the man not to hear him anymore, Sonny slowed down, and Jake got to catch his breath and listen.

"Just a dumb story. Made up by the people who settled here back in the seventeen hundreds. The only theory I ever believed is that parents told it to little kids to keep them safe. If they thought there was a crazy, screaming beast out here, then they wouldn't wander through the woods at night and run into a real threat, like a bear or a wolf. And just like some people believe in vampires and witches, some nutcases in Jersey believe we have our very own devil right here in the Barrens."

"What's he look like?" Jake asked. He hadn't meant to, but his words came out in a hushed tone, almost a whisper. The woods were definitely creepy at night. Despite Sonny's explanation, he really could imagine something otherworldly lurking in those ancient trees. And that guy on the hill had just seemed so *sure*.

"Why? You wanna keep an eye out for it? How about going on elf patrol tonight too?" Sonny cuffed him lightly on the shoulder, roughhousing, which Jake loved. They both started to laugh. "There's a lot of rabbits out here. Maybe you can keep an eye out for the Easter Bunny?" Sonny gave him another small push. "Huh? What do you say, tough guy? Can you keep us safe from the Easter Bunny?"

Jake shoved Sonny back, laughing even harder. "Knock it off, Dad!" he said, even though he wanted it to continue. They playfully teased and pushed each other down the trail as they made their way back to camp with only the lightning bugs to keep them company, their phosphorescent flashes of green growing ever brighter as the early evening twilight gave way to night.

Jake didn't bring up the story again, knowing Sonny well enough to realize when a topic was closed. When they got home from their trip, though, of course, he did a Google search on the Jersey Devil. He couldn't help himself. That creepy old guy and his warning were stuck inside his head. When he'd been little, if Sonny or Wendy told him that something was silly and nothing to worry about, he believed them. As he grew older, his parents' magical powers began to fade. Once he felt unsettled, their words and assurances no longer soothed and distracted him so easily. By ten, he'd discovered both his need to find things out for himself and the ease of researching any topic imaginable on the Internet. He found site after site dedicated to the Jersey Devil.

At first, he was mesmerized by its image. Many artists' renderings of it were easily pulled up online, drawn from the descriptions of those who claimed to have encountered it, mostly in the Pine Barrens. It looked like an experiment in genetics gone horribly wrong. Its face was horselike, its head topped with two curving horns. A huge pair of wings grew out of its back, leathery and as bony as a bat's. Its arms were oddly small, but protruding from what Jake imagined to be these almost useless-limbs were disturbingly clawed hands. Its feet bore cloven hooves, and it boasted a long, forked tail. It looked sinister and bizarre and like nothing Jake would ever wish to encounter in the woods.

He kept hearing the odd old man's voice: *You never told your boy the story?*

He scrolled down, leaving the eerie pictures behind, and began to read:

It was said that a woman, known only as Mrs. Shrouds of Leeds Point, New Jersey, had twelve children. After giving birth to what she clearly hoped would be her final baby, the exhausted mother stated that if she ever had another, it would "be a devil." In 1735, Mrs. Shrouds did indeed go into labor with her thirteenth child. The infant was born normal but changed form soon after its arrival. What had been a beautiful baby boy turned into a creature with hooves, a horse's head, bat wings, and a forked tail. It growled and screamed at everyone in the home before flying up the chimney. Later that evening, it was seen circling the villages before it headed for the darkness and shelter of the pines.

Every morning, the creature returned to Mrs. Shrouds, but she stood firmly at her closed front door, never letting it inside, ordering it to leave her alone, as if she had played no part in its existence. After a few weeks of this ritual, it got the hint and never returned.

"That poor guy," Jake whispered. "That poor, poor guy." He wondered why the father wasn't mentioned in the story but guessed that he hadn't cared about the beast either, just gone along with his wife. At the time, Jake couldn't imagine having a parent who simply tossed him aside. He knew he meant the world to Wendy and Sonny, and they to him. He never questioned their connection or imagined a life without their presence.

After Wendy's departure, Jake began drawing pictures of the Jersey Devil in his school notebooks. At first, he was just doodling in the margins of his papers, but then he began to draw the creature obsessively. Rather than algebra equations or notes on *A Tale of Two Cities*, he filled his Marble composition books with picture after picture of the beast, shadowy, desperate, and fierce. No, it didn't take a scholar to get the connection. Jake didn't have a mother any more, but in the Jersey Devil, he'd found a kindred.

Jake's thoughts were interrupted by the sound of footsteps and obscenities uttered in a drunken voice. He looked down from his bunk, grateful he'd taken the top one, to see an officer unlock the door of his cell and push a large man inside. His new roommate reeked of vomit and whiskey. Jake quickly rolled over, pretending to be asleep. The man took no notice of the fact that someone else was in the cell with him and collapsed on the bottom bunk. The springs of the thin mattress groaned comically. After yelling and proclaiming his innocence for a few moments, the new inmate was soon snoring loudly. Throughout the night, he'd mutter in his sleep, "Monique, baby, I did it for you! It was *all* for you!" Sometimes he'd cry, shaking the entire bunk, and Jake thought it would have been funny if his cellmate's voice hadn't sounded so wounded.

Between the stench and snoring of his fellow inmate, and Jake's thoughts, which were the most self-aware they'd ever been, it was the longest night of his life. He vowed during those sleepless hours never to know another like it. What he didn't know yet was whether that meant he was finally ready to shape up or whether he was simply determined never to get caught again. The only thing he was certain of was that he was done pitying himself. Whatever path he took next, he was going to admit that he'd chosen it. It was finally time to grow up.

Vivian

The gifts of affection most teenaged girls received from their boy-friends to mark significant life events were flowers or cheap jew-elry, but on the occasion of her first criminal hearing, Jake sent Vivian a really good lawyer, wrapped up in a dark blue pantsuit. Ms. Dunlap wore a double strand of fat pearls around her neck, and a look of fierce confidence. As soon as her mom met this at-torney from the Donnely team, Ivy quickly dismissed the one she'd found randomly in the yellow pages in the frantic moments before she'd driven to the police station. Vivian watched, exasperated, as Ivy began sobbing with gratitude when Ms. Dunlap told them her fee would be picked up by the Donnely family, only to stop the waterworks just as abruptly when a realization hit her and she said, "If you'd never associated with that thug, you wouldn't be in this awful mess! I mean, really, it's the *least* they could do!" Vivian bit the side of her cheek when Ivy called Jake a "thug." She wasn't stupid enough to try to come to his defense against her mother now. After her outburst, Ivy dabbed at her eyes, apparently trying to assume her normally dignified manner.

"I'm sorry," Ivy said to Ms. Dunlap. "It's simply been the most trying two days of my life."

"There, there," said Vivian's attorney soothingly. Her voice was deep and velvety. Had she not become a lawyer, she could have been on the radio, thought Vivian. One of those late-night hosts who played soothing songs and told her insomniac callers that no matter how dire the situation was that was keeping them awake, everything would be OK. Yes. There, there indeed.

"I've been going over all the information you brought to me, and I can see you have a great kid here," Ms. Dunlap began. Vivian wondered if she was ever going to address her, the actual defen-dant. And…what the hell? Was that *thing* in her hands actually what she thought it was? Oh, God, it really was. Her attorney was hold-ing Ivy's monstrous scrapbook of all of Vivian's accomplishments since kindergarten. The cover had a picture of her at age five, front teeth missing. Even more degrading, Ivy had drawn a big star around it with sparkly glitter glue. Vivian raised an eyebrow at Ivy, shorthand for, *Seriously, Mom?*

Ivy caught the look and shrugged. "I'm sorry. I just didn't have time to sort through it all." Vivian noted that Ivy's apology was directed at the attorney rather than her. Not that she felt she was owed an apology in *this* situation of course, but Ivy had barely engaged Vivian since her arrival at the police station. Vivian had prepared herself to deal with her mother's rage, to see that crazy vein throbbing in her neck, to be deafened by some yelling. She thought there would at least be some wailing about how she was throwing her bright future away, but no, there was only Ivy—speaking about her to police officers, talking about her to the lawyer. Talking around her, about her, over her, but rarely directly *to* her.

Again came the attorney's silky voice, and Vivian marveled at its ability to smooth out the worry wrinkles on Ivy's brow.

"Not to worry, Mrs. Ellis. I am being paid to sort through things for you. I am being well compensated to decide what the most important factors are in this case. What to include, what to leave out." Vivian's lawyer smiled and opened the huge homemade book to one of the many places that she had bookmarked with a Post-it.

"For example," she continued, "I won't be including *this* article in your defense, although I found it charming and it did help me to understand you better."

Vivian's lawyer-on-loan turned the scrapbook to face her. Aside from the preliminary introductions, this was the first time Vivian had been addressed by her. Vivian attempted a polite smile and then looked at the open book in Ms. Dunlap's well-manicured hands.

Of course. The Little Miss Chaos article. Funny, Vivian hadn't looked at her memory book in years, even though she knew that Ivy faithfully recorded every accomplishment in it, big or small.

Her mom kept that book current; she had to give her that. It was harder to completely loathe Ivy when confronted with the hugeness of that book, the gargantuan proportions of her mother's pride.

Harder still for Vivian was confronting the photograph that had been in the paper all those years ago. Her dark curls were a wild mess from being windblown on the beach, her tiara was crooked, she still clasped, in a chubby fist held triumphantly in the air, the wooden spoon she'd used to bang on all of those pots and pans, and her dad—her absurdly young dad, wearing an expression of delight and love for her—clasped Vivian in his arms.

Involuntarily, Vivian's hand touched her face, a memory resurfacing. After that photo had been taken, her dad had kissed her cheek.

"Little Miss Chaos, you are perfect," he murmured in her ear, his voice deep and soothing as always to her restless spirit. "Don't ever forget that your daddy loves you, and you are perfect. Always be who you are."

Her self-confidence had been born in that moment. All that she would ever be began then. Oh what the hell had she done? What had she been thinking getting into that car with Jake? Why was she trying so hard to throw everything away?

Vivian took a breath and was surprised when it got caught in her throat. She forced a smile and said, too brightly, "Yes! That was an amazing day. I can barely remember it, though. I promise I won't be at all chaotic today. I will do everything you say." Vivian's hands started to shake. "Do I have time to run to the restroom for a sec?"

She obviously wasn't fooling her astute lawyer, who quickly closed the memory book. "We don't meet with the judge for two more hours, dear. I have a pile of accomplishments to parade before her and only one offense, for which you were not responsible. Take all the time you need, Miss Ellis."

As she ran to the restrooms, she heard Ivy call out, "Do you need—"

"No!" Vivian yelled. The last thing she wanted was an attempt at comfort from her mother. She made it to the bathroom just as her body was wracked with sobs. It was mercifully empty. She pressed her forehead against the wall nearest the sinks, leaning into it for support.

"Dad," she said softly, just for herself to hear. "Dad, I can't do this without you."

And just as suddenly as she had started crying, she stopped.

The realization hit her that none of this, not the crazy Camaro theft or the weeks and weeks of secret beach dates or letting her music slide or even Jake himself, absolutely none of this would have happened had her dad still been alive. She knew she sounded like Ivy now, but she didn't care. She had grossly underestimated the impact of her father's death on her, on her dreams, on every decision she'd made since his passing. That picture—oh, that picture of him holding her—how safe she'd felt in his arms, in his presence! In her longing for him now, she realized when she'd lost him, she'd lost the one person who understood her best. He'd helped her explore the reckless part of herself in a reasonable way. He taught her to ride a bike but didn't encourage her to break the speed limit. He saw she had musical talent and never once, despite his own very stable job, never *once* did he try to talk her into going down a path with less risk. He took her to see musicians who were making it. He showed her she could have anything if she wanted it badly enough, if she worked at it hard enough. *Always be who you are*, he'd said. She barely recognized herself now.

"I miss you, Dad," she said out loud, but now her voice was calm. "I miss you, and I still want Princeton. I still want my music, and I still want a big life."

Jake. Yes, she still yearned for him too, and she still loved him, but she understood now. She had to end it.

She washed her face with a rough restroom paper towel and smoothed her hair. When she rejoined her attorney and Ivy, she knew she would do anything it took to get her future back.

CHAPTER FOURTEEN

Hailey

Normally, she was able to deal with annoying customers. The ones who wouldn't pull away from her window without checking to see if she got their order right. The ones who put their cars in park and examined each box of donuts. To make sure she put in the chocolate cakes and not the chocolate frosted. The ones who would let the drive-through lane get so backed up that her boss would yell at *her* about it. As if it was her fault.

"It's all in there," she was used to saying brightly, with a cheerfulness she absolutely did not feel, at least a half a dozen times a day.

"Oh, yeah, OK," some of them would say distractedly, deciding to trust her, putting their cars in gear again, and slowly gliding away. But others were stubborn. Today, she had a guy who not only wouldn't stop checking his five boxes of donuts and each of his three bags of breakfast sandwiches, but who also wouldn't acknowledge that she'd spoken to him.

Hailey drummed her fingers on the cash register.

"Sir," she said again, leaning out the window, "really, your order is accurate." Again, no response. She was sitting on a stool, an envelope in her pocket jabbing her in the back. She had no idea why she'd brought Mrs. Ellis's letter to work with her, along with that ticket. That crazy plane ticket. Whenever there was a lull at the window, she'd take the letter out and reread it. Then she'd stare at the destination: New Orleans.

Someone behind the man who was completely OCD about his donut order leaned on a horn. The man extended his middle finger and began checking his fourth box. Hailey really needed to get back to that letter, to process everything and decide what to do. She noticed that the man had rolled up his window, showing that he had, without a doubt, heard her. Something in her snapped, and she tapped on the glass. This got his attention. He slowly rolled his window back down.

"Yes?" he said curtly. And it was then that Hailey allowed words, glorious in their arrogance and fury, pour from her mouth.

"Listen. I'm an intelligent person who can accurately fulfill all of your breakfast wishes. One day you'll see my name on the *New York Times* best-seller list. Trust me—all sixty of your very important donuts and your eight egg-white flatbreads are accounted for, and I did remember to put the coconut syrup, skim milk, and the three Splendas in your decaf coffee. Now, you're gumming up the works. This is a drive-through, so drive through—"

She stopped. She struggled for a moment not to say it, but as impulse control was not her strong suit, the word tumbled out anyway and sealed her fate: "*Asshole.*"

She got canned that day. It was three days before winter break, which made her decision easier. Sitting in her car in the Dunkin' Donuts parking lot for the final time, she unfolded the letter from Vivian's mom.

Dear Hailey,

    By now, you've probably heard about all of the trouble that Vivian has gotten herself into, and I am asking for your help. I think a change of scenery would do us both good, but we are barely speaking. If you would be willing to come on this trip to New Orleans with us, I'm sure it would lighten the mood considerably—

"Ha!" Hailey shouted, involuntarily, when she got to that line. Vivian really *wasn't* talking to her mom if Mrs. Ellis still thought they were tight. Wow, it had been weeks since their falling out. Weeks, jail time, and the destruction of Vivian's golden reputation stood between that friendship-ending moment and this letter. What was going on in that house? In Vivian's life? Most importantly, did she still care? She sighed and reread the rest of the note.

    would lighten the mood considerably. Of course, you'd want for nothing. To show my gratitude for your willingness to spend your winter break away from family, we will show you the best New Orleans has to offer. You'll eat at the finest restaurants, hear the most amazing music, and get to know what I think is the most unique city in the country. We'll show you the time of your life, if you'll only say yes and help me get Vivian back on a good path. I've already spoken to your mother, who said she is excited for you to have this opportunity, but I wanted to reach out to you personally. Please, Hailey, won't you say yes? Thanking you for your consideration. Laissez les bon temps rouler!

Whatever the hell *that* meant. She took Spanish, not French like Viv. She'd look it up later. The letter was signed with "warmest regards" from "Ivy." Hailey noted that they were now on a first-name basis. She had never been invited to call her anything other than "Mrs. Ellis" until today. Until she needed something from her.

She stared at the round-trip ticket in her hand and thought about how relationships were very weblike. Just when you thought they were over, if the connection had been important, taking a single step, just putting one foot back in, made it all too easy to become freshly entangled, and perhaps the more one struggled against it, the more stuck one got. Maybe there was no such thing as a clean break in a relationship that had been real. Maybe getting involved again was inevitable anyway. Should she really fight this?

She thought about spending endless amounts of time with her estranged friend and her intense mom, and her jaw clenched. Could she really endure their company for her entire winter vacation? Then she glanced up at the donut shop where she was no longer an employee and shrugged.

"I have absolutely nothing to lose," she said out loud, her eyes lingering over key phrases in the letter: *Unique city...finest restaurants...amazing music...you'll want for nothing...*If she *was* about to get entangled in a web again, why not let it be one that scored her an all-expenses-paid vacation? She folded the stationery carefully and put it back into its matching envelope, her nose wrinkling at the cloying smell of Ivy's perfume. She'd always hated that odor. What had Vivian said it was? Some Southern flower? Honeysuckle? Whenever she went over to Viv's, Ivy's perfume hung heavily in the air, whether she was home or not. If the entire state of Louisiana smelled like that, she would always be on the verge of gagging. She sighed. If she didn't kill herself or one of them on this trip, it would be more than a small miracle. No, it would be a water-into-wine kind of phenomenon. But money was always tight in her family. The farthest she'd ever been from Jersey was on a school trip to Philadelphia. She'd always longed to see more of the world, and she had to agree with Mrs. Ellis. This *was* an incredible opportunity, and a free trip was a free trip, right? *Right?*

Sonny

How was Jake going to take it when he found out that Wendy was moving back in? At least, he *assumed* she was moving back in as she hadn't left since that day at the beach and the night that followed. She'd say things like, "Really, I should head back now." And he'd say something like, "What's your hurry? We've got a lot to sort out. Let's see Jake through this first." Then, they wouldn't talk at all, and her presence did more to erase the pain and hurt she'd caused than all her years of letters ever could.

Sonny was a simple man with simple needs, and he felt in his gut that he needed Wendy just as he needed air and sunlight and to pilot his plane every summer. Now that Jake was experiencing his first love, maybe he could understand Sonny's willingness to forgive more. Or would Jake see Sonny as a wimp, a loser, a man with no backbone or self-control?

Sonny also realized it was a testimony to how much he loved his kid to spend so much time worrying about Jake's opinion. His boy had a criminal record now. Yeah, Jake should be worried about *his* opinion and *his* rage, not the other way around.

Those fancy lawyers had done a bang-up job for sure, though. They got the judge to buy into that "opportunistic theft" angle the Pezzano attorney had been going on about that night on the news. The thing didn't even go to trial, as they chose to plea out and Jake had no prior record. But the judge didn't let Jake walk out the door whistling, either. Sonny got to enjoy this secret time with Wendy because Jake was sentenced to probation and one month of community service. Every day for the next thirty days, he was to work at a soup kitchen in Spring Lake, serving meals to the homeless, who no longer had the summer sun to warm them or the generosity of tourists to keep them fed. He was staying on the grounds with the other volunteers, many also working off a sentence of some sort, helping to prepare and serve three meals a day.

"This is my favorite sentence to give young people," the judge said, looking into Jake's eyes until he was visibly squirming in the orange jumpsuit he'd been given for his overnight stay. The running shoes they'd returned to him and allowed him to wear to his hearing squeaked once, loudly, on the floor, and Sonny felt pity for Jake as his face flushed crimson. His red cheeks and bright clothes would have been comical had the situation not been as dire.

"You spend some time at this shelter, young man," the judge continued, "and maybe you'll lose the self-centeredness that made you steal a car for a joyride. So full of getting what you wanted that you didn't even take note of a *child* in the backseat. You will *work* there. You will *live* there. You will *help*. If that doesn't change you for the better, I don't know what will. Any more trouble from you, and you *will* see the inside of a jail for much longer than one night."

Jake looked sick, but Sonny felt deeply grateful. His son's life wasn't over. He looked at Wendy, who was sitting next to him, and saw relief in her eyes too. He squeezed her hand. No, Jake's life wasn't over, and it felt as if his was finally beginning again.

Jake

"It was amazing of you and your parents to help me like that," Vivian said. "Really amazing." Jake noticed she was wearing the T-shirt that said *Dare To Be Great!* The one she'd had on that first night he'd surprised her after work. He could still remember the rush of victory that surged through him when she climbed onto the back of his bike. Instead of dialing 911 and ratting him out to the cops, she'd gone on a *date* with him. No, he hadn't deserved her then, and he didn't deserve her now...or ever. All he represented in Vivian's life was a lapse in good judgment. He was a living testament to her temporary insanity, and he knew from the determined look on her face that she'd finally recovered. Please, God, let her make this quick.

"The way that lawyer used just the right words to make me seem so young and innocent? Pure magic." Vivian smiled while she spoke, but her eyes looked sad to Jake. He took it as another bad sign that she wasn't screaming at him for screwing up her life. The last time they'd been together was in the back of that police car, and he'd been a self-centered, raving lunatic. For their reunion to be this calm felt ominous, like the distant but unmistakable sound of far-off thunder. The downpour was coming, and the lightning too. He could feel it.

"You know I'm really, *really* relieved for you," he said, deciding to make things lighter, his instinctual urge to cheer her winning over his reluctance to postpone the inevitable, "but I wouldn't call her a miracle worker, Viv. You're obviously young." He arched an eyebrow at her mischievously before continuing. "And despite my best attempts, we both know you're still innocent." He pretended to wince when she punched him in the arm.

"Really, she could have been a monkey," he said. "All anyone needed to do was stand you up in front of the judge and point. 'Here she is, Your Honor. Here she is.' Everything about you screams *not guilty*, Viv."

Her smile grew wider for a moment, and Jake's heart began to beat faster when she slipped her hand into his. Stupid, stupid hope, he thought, as he felt it ignite inside of him. Its flame was small, but he felt it inching forward, threatening to scorch the certainty he'd had that Vivian was going to end them. Could he be wrong? He revised the prayer. Please, God. Let me be wrong.

"I'm not describing this well," she continued, still holding his hand. "Let's put it this way. I'm no little kid, and I haven't been naive in a long time. That lawyer you let me borrow made me seem book smart but dumb in life—you know what I mean?"

"I've never been accused of the first, Viv, but the second charge against you? You know I get that one." He paused, staring into the amber eyes that always made him think of the sun as it rose and set on the beach, golden and warm, no matter if it was opening the day or closing it. "I'm sorry. It must have been hard for you to look stupid in any way."

He felt even more crazy hope when she squeezed his hand. "So how's all this working out for you?" She used her free arm to make a sweeping gesture of the huge church auditorium they were in, where he was performing his community service, feeding breakfast, lunch, and dinner to the homeless people he regularly saw sleeping under the boardwalk, now that he was paying attention. He wondered how many times he'd jogged right by, never noticing all the people with no place to go. "This is quite an operation," Vivian said.

"Yeah, it *is* impressive," Jake agreed. "We just got breakfast cleaned up, and in about an hour, it all starts again."

"You must be tired," Vivian said. She had come to him between shifts, and they were sitting on one of the long cafeteria-style benches. She moved closer to him, and that single flame of hope he felt began to blaze. Jake could feel the heat of it in his chest now. She wanted to know about his life here. That didn't seem like someone trying to sever a connection, he didn't think, but he was determined to stay calm. Or to fake calm, anyway.

"Nah," he said, nonchalantly. "I feel really good here. The lady that runs the place? Everybody calls her Sister Celia, even though I don't think she's a nun. She says she'll kick any one of us to the curb if she hears us calling anybody who eats here 'homeless.' She says to call them 'guests.'" Jake sat up straighter as he talked. Even though this was his punishment, and he had to be here, it hadn't taken him long to feel proud to be here, to be a part of something bigger than himself again. "She won't let anyone stand in line, and that's why she needs so much help. She says that 'guests are served,' so we take their orders and bring them their meals."

Vivian nodded thoughtfully. "You show them respect."

"Yeah," said Jake. "Sister Celia says that self-worth is what everybody gets here. That and clean slates. She says every time you walk through her door, you have one. Told me I had one too, no matter what I'd done. Yeah, Sister Celia's a big believer in second chances."

As soon as they were out of his mouth, he winced at his words. He hadn't meant for them to be loaded, to apply to him and their situation, but they'd just spilled out, and now they felt heavy in the space between them. The space that Vivian herself had made smaller when she slid across the table and leaned in closer to him.

The hope that had been burning inside of him was quickly extinguished when Vivian withdrew her hand.

"Jake…oh, Jake. I'm here to say I'm sorry. I'm here to say I'm *so* sorry that I can't do this anymore. I love you, but—"

"Shhh, Viv." He embraced her. It was hard to have her back in his arms but worse to look into her eyes. So he looked over her shoulder, out the window, across the boardwalk, at the ocean as he talked. Please, God. Help me do this right.

"From the start, I've always wanted what's best for you," he said into her ear. He closed his eyes for a moment, breathed in the scent of her hair, and swallowed once, hard. "And from the beginning, I knew that wasn't me."

He felt her squeezing him harder and harder as he spoke. Then he felt her lips on his, and this last kiss was nothing like their first. It was harder, fiercer, like slamming a book shut when you didn't like the ending, instead of the feeling of cautiously opening it to see if you liked what was inside.

With regret, he released her and watched her run out the door. His face was wet, with her tears, he realized, not his. He wondered idly why he seemed to have lost the ability to move. All hope gone now, he stared after Vivian's retreating figure, growing ever smaller as she made her way to the bus stop. Numb and staring, he stood for he didn't know how long, until the distinctly deep voice of Sister Celia called out from the kitchen:

"Jacob Donnely! It seems your guest has gone home, and we have a lot more coming. Now get back here, son, and get to work!"

⚊⚊

Part of getting back to work that day involved learning CPR.

"Just in case," Sister Celia told Jake and the twelve other young men and women who were doing their community service under her watchful eyes. "I learned the rough way that when you work with people who live hard lives, you've gotta be prepared for anything." She paused, scanning the room, and Jake followed her gaze. First her eyes stopped on a restless young woman, rocking back and forth in her chair, its back legs bending dangerously.

"You want to quit that now, miss!" Sister Celia said, and the young woman, her hair dyed a deep blue black and wearing eyeliner to match, blushed. "Thank you for your attention. This is important."

Next her eyes fell on a thin man who, Jake knew from a few late-night conversations, shared his love of motorcycles and was twenty years old. "Young man!"

Jake saw Sister Celia consult her roster. She'd told them all to forgive her for taking a long time to remember their names. She was able to recall on a daily basis the dozens of names of her "regular guests," and she said that sometimes it seemed her brain "just couldn't hold anymore." Jake knew that whenever she called him by name she'd probably asked someone else what it was, or she'd looked on that roster.

"Jackson!" she finally roared.

Jake felt a surge of pity for the guy as he tore his gaze away from the window that looked out to the ocean.

"Ma'am?" he said meekly.

"It is time to listen."

Jackson bowed his head in defeat. Jake had learned that he'd been caught vandalizing the community college he'd flunked out of, and the guy was huge, too, six feet five. Sister Celia was barely five feet tall, but there was something about her that seemed to tame even the wildest of beasts. From the moment she corrected Jackson, he kept his eyes on the presentation.

"I learned the hard way," Sister Celia continued, "that a lot of people who drink too much end up with weak hearts. Watched a man drop right in our dining hall. I called nine one one, but before the ambulance got here, he was already gone."

Jake was sure she had everyone's attention now. The room was still.

"I pray every day that never happens again, but we've got to be prepared." Sister Celia walked to the door, opened it, and put her head around the corner. "You can come in now. They're ready to listen."

A woman dressed in light green hospital scrubs entered the room, carrying two large black cases. She unzipped them, pulling out two floppy mannequins she introduced as Rescue Annie and Rescue Andy. For the next two hours, Jake learned of chest compressions, rescue breathing, and the ratios between the two. There was a rhythm and a sanity to it that he liked, despite the pretend life-and-death circumstances.

When his turn came to practice, he got Annie, and he felt an urgency to do well. From the moment he'd met Sister Celia, he'd wanted to prove himself in her eyes. He wanted to become someone whose name she'd learn and never forget.

"You're a natural," the nurse said as Jake compressed the mannequin's chest thirty times as seriously as if it really did contain a stalled heart that had a chance to beat again.

There was something about Sister Celia and the mission she was on that made him try harder at everything. He was grateful to be a part of it, grateful that he had something like this to think about instead of obsessing over losing Vivian. Twenty-five…twenty-six…twenty-seven…It was almost time to start the rescue breaths. He felt for the first time how good it was to be competent at something important. No, nobody would go down and not get back up again on his watch. That was for sure.

Vivian

She got home just in time to see Einstein snacking on Jake the Fish. In her haste to get to Spring Lake, she'd forgotten to shut her bedroom door. As she walked down her hallway, she saw it was wide open. Her sock got wet when she stepped inside her room. There was some gravel, blue for the sea, scattered on the floor. The bowl, protected by her thick carpet, was still in one piece, but her fish, sadly, was not. Einstein was sitting calmly on her bed, one beautiful feathery fin still hanging from his mouth. Vivian slapped her hand to her own mouth in horror. Einstein quickly swallowed, making room for the rest of his snack, and before Vivian could react, the last fin disappeared.

There was no point in calling him a bad cat, because he wasn't. He was simply following his nature, just being a cat. It was *her* job to shut the door, to protect what she had. No, he wasn't an evil creature, but Vivian couldn't bear the sight of him right now. She took her hand and shooed him from the bed. Einstein bolted, and Vivian closed her door.

"Oh, Jake, I'm sorry," she said to the bowl that was empty, except for the little plant and the tiny ceramic motorcycle. "I'm so, so sorry." Then, like the seventeen-year-old girl she was, she sat with her back against her door, hugged the bowl to her chest, and sobbed.

Three days later, her plane touched down in New Orleans. Normally, the sight of the swampy land beneath her filled her with childhood memories and delight, but now she felt dread. This trip to the land of joyful jazz and soul-heavy blues, of subtle creole delicacies and eye-watering Cajun spices, this city where Saint Louis Cathedral was just around the corner from the voodoo shops, this journey to her beloved land of extremes, was no brief respite from the harsh northeastern winter. No, this was a call from her mother to abandon the Garden State, a call to consider her birthplace her true home. Ivy wanted her away from the scene of her crime and, most of all, forever away from her criminal.

She had yet to tell her mom that it was over with Jake. She didn't want to give her that satisfaction, and it also pained her to admit that the whole thing seemed mutual. She couldn't really say she'd broken things off because when she began to waver, Jake helped her. He *helped* her to end it. She could still feel his warm breath in her hair, his words in her ear: *I've always wanted what's best for you, and from the beginning, I knew that wasn't me.* And that parting kiss had been so lovely that it felt like a form of torture. As always, his lips tasted like the ocean he loved, salty and yet heartbreakingly sweet too. Since that awful day he'd almost passed out on his bike, she knew he'd become diligent about eating fruit at regular times. She'd obviously caught him right after he'd had a peach.

For all his bravado, his I-don't-give-a-fuck attitude, his actions that day showed someone who, in fact, cared a lot. He was taking far better care of himself, and he wasn't merely going through the motions of the judge's sentence. He was obviously engaged in the task before him and trying to do the best work he could. Before she'd let him know she was there to see him, she'd watched him through the window for a few minutes. Jake was busy carrying stacks of plates, most empty, some with remnants of bacon and eggs on them, to the kitchen. After he cleared a table, he'd wipe it clean, whistling all the while. Occasionally, he'd stop to take direction from the elderly African American woman who seemed to run the place. Sister Celia, she found out later. She seemed to genuinely like him, and Jake's eyes lit up as they spoke to one another. Watching him, unafraid to work, doing something good for a change, she realized that if he got his act together and kept it together, there wouldn't be a girl alive who wouldn't want him.

But who knew how long that would take? She had to be strong. She also had to admit that it killed her that he hadn't fought for her.

She felt Hailey's hand on her shoulder. For the duration of the three-hour flight, she'd said as little as possible to either her mother or her ex-best friend. (Or her ex-ex-best friend? She had no idea where they stood.)

"Hey, Viv? It's time to get off."

Did she see concern or contempt in Hailey's eyes? Both feelings creased a person's brow, made the eyes narrower. And did she even care? She took her place in line behind Ivy and Hailey, and they began taking the slightly off-balance shuffle steps of a group of people awkwardly weighed down with only one carry-on each, into which they'd shoved too much.

"Welcome to New Orleans," the pilot said. Ivy thanked him, and within thirty minutes, they were outside with their luggage, hailing a cab, and Vivian could barely breathe.

In the past, the thick air of Louisiana, heavy with both humidity and history, had always settled over her like a familiar blanket, soothing, warm—pure comfort. But today was different. The minute she felt the heat of the city where she'd taken her first breath, her heart began to pound. No matter how deeply or desperately she inhaled, she felt as if her lungs were rejecting the swampy air. She couldn't seem to fill them all the way, no matter how desperately she tried. It wasn't a panic attack. She knew that. She simply wasn't used to the below-sea-level altitude and the humidity of New Orleans anymore. When the cab rolled up, she felt deep relief, its air conditioning providing her with immediate comfort. As the city that she would always love came into view, beautiful and yet alien to her now, she knew one thing was certain: this was not her home anymore.

CHAPTER FIFTEEN

Hailey

When she returned from the restroom after indulging in the bread basket, she discovered that her napkin had been re-folded into a fan. As she sat back down, a waiter she hadn't even realized was close by was suddenly at her elbow, picking up her artfully folded napkin. With one flourish, he snapped it open again. Hailey smiled in wonder as she watched it glide over her lap. When she turned to thank him, he'd already disappeared.

She looked across the table at her former best friend and her slightly crazy mom and thought, I was right. This *was* worth the hassle. I could put up with this pair for the rest of my life in exchange for more dinners like these. And she hated to admit it, but she was growing fonder of them both by the minute, her heart beginning to thaw toward Vivian, to entertain the thought that perhaps Mrs. Ellis (Ivy, she corrected herself, having been reminded a half dozen times today to call her Ivy) wasn't *completely* nuts. It hadn't been all that long since Vivian's dad had died, and her freakishly smart and talented kid had just escaped the slammer. Maybe she was holding it together better than most, considering. Funny how luxurious gifts can turn this girl's head, she thought. *I'd completely hate myself if I weren't so fucking happy.*

They were in what tourists referred to as the Garden District of New Orleans and what locals called "Uptown." Hailey didn't care what anyone else called it; it was perfection. The streets lined with massive oak trees, the historic Victorian homes, including Anne Rice's. (God bless America, she'd walked right by Anne Rice's house!). And the restaurants: be still her food-obsessed little heart, *the restaurants!* Mrs. Ellis was treating them to a meal at Commander's Palace, the former stomping ground, she said, of Emeril Lagasse, who had first risen to fame there as the five-star restaurant's executive chef. Yes, Ivy was turning out to be a rather fabulous tour guide. The first exotic item Hailey sampled from their menu was turtle soup.

She couldn't believe it when Ivy started off their meal by ordering it for all three of them. "Hailey, trust me, it's amazing," she said. "If you don't like it, slide it over to me or Viv. We'll gladly finish yours, and you can order something else."

Even Vivian, who had been sullen for the entire plane ride and for most of their first three days in the city, surprised Hailey by nodding at Ivy's words. "Hailey, it's superdelicious. Come on. Try it." Her eyes, a bit swollen and red, showed a hint of their former mischievous sparkle. "I *dare* you."

Ah, like old times, silly elementary-school games. *I dare you to jump in that puddle, to lick the swing set, to pet that stray dog, to eat the turtle*...A laugh escaped Hailey. It was all in good fun, and she probably *would* order something else, anyway. It wasn't her money, so who cared? *Laissez les bon temps rouler. Let the good times roll,* as Mrs. El—Ivy had said.

When the soup arrived in three shining silver bowls, it took two waiters to serve it. One placed a bowl in front of each of them, and the other quickly poured a shot of sherry into each person's serving.

"Aren't they going to card us?" Hailey cracked.

Vivian laughed. "No stalling!"

Hailey closed her eyes and picked up her spoon.

It was, hands down, the most singularly delicious thing she had ever tasted. She kept her eyes closed as Ivy began to speak.

"Turtle meat is intense, yet delicate. Dark, rich, thick…practically indescribable." Hailey was struck by the drawl that was suddenly in Ivy's voice. She'd never noticed it before. It was subtle and hypnotic, very much like the soup that she discovered she couldn't stop eating.

"It does *not* taste like chicken," Ivy continued. "It doesn't taste like anything but itself." She paused to sample her own bowl, and Hailey could tell that the sigh that escaped Ivy's lips afterward was one of deep contentment. "Oh, the spices are easy enough to identify," she said. "Oregano. Thyme. Black pepper, freshly ground. Onions and garlic, minced. Fresh lemon juice and parsley."

The rhythm of Ivy's words sounded like an incantation, and the spell she cast helped Hailey to slow down and really taste her soup. She usually crammed everything into her mouth as fast as she could. She couldn't remember the last time she'd taken her time and savored something. She glanced at Vivian, who was slowly eating her own bowl, a look of reverence on her face.

"Turtles have been around since before the Jurassic period," Ivy said, after indulging in another spoonful. "So what you're tasting right now, Hailey, is refined, yet prehistoric. It's a primal experience, and, if you like it, that's what you're responding to, just as much as anything else."

Ivy seemed to lose herself in her own bowl then, and the three of them ate in contented silence. The bulimic, the widow, and the jailbird, thought Hailey, as a jazz trio that had been strolling through the restaurant to treat all the diners settled into the corner behind them and began to play. The opening notes of "What a Wonderful World" washed over them, and she was inclined to agree with the sentiment. As bizarre as this all was, it was also quite possibly the best moment she had ever known.

She took another bite of soup and promised herself that she'd made her last trip to the restroom. She'd relieved herself of the bread she'd indulged in at the start of the meal. But to lose this soup? Well, that would be a sin. She was determined to keep this experience down.

Ivy

She had carried her longing for the South for so many years that she often dismissed it, like minor, but chronic, back pain. But the minute she felt the muggy caress of a ninety-degree day in December, the entire state of Louisiana as luxurious and languid as her own personal sauna, she knew that she had never been merely homesick. For the last fourteen years, Ivy had been gravely ill with her need for New Orleans. After treating the girls to a few days in the heart of the French Quarter, she stood on her old front porch, her finger pressing the doorbell.

"Back in the fold!" her mother exclaimed, when she threw open the door of the huge shotgun house on St. Peter Street that had been in their family for four generations. Legendary Southern hospitality on full display, Ivy noted that her seventy-five-year-old mother gave Hailey almost as long and as warm a hug as she gave to her own granddaughter. A pitcher of sweet tea with slices of lemon floating lazily on its surface was sweating on a table on the back porch where her mother encouraged them to sit and relax. She could smell gumbo on the stove, and there were éclairs she recognized from Le Madeline's in the Quarter on a bright white plate. Lively zydeco music played on her mother's huge, old-fashioned stereo.

Ah, Ivy thought, we're at a celebration. Viv and I are the wandering sheep returned, and we just happened to bring along an extra lamb. Well, it looks like she's family now. Ivy felt a wave of shame at the way she'd never invited Hailey to call her anything but "Mrs. Ellis" until this trip came up. If you're away from your people for too long, she thought, you forget their ways. While never rude to Hailey, she was always reserved. The warmth she'd learned at her mother's table, a distant memory. Ivy realized that she'd never felt entirely accepted in New Jersey, or maybe *she* hadn't been accepting of *it*, but either way, she'd put up a wall, never welcoming anyone into her world. Watching the effortless kindness of her mother, she could see that she had chosen a very cold way to live.

"Come here, *chère*," she'd said to her daughter's best friend. Ivy noted Hailey's eyes growing huge as she was hugged by a complete stranger. People didn't usually embrace at first meetings in the northeast, and Hailey's arms hung stiffly at her sides. But Ivy's mother did not give up.

"I'm just gonna squeeze you till I get somethin' back!" she said, and Hailey laughed and gave in, hugging Ivy's mother warmly. Oh, Mama, Ivy thought, as she settled into the flowery couch cushions covering the wrought-iron porch chairs and took a grateful sip of sweet tea, I think I've missed you and New Orleans in equal measures.

She felt another twinge of guilt, thinking of how little she'd called her mom as the years marched forward in Belmar. It hadn't taken her long to get out of the habit of maintaining their close connection. Once Vivian was school age, their visits South dwindled to just once a year, and the mother/daughter phone calls started to occur only on holidays and birthdays or whenever some tragedy or emergency struck. Her mother tried to keep up her end, calling Ivy just to chat once a week during the early years of her marriage to Will, but when Ivy became a busy young mother, she let the calls go to voice mail more times than she cared to admit. Each year brought fewer calls, until their connection reached its current, sad state, so it amazed Ivy how quickly they fell back into the familiar rhythm of family. Except for Vivian.

Ivy watched with concern as Hailey, obviously at ease after the hug, sat chatting comfortably with her mother, and Vivian hung back, taking only half a ladle of gumbo, one small bite of her éclair. She smiled a lot at her grandmother and answered all of her questions politely, but she started no conversations of her own.

"She's very tentative," Ivy's mother said after the girls took her suggestion to take a walk around the block.

"Yes, I know, but it's better than she was after the charges were dropped. I would either hear her crying alone in her room, or she would sit around the house emotionless. Practically catatonic. It scared me."

"And the boy?"

"She doesn't mention him."

"Probably a bad sign."

"What do you mean?"

Ivy's mother took a sip of her own sweet tea and sighed. "Things you don't talk about tend to stay stuck inside," she continued, "in both your heart and mind. At least she's got her friend. Seems like a nice young woman, that Hailey."

"That's the thing," Ivy said, drumming her fingers nervously on the arm of her chair. "They hardly talked the whole way down here...two teenaged girls barely speaking. And you know that's a long flight. There's something going on with them too. I just have no idea what it is."

"So tell me, my sweet Ivy, when did you lose your daughter's trust?"

"What do you mean, Mama?"

"You knew nothing about the boyfriend who led her astray for months, and now you don't know what's going on with her best friend, either. This goes way beyond being out of the loop, my dear."

Ivy dipped a crusty slice of French bread into her bowl of gumbo, took a small bite, and chewed on it thoughtfully. She decided it was stupid and prideful to hold anything back.

"I snooped around and read her journals."

Her mother's brown eyes, warm as the melted chocolate on the top of their éclairs, gave her a look of empathy. "You were wrong, but you were worried about her, *oui?*"

"Exactly."

"That's one of those things she won't forgive you for unless she becomes a mama of a teenaged girl acting crazy someday. You never apologized?"

Ivy dropped her bread on the floor. "How did you know that?" Before she recovered enough to pick it up, her mother had already done it, wrapping it up in her napkin to throw away.

"Vivian has made extremely bad choices," she said, holding out the bread plate and offering Ivy another slice, "and yet she carries herself as the one who's been wronged. She's usually more sensible than that. She's stuck in the past, stuck in thoughts of the boy, and she needs you to be truly sorry for your role in all this madness before she can move on."

"How can you figure all this out in the first half hour of our visit?" Ivy exclaimed, accepting the new piece of bread.

"Oh, baby, I'm *old*!" Her mother shook with laughter. "I'm old, and part of the irony of old age is that you can finally see things for what they are, but nobody wants to hear about it. You're wise at last and can cut through all the static, but everyone who could benefit from your life experience is too busy rushing around making the mistakes of *their* lives to bother asking you how to avoid them." She paused to take another sip of sweet tea. Her eyes sparkled mischievously. "And also, Vivian calls me now and again, which is more than I can say for you."

"Well, when everything settles down, I'm going to do better," Ivy said, in a rush of conviction. "I'll call once a week again, just to shoot the breeze, just to see how you are." Ivy laughed and shook her head. "Forget that, Mama. I need you to tell me how *I* am. Oh, if only I'd been smart enough to call you when I first started having trouble with Vivian!"

"You won't need to call. You can just stop on by. You're coming home. That's what this trip is all about."

Ivy didn't miss that her mother was making statements rather than asking questions.

"I don't know yet."

"With Will gone, what else is left for you up there?"

"Vivian, obviously."

Ivy's mother reached out and took her by the hand.

"Baby, the hardest thing I ever did was let you go, and I had to do that when you weren't much older than Viv."

"Why would I do it any earlier?" Ivy felt her mother squeeze her hand gently.

"Because she's already left *you*. That's what's obvious, here, Ivy Caroline. You need to give her space if you ever want her to come back in close."

"What if I can't?"

"Well, then, my darling, you've truly lost her for good."

CHAPTER SIXTEEN

Wendy

S he stared at her reflection in the bathroom mirror: thin, wan. Still sober but aching for a drink. *Any* drink. She'd caught herself rummaging around in the medicine cabinet in the middle of the night, all self-possession gone, looking for cough syrup after she'd woken up sweating. When would the withdrawal stop already? Since the initial week of pure hell, she was having more good days than bad, but there were times when the urge for alcohol would simply knock her flat. She hadn't gone for one of Sonny's beers yet because she wanted to be better. She wanted this to work. No one would notice if she downed a bottle of Nyquil or Robitussin, and it might get her through this night. In this moment, she'd do almost anything just to get through the night. Poor Sonny, she thought. He always trusted her too much. What was that joke she'd learned during that year her parents paid for a pricey stint in rehab? Oh, yes, yes, of course: *How do you know if an alcoholic is lying?* Pause for effect. *Her lips are moving.* Ba-da-bing!

It was a painful sort of funny, the way desperate truths usually are, and she and her fellow addicts had shifted uncomfortably in their seats as the joke made them all roar with laughter while also feeling punched in their guts. That treatment center had been experimental, to say the least, and Wendy knew it was her parents' final rescue attempt with her, as nothing ever stuck. Hiring a comedian to come and make cracks about their addictions at the end of their recovery was thought of as a "cathartic exercise." But of course it turned out that she hadn't really recovered after all—again.

After that failure, her parents dubbed her "hopelessly weak willed" and tried taking the tough-love route, refusing to answer or return her calls for months. The funny thing was, their toughest love didn't feel all that much different from their regular love. It was only slightly more distant.

Oh, that joke was haunting her tonight as she thought about how close to the edge she was, and how Sonny, sleeping peacefully in the bed they now shared again, was completely unaware. He'd so quickly accepted her back into his life, and she knew this meant that he loved her still and trusted her not to screw things up this time. Because she presented a picture of someone getting her shit together, he chose to believe in her. After everything she'd put them all through, *why* did he still believe in her?

Damn it! There was nothing in the medicine cabinet but some aspirin and vials and vials of insulin. She'd forgotten that, before she'd left for AC, she'd set up Jake's deliveries to come in three-month blocks, so he was never in danger of running out. She realized that Sonny and Jake probably didn't bother treating niggling things like coughs when they had more serious concerns. It made sense, but that also meant that she had two choices. Go back to bed, or pop open a beer.

She knew the reason she was a wreck was because Sonny had invited Jake for dinner tomorrow. He thought it was time they tell him about their reunion. The thought of playing at having a family meal with the son who rightfully loathed her made her long for numbness. That rehab comedian had another crack that also kept running around her head. He said alcoholics liked to trick themselves into believing that booze was like therapy, "a bunch of answers in a bottle." But Wendy knew that it was really forgetfulness in a bottle, all the sharp edges of life dulled for a bit. Having Jake find out that Sonny had just let her slip right back into their home? That was the pointiest of edges, and she longed to file it down.

"Best to let him know before he's on his way back here to live, don't you think? Give him time to get used to the idea." The smile Sonny tried to give her when he said this pained her. She knew it was meant to be reassuring, but the smile never hit his eyes, which looked as anxious as she felt.

Wendy walked out of the bathroom and glanced at the clock on the wall above the kitchen sink. It was after midnight. Today, then. Jake was coming for dinner today.

"I'll make his favorite," she'd told Sonny.

Sonny arched a skeptical eyebrow at her, knowing Jake's favorite dish was penne a la vodka. Not surprisingly, most of Wendy's recipes included alcohol of some sort: amaretto chocolate pie, Sam Adams Chili, and the list went on and on. "I thought we'd all go out," was all he said.

"I think I'd feel better cooking us a meal. Sitting around this table again. Maybe having a real conversation."

Sonny kissed her on the cheek. He was leaving early to hit the gym before he started his day at Saint Catherine's. "Well, it'll be delicious as always. Looking forward to it, babe."

At the memory of how he'd looked when he'd left yesterday morning, and at the trust she'd felt in that kiss, she wondered how she could have ever left him behind. He worked hard, he was the most amazing dad and partner, and she was still as attracted to him as she had been when they were first married. Despite all she'd put him through, he somehow still looked a decade younger than he was. Yes, she'd had everything—*everything*—before she let drinking derail her. And close as she was to having everything back again, it didn't feel solid. Always, the gifts of her life felt like grains of sand, merely passing through her fingers. And now she was back at the beach, scrambling to scoop up all the wonderful things she'd stupidly let go of, trying to put them back into her bucket before it was too late.

Sonny seemed to want nothing more than to be a permanent part of her life again, but Jake's love felt impossible to win back. *Yeah, Wendy,* said a scathing voice in her head, *you fucked everything up royally, didn't you?* That was the voice, forever berating her—the one that she couldn't evict. That she tried to silence with wine, vodka, cough syrup, whatever. *You are a worthless fuck-up, Wendy,* it said. *Worthless Wendy, who deserves nothing, who is nothing. Worthless, worthless Wendy.*

"Shut up!" she whispered fiercely. She would have screamed it had Sonny not been sleeping. Why couldn't she get that voice to stop, and who did it belong to anyway? She turned on the faucet and splashed her face with water. Then she threw open the refrigerator and grabbed a can of Sonny's Miller Lite.

She stood there, holding it for a few minutes, her hand shaking. She felt hot and pressed the cold can against her forehead. She put it down on the counter. Picked it up. Put it down. Picked it up.

She popped the tab. Leaning her face over the small opening in the can, she closed her eyes and inhaled deeply. Then, still trembling, she shook her head and poured the beer down the kitchen sink. *I finally know what I've got,* she said in response to the cruel voice in her head. *I finally know what I've got, and I'm not going to lose it again.* Then she walked down the hallway to the bedroom and crawled back under the covers, molding her body into Sonny's like a spoon.

Jake

The house smelled amazing when he walked through the front door, and familiar too, although he couldn't immediately place what it was that Wendy was making. His dad had given him a heads-up that she was still around, but it came as a shock anyway to see her in his home, stirring that delicious-smelling something in a large saucepan. He had to remind himself that he was nineteen and on a one-night leave from his community service, not the thirteen-year-old kid he'd been when Wendy had last cooked him dinner.

"Hey," was all he said when he came inside. No smile.

Wendy nodded at him. "Hey, Jake. Thanks for coming. Hope you're hungry." She looked nervous, maybe even scared. Good.

"Where's Dad?"

"Running late. He called a few minutes ago. Father Giraldi needs him at the chapel." She picked up a shaker of sea salt and ground a little bit of it into the pan. She met Jake's eyes. "Some shingles came off in the storm that passed through this afternoon."

"I don't buy it," he said, looking at Wendy with a coldness he didn't try to hide. He knew it was cruel, but he wanted to make her squirm. "He probably expects us to talk."

"Well, there *is* a lot to say," Wendy answered, furiously stirring and stirring whatever it was that she was cooking, but managing to hold Jake's gaze.

He shrugged. "Not really."

"OK, Jake," Wendy said, her eyes drifting down to the pan. "OK."

Jake plopped down on the sofa, putting his boot-clad feet on the coffee table that looked as if Wendy had recently dusted it. It was shiny for the first time in years and smelled of fake lemons. He and Sonny weren't pigs; they swept and dusted every other week or so and kept the dishes out of the sink. But there was always something sad about the place after Wendy left. She'd taken the time to do the detail work they neglected, making everything shine. He begrudgingly had to admit that the house looked as great as it smelled. She'd turned on lamps he'd forgotten they even had. He and Sonny usually just flicked on the switches on the walls for overhead light. Tonight, Wendy had all the dark corners illuminated. But if she thought a meal, a squirt of Pledge, and a few new light bulbs were going to make him forget about the last six years, well, she must still be drinking. He glanced up at her again. *Was* she still drinking? He pulled out his phone and texted Sonny:

WHERE R U? This BLOWS!!! Leaving if u aren't home soon.

Within sixty seconds, his phone vibrated with Sonny's answer:

On my way. Stay where you are. Show some respect.

He was kidding, right? Show some respect? Why? Because she'd shown so much to them? What the hell was wrong with his dad? Why was Wendy still here? None of this made any sense. None at all.

In a fit of madness, he texted Viv. It was the second time since she'd left that he'd been weak and contacted her. The first time he'd texted, he asked for her New Orleans address. He'd wanted to send something to her, a parting gift of sorts:

I mailed u that thing, Viv.
Just wanted u 2 look for it.
After that, I won't bother u again.

He started to put the phone away but thought he'd better say one more thing:

Promise.

He shoved his cell back into the pocket of his jacket. His stomach was growling, which annoyed him. He wished he could refuse to eat, but since skipping meals wasn't an option for him, it looked as if he was definitely going to be breaking some bread with the enemy. Man, this really did suck.

Wendy put a large tray of appetizers on the gleaming coffee table from which he stubbornly refused to remove his feet. Next to the food, she placed a container of fancy toothpicks, like the kind he imagined you'd see in fruity drinks on cruise ships. She'd gone all out—that was for sure. There was homemade bruschetta that he remembered her making every Christmas Eve. That had always been a favorite of his dad's. There were fat green olives stuffed with things he'd never encountered in an olive prior to that moment. Some were filled with almonds, some with jalapenos, and some were almost bursting with blue cheese. There wasn't one common pimento in the lot of them. She'd also taken the time to cook scallops and wrap them in prosciutto. When he was sure she was busy at the stove again, he furtively popped one into his mouth.

Damn. It was good. *Really* good. He tried the bruschetta. Also amazing. What game was she playing? As he wondered, he grabbed a toothpick and jabbed at a blue-cheese-stuffed olive with a fierce grimness. He bit down on it so hard that his teeth hit wood, snapping the pick in two. He spit the remaining splinter into a napkin before finishing the olive.

If Wendy hadn't been the one who'd prepared the food, he'd be pretty happy right now, in a home that actually felt welcoming for a change. Pillows plumped, good things bubbling on the stove.

What was that smell anyway? It was driving him crazy it was so familiar. He glanced at her over his shoulder. Wendy was carefully measuring out a teaspoon of crushed red pepper. Then it hit him. Vodka pasta. He'd asked for it for every one of his birthdays after the first time she'd made it for the family. The cream and butter made it rich. The vodka and pepper flakes gave it a kick. The crushed tomatoes were what "gave it balance," he remembered Wendy saying long ago, when he was little and used to watch adoringly as she prepared it.

He also remembered seeing her filling a little shot glass while she cooked. Tipping her head back, getting sillier and sillier as the pasta bubbled on the stove.

"Funny, Mommy," he remembered saying once. "Funny, funny Mommy."

Or drunk Mommy. Yeah, that was more like it. Or alcoholic Mommy, or dangerous addict Mommy. How clueless he'd been! Jake glared at Wendy, who caught him staring. There was no shot glass in sight now, but it didn't matter. It was still too much. His stomach was full enough. Blood sugar in check. Without a word, he got up and walked out the door.

He passed Sonny on the way out.

"Where are you going?" his dad asked, his voice deep, angry.

"Back to work," Jake answered. "You got a problem with that?"

Sonny

He'd had it. Jake had been babied long enough. He grabbed his skinny nineteen-year-old by the collar and dragged him back to the door.

"What the *fuck*?" Jake roared.

"*You* answer that question first," Sonny yelled back, feeling heat rise to his face. It was as if someone had lit a match inside him, and he was dry grass on a hundred-degree day. He was finally giving himself permission to show the anger he'd kept buried for Jake's sake. But ever since he'd answered that call from the police station, he'd felt a shift inside. And from the minute he saw Jake behind bars, he realized that he was done.

He was done keeping his emotions in check for his son. He was done pitying him for having no mom, and, yeah, even for being sick too, because it was clear that his pity had done Jake harm. He was finished expecting nothing from him. He realized one thing after seeing his mug shot on the news—as a parent of a teenager, there was no such thing as getting nothing from your kid. You got extremes, the good and the bad, and in his pity, he'd been as useless a parent as there ever was. His philosophy as a dad had been along the lines of, "Leave the poor kid alone." Yeah, that had worked out just great. But even though he'd acted otherwise for years now, he'd always cared deeply. It was time to show it.

In spite of the freezing winter day, he had to unzip his jacket. His heart was really thumping along now, as if he'd just run five miles on the treadmill. He stared at his son, watching him swallow and shift from foot to foot. He looked nervous, and Sonny knew that he'd made an impression. *Good.* He'd be damned if he'd let Jake leave. Yeah, sure, this dinner was going to be strange, but it was going to happen. Sonny needed it to happen. And he was also done pretending he didn't need anything out of life. He wanted Wendy back, and it seemed as if he had her, so Jake would just have to deal.

"Go inside *now*, Jake," Sonny said, turning for the door.

"I'm not going to sit around that table, pretending the last six years didn't happen, Dad! I'm *not!*"

Sonny turned around again, feeling weary in spirit, but strong of will. "No one's asking you to do that."

"Then why my favorite dinner? I feel like she's trying to cook her way back into my life. It's lame, Dad. Lame."

"You can think whatever you want. Have any opinion you choose," Sonny said. "But you *will* go inside and eat the meal your mother prepared. Lame or not. Feel free to leave right after, but you can't make a judgment based on a moment you walked out on."

"Does that go for Wendy, too? She walked out on a lot of moments, didn't she?" Jake's eyes flashed dangerously, and Sonny caught a glimpse of the out-of-control delinquent that had kicked the hell out of that Camaro. The kid he'd refused to see. He'd always known Jake was hiding things from him, but he pretended not to know. He'd really made mistake after mistake.

"The difference is, Wendy isn't judging us, Jake," he continued. "She's begging us to forgive her, yes. But judge us? She wouldn't dare."

They stopped talking when the front door slowly opened. Sonny couldn't help but smile when both the smell of that great sauce and the heat of the kitchen hit him in his already warm face. He looked at the woman he was inexplicably still drawn to as she stared anxiously at their son, nervously biting her bottom lip like a child.

Seeing Wendy standing there, vulnerable and split open, Sonny thought that maybe when they'd all lived together he'd really had two children. And he loved them to a fault, but it was time for them both to grow up and for him to treat them as the adults they were.

"Guess dinner's ready?" was all he said.

Wendy nodded. "Yes, please come inside."

He caught Jake's eye again. "After you," he said.

Jake gave Sonny a final glare, squared his shoulders, and walked roughly past him through the open door.

CHAPTER SEVENTEEN

Vivian

Her phone vibrated with Jake's text while her mother was forcing her to tour the University of Mississippi, in Oxford, an oak-tree-lined college town named for its highly esteemed cousin in England. It was a heck of a drive from New Orleans. Over five wasted hours of Vivian's life. And Ivy's taste in music was sketchy at best. She tended to only listen to whatever was on the local Top 40 station, which drove Vivian nuts. Almost every song was in 4/4 common time. Four beats per measure with four basic themes: falling in love, falling out of love, being torn apart by love, or being made new by love. Blah, blah, blah, *blah*. Give her some up-tempo blues in 12/8 time with a survival theme over that dreck any day. How could Ivy and her music connoisseur of a father ever have ended up together? But as she viewed everything about this trip as justifiable punishment for her crimes, she endured all the driving to and from schools and the bad music on an endless loop in stony silence.

Her mind kept wandering back to the boy in the backseat of the Camaro. Still plagued by the memory of his blue eyes, wild and bright with terror, she felt she deserved a lot more torture than this. Relieved as she was that her good-girl status had helped her to escape squeaky clean from all the charges, she often thought that doing community service like Jake would have been a relief. Maybe having a stain on her record wasn't something she should have wished so much to erase, but to face and correct.

So this was the fourth campus she'd been told to "consider," as Ivy put it. Loyola, Tulane, and the University of New Orleans were the first three schools on Ivy's list. Yes, there was a master list with appointment times and information on what made each school impressive. Ivy kept rambling that their family connections could get Vivian into Country Day, an elite private high school in New Orleans, for the remainder of her senior year, and then she could "just slide on in to one of the best schools in the country."

Slide on in? Her mother's expressions were becoming more distinctly Southern by the second. Ivy's drawl had also made a definite reappearance, and Vivian noted that she crackled with energy, and something else she hadn't quite placed yet. She barely recognized this lively woman. After her dad had gotten sick, all travel stopped, and it had been over two years since they'd visited their hometown. Was her mom usually this way when she got back to her roots? Her dad had always been so full of fun that if Ivy had possessed some of that same vibrancy, well, Vivian guessed his had always overshadowed hers.

As for transferring to Country Day for her final two semesters as a high-school student, well, to be blunt, that would only happen over her dead Jersey-girl body. Everyone had an off-ramp, a place to call home, and hers was exit 7A. Ivy could drag her to every school in the tristate area, but Vivian was having *none* of it. Hailey, though, that was another story.

Her (old? former? new-again?) friend seemed overjoyed to be tagging along on all these campus tours. She'd found something to admire at each of the first three universities, but she kind of lost her mind at Ole Miss.

"Oh my God...Oh my God...Oh my God," she kept whispering, almost in a fugue state, when they hit the English department. A big flaw in Ivy's plan was that every school was on winter break, so their tours were being run by the skeleton crew of students not lucky enough to have someplace homier to go for the holidays. The vaguely gloomy people left to show them around pretty much just threw open the gates to the hallowed halls, said, "Voilà," and then left them to their own devices. This should have allowed whatever misconceptions they had about the schools they were touring to go unchecked. However, Vivian, determined to remain unimpressed, used her iPhone to access Google in an attempt to blow apart some long-standing myths about each university.

Hailey's over-the-top reaction to Ole Miss was a response to Ivy pointing out that one of the most celebrated students to ever grace its halls was Faulkner, one of Hailey's literary idols.

"Yes," Ivy was saying, ruffling through her papers, "here it is, right in the packet they gave me: 'The city of Oxford served as the inspiration for Nobel Prize winner and former Ole Miss student William Faulkner's fictional Jefferson, the locale of many of his novels.' Impressive, no?"

"Oh my *God*," Hailey said again.

"No," said Vivian.

Ivy put a hand on her hip. "What do you mean, *no?* How can you not be a little daunted by the talent who wrote *The Sound and the Fury?*"

"I mean," said Vivian, "it's not impressive, because it's misleading propaganda." She waved her phone at Ivy and Hailey. "I looked it up. What all the Ole Miss ads *aren't* going to tell you is that Faulkner dropped out of this place after only three semesters."

Hailey, obviously not giving up her awe easily, shook her head. "But still," she said, "he was here for over a year, in this space, *writing*. He's the one who said, 'The past is never dead. It's not even past.' Think about that for a second. If that's true, he's still here, in a way. Being here would be like going to school *with* William Faulkner. "

"But," Vivian said, "most of the words you admire weren't written here, and the stuff that was wasn't even appreciated! Ha! Look—it says that he 'once received a D in English while studying at Ole Miss.'"

"Vivian, you are exasperating," Ivy said, taking the phone Vivian offered her and skimming through the article. "And Wikipedia's a pretty sketchy source, isn't it?"

God, her mother was annoying. Vivian snatched her phone back. "Wikipedia's a lot more reliable than the papers you picked up from the university," she said coldly. "They'll spin things any way they please to make themselves look good. And," she added, letting the words tumble from her mouth without thinking, "if Faulkner scored a D here, what do you think *you'll* get, Hailey?"

"I will most definitely receive straight As," Hailey said grandly. "Obviously, only unappreciated geniuses get Ds."

Vivian smiled, admiring the comeback. She'd regretted the words the minute she'd said them and was grateful Hailey wasn't holding them against her. She was sick of all this silly running around when her mother knew the only school she cared about was Princeton, that all her backup choices also kept her close to Jersey, to the beach, and yeah, *OK*, of course she got it. It kept her too close to Jake. All of this—the trip itself, her longing to get back home, the way her mother had a knack for driving her completely crazy—was making her feel mean and petty today. And then she had to go and take it out on Hailey, who was good enough not to take it personally. Yes, there was a reason this girl had been her best friend since the first grade.

"I'm sorry." She grabbed her friend's hand tentatively, gave it a squeeze, and then quickly released it. "For a lot of things." She flashed a smile that felt wicked. "Of course you'll get Ds too, if you come here. The glorious Ds given to only the greatest giants of literature."

"And then I can pull a Faulkner," said Hailey as she scrolled through the information Vivian still had pulled up on her phone. "It says he 'then settled in New Orleans to write his first novel.'" She gave a contented-sounding sigh. "Oh, Viv, this place is a hotbed for writers. Why didn't I consider any schools away from home before?"

"Because of our world-domination plans? Maybe it's easier for us to stick together in order to rule and whatnot?"

Hailey laughed. Ivy nodded at them both and kindly strolled ahead. Vivian was glad her mom wasn't completely clueless to the fact that she and Hailey could use the private time.

"I've missed you, Viv."

"Yeah. Same here."

"I just...I just..." Hailey's arms were folded across her chest. She looked as if she was hugging herself as she rocked back and forth on her feet. Her excitement like sparks of static electricity in the air.

"You just what, genius?"

Hailey put her arms at her sides and stopped fidgeting. "I just feel more *alive* here than I ever felt in Jersey. I had no idea what anyplace else was like. I know it in my gut that this is where I'm going to school. It's like a magnet, you know? Places pulling at you. Destiny calling. If you feel dead inside wherever you're living, it's time to leave. I never realized it until this trip, but I never feel *right* in Belmar. I was born there, sure, but maybe all that place ever was to me was a geographical accident. Becoming best friends with you a million years ago, getting dragged on this trip—that's what isn't accidental. That, my friend, is fate."

"So what does it mean that I can't wait to get the hell out of here?"

"My mecca's your misery, I guess?"

"Exactly."

"Different magnets, different desires, different pulls." Hailey leaned against the wall behind her, bumping her head into a large bulletin board full of homemade ads, begging for roommates, recruiting students for clubs, so many opportunities and adventures for the asking, one ad overlapping the next in a cacophony of neon-colored flyers. Vivian laughed as Hailey rubbed her head where she'd watched her bang it into one of the many thumbtacks.

"So which magnet are you responding to, do you think?" Hailey asked. "Jersey itself? Princeton?" She paused, grimaced. "Jake?"

"You know, you don't know him at all."

"I'd argue that you don't either. It's only been a few months, after all."

"They were big months, Hailey."

"OK, I can accept that. Meeting him was for you, I think, what being at this college is for me."

"A turning point."

"A fork in the proverbial road."

"A call to act."

"To change."

"To live."

"Obviously, though, Ms. Jailbird, some mistakes were made."

"Which I've learned from."

Hailey looked at Vivian with an intensity that made her squirm. "Have you? How do you know? Is it safe for you to go back there and even find out?" She paused but kept looking at Vivian in a searching way. "I know you'll hate me for saying this, but maybe your mom is right. Maybe, despite your magnets and your misery, you should try to stay here for a while. Try to make it work."

"I know it's safe for me to go back, Hailey, because Jake and I broke it off."

"I'd say I'm sorry, except—"

"That you're not."

"No."

They were back at this impasse again, but this time it didn't bother Vivian. "Well, Hailey, whatever's pulling me—and I'd like to think it's mainly Princeton—I like imagining you doing your part on this side of the Mason-Dixon Line, working hard to ensure our eventual rule."

Hailey smiled. "Yes, we'll spread our influence around, reach more people this way."

And that's when Vivian's phone vibrated. Hailey was still holding it.

"Who is it?" Vivian asked.

Hailey shook her head. "Jake. I guess you hear from him every day?"

"This makes twice since we left. Like I said, we broke up."

Vivian took note of Hailey's skeptical expression as she took back her phone. Deciding not to text back, she dropped the cell into her purse. On the long ride back to New Orleans, she'd muse over what Jake could have possibly sent to her.

"Well, we'd better go find Ivy before she fills out an application for you," Hailey said. "It's obvious you won't be going to school here."

"You're right about that," Vivian said. "But it's really not about Jake."

"I absolutely believe every word that you're saying," Hailey said, her right hand in the air, as if she was taking some kind of oath.

Vivian playfully shoved her friend back toward the offending bulletin board. "And you *should*!" Vivian laughed.

"Oh, I do, Viv. I really, really do," Hailey continued in her mock-earnest tone.

"If you're going to be a successful writer," Vivian said, "you really need to learn how to be a better liar."

"I'll work on it," said Hailey. "I'll do my best."

"But first, let's grab an application for *you*, shall we?" Vivian watched a little wistfully as the sour expression Hailey always wore when they spoke of Jake disappeared, her whole face lighting up at the mention of filling out her Ole Miss forms. Damn, thought Vivian, I'm going to miss you, Hailey. "We're really in your new home sweet home, then?" she asked, faking cheerfulness.

"Damn straight, Viv," Hailey said. "My destiny awaits. Follow me."

CHAPTER EIGHTEEN

Jake

If he looked at it as just a free meal, he'd survive it. He stared at the big pasta bowl Wendy placed in front of him filled with vodka penne, breathed in its rich smell, took a heaping spoonful of parmesan, and shook it all over his dinner. While he watched it melt, he remembered that Wendy never bought the cheese preshredded, always taking the time to grate it herself. He could still see her as she was years ago, with the grater in her right hand, her left patiently gliding the wedge of cheese back and forth, back and forth across it, the fine shreds of parmesan falling down as gently as snow. When he was very little, she'd usually break off a small piece and pop it into his mouth. As he grew older, she would save a corner of it, putting it into his outstretched palm as he ran by her after school, usually on his way to the shore.

He shook his head. He needed to get some control over his brain. The part of it that remembered Wendy as his mom, the section he was able to bury when she stayed in Atlantic City where she *belonged*, well, that fucking part was still eight inside and loved her still, no matter how hard he tried to fight it. And it was that sappy, stupid part of him that was in a wrestling match with the saner section of his mind that knew better than to forgive or to trust her again.

He glanced at Sonny who was twisting the pepper mill over his own plate of pasta. Coarse, black pieces of spice rained down on his noodles, looking gross to Jake, like whiskers in a sink. His father's expression was calm, but unreadable.

What are you thinking, Dad? Jake thought. *Why* is she still hanging around? Maybe she'd lost her job or something. Sonny had filled him in on the lawsuit at the Trop after Jake saw a piece about it on the eleven o'clock news he used to watch for mentions of his own exploits. There had been three more interviews with his mom and the other waitresses since then, and the case kept getting mentioned in the *Asbury Park Press* as well. Wendy, without knowing it, had stolen his thunder. If she'd lost her place to stay because she'd spoken out against the Trop, well, Dad was way too good a guy to toss her out. Yeah, that was probably it. Hopefully, the case would be closed soon, Wendy would either go back to that job or find another, and that would be the end of it.

Wendy kept walking around them, putting more things on the table. She placed a bottle of crushed red pepper in front of Jake. He always liked his penne extra spicy. As she put the bottle down, he caught sight of a familiar scar on her arm. He bristled, trying to shove the memory of their turtle-saving days aside. But images of her tying that goofy cape he used to wear around his neck, and of their road trips and their rescues, insisted on flooding his brain. He wished somebody would talk already. At least, somebody that wasn't *him*. If he started talking, who knew what might happen? If he told Wendy how much he'd hated her every day, every second, since the moment she'd left? He might completely lose it. No, he'd better stay quiet.

He shook his head vigorously no, when Sonny asked if he wanted the pepper shaker too. It was taking more self-control than he knew he possessed to play the normal game along with him, but that seemed to be what Sonny expected, no matter what he'd said outside. It was surreal, and it was his penance of sorts, Jake guessed. If he hadn't just gotten out of that orange jumpsuit, he wouldn't sit here and put up with any of this. But getting caught really did suck, and the repercussions were many. He had no clout around here anymore. If what Wendy had done was terrible, well, at least she'd never ended up in jail. She'd never publicly tarnished the Donnely name. In fact, these days, she was making the family look really good, publicly fighting for the rights of herself and all of the other waitresses too. No, he had no high ground to stand on, which is why he had to sit, in this chair, and eat a bowl of noodles prepared by the mother he'd hardly spoken to since he was thirteen. Crazy.

The fact that she usually made this recipe for holidays and birthdays, not just a random Wednesday night like this, didn't escape him. What, exactly, were they celebrating?

"Dig in," Wendy said. "No point in letting it get cold."

Jake did as he was told. He hoped he'd lost his appetite for her cooking or that she'd lost her talent for it. He wanted to hate it. He tried to hate it. But he only ended up hating himself when an involuntary moan of pleasure escaped his lips after that first reluctant bite.

"It's good, right?" Sonny said to Jake, in between mouthfuls.

Jake just shrugged and kept on eating, trying to keep any other signs of enjoyment to himself. There was a loaf of French bread on the table. Jake went ahead and took it. At least he wouldn't make any goofy noises of pleasure over bread. He broke off a large, crusty section. Still warm. Damn her! What game was she playing? He roughly dragged his bread through the delicious sauce, took a huge bite, and chewed it all rather violently. Across from him, Sonny was already finished with his first helping. He'd basically inhaled it, and as soon as he swallowed his last forkful, Jake saw him back in the pasta bowl, dishing himself another monster serving and then grinding the pepper mill again, giving part two of his dinner its five-o'clock shadow.

Even though he was trying to ignore her, Jake couldn't help but notice that Wendy was barely touching her meal. Her eyes were darting nervously from father to son and back again. Jake regretted looking her way. She was pale, and the dark circles under her eyes were pronounced. He thought of all the people with drinking problems he served every day, the stories they told, the rough lives they'd lived, or created, all by themselves. Sister Celia said they all had something unspeakable inside and that this unsayable thing was what they kept trying to drown with alcohol. "It's rough for them to name it," she said. "Until they do, they have us."

Jake found he was able, somehow, to have compassion for everyone who sat at those long tables and not to judge them, to ask them if they wanted hash browns or home fries with their pancakes, and if their syrup dispenser needed refilling. Had he ever bothered to ask Wendy what her story was? During all her days in rehab, had she ever hit on whatever the unspeakable thing was? Had she ever named it? He felt a surge of pity for her and then got it under control. Despite all he was learning, he needed to keep hating her. It was his fuel and his reasonable explanation for his own insanity. He looked away again.

"It did turn out then?" was all she said.

"Oh, it turned out great all right," said Sonny, and Jake couldn't believe the huge smile his dad gave to her then. To him, it looked goofy, but it did the trick to calm Wendy, who smiled for the first time since Jake had arrived. "Thanks, babe," Sonny said, "this is a treat."

Babe? What the…? It was Jake's turn to look from one person to the next, from Wendy to Sonny and then back again. It didn't take a Vivian to figure out the score.

"Well," he said, wiping his mouth furiously with one of the linen napkins he hadn't seen since Christmas Eve 2000, "this is just *awesome*. Really. Congratulations and all that."

"Sit down, Jake," Sonny said, pushing his chair back from the table with a scrape.

"No. I've done enough sitting, and I'm guessing my screw-up is what brought you back together, so, you know, I've done my part, right?"

"Sonny," Wendy said, with a warning tone in her voice. "Telling him—wasn't that the point? He's figured it out, so…if he wants to leave…" Her voice trailed off. Jake could feel her looking at him, could feel her silently pleading, but he refused to meet her eyes. "He should have that right," she said, finishing the thought.

Jake knew that if he looked at her, if he really looked at her, he'd either scream his brains out, or even worse, he might cave, just like Sonny. The part of him that would always love her no matter what she did, the part that was dangerously close to trying to understand her, couldn't win. No matter what, she'd abandoned him. It shouldn't be this easy for her to waltz on back.

"See you around, then, Dad," he said. "I sat through the moment and all that. And I've made my judgment." He gave a curt nod, glanced over at his mother. "Wendy."

She slipped a plastic container into his hands as he passed her, which she must have filled and set aside before he'd come back with Sonny. The top of the lid was beaded with condensation, the pasta still hot. It warmed the tips of his fingers. Without a backward glance, he slammed it down on the table and walked out. This time, no one was stupid enough to stop him.

Vivian

Her grandmother handed her a small package with a New Jersey postmark.

"No return address, *tit monde*," she noted, her voice sounding more concerned than Vivian was used to hearing it. *Tit monde* meant "little one," her baby nickname. Hearing it again was like crawling beneath a favorite blanket in a cool, dark room with lullabies playing.

"Thank you, *ma grand-mère*," was all she said, knowing her grandmother was longing for her to speak a little French Acadian again, to use the Cajun term of endearment that Vivian had long ago abandoned. It had stopped feeling natural to her after so many years away.

She turned the package over and over again in her hands, not wanting to open it until she had some privacy. It was still early, and it had rained in the night. Vivian felt like a child again, watching the street dry after a night rain in the same window seat with the same overstuffed red cushions, her grandmother sitting next to her, sipping her chicory coffee, its scent nutty and sweet. The sunrise and the heat that came with it were already burning the remaining condensation off the concrete, steam rising in the air.

It looks like special effects on a movie set, she thought. And it did—so much so that it was hard to believe Saint Peter Street was a real place, rather than something in a dream she'd had when she was two. She'd truly forgotten what a *sight* this place was. She smiled when she noticed a bright green tree frog, its feet splayed, sticking to her grandmother's screen. On a walk she'd taken with Hailey, they watched an armadillo cross the street. Hailey had gone kind of nuts with excitement, having never seen one before. At the memory, Vivian shook her head, amused. She was glad she'd gotten up early. The last of the condensation quickly evaporated, reminding her of the feeling of waking up from a vivid dream that simply slipped into the ether once consciousness hit.

Everything about the Deep South felt significant somehow. She knew that was one of the many things Hailey was responding to about Louisiana, and during their trip to Ole Miss in particular. This part of the country had a way of feeling important, its struggle to overcome its past as weighty as the swampy air Vivian now found hard to breathe.

She felt a gentle kiss on the top of her head.

"I'll leave you to your thoughts, *ma tite fille.*"

"I'm sorry," Vivian said. "I'm not much fun this trip."

"*Tout va bien,*" her grandmother said.

All is well, thought Vivian, quickly translating the French. She realized that Ivy must have pushed her to choose the language in school for this very reason. She was glad she could still understand the Cajun French phrases that peppered her grandmother's speech.

"At least I hope so," she said, eyeing the package with a nervous look. "Your mother will have a fit if that's from who I think it's from."

"I know," Vivian said, tearing her gaze away from the package to look up at her grandmother, but she was already walking toward the kitchen, no doubt to start making preparations for breakfast, as she was the most gracious of hosts.

As soon as she was alone, Vivian tore off the wrapping. She didn't know if she wanted to laugh or cry. Jake had burned her a CD: Bon Jovi's *New Jersey.*

Vivian decided to laugh. No, subtlety had never been his strong point. There was a note in the package too. In Jake's impatient script it read:

Things I'm Sorry For—
Robbing you.
Almost crashing my bike with you on it.
Tempting you with that stupid car.

Landing us both in jail.
Completely screwing up your life.
Not trying to be a better person for you.
This note. I won't write again. Just don't forget me, Viv.

Oh, and give Bon Jovi a chance, OK?
—Jake

When she got to the end of the note, she was no longer laughing. It was tender of him to mail this to her, but it was cruel too. Even though he didn't mean for it to be, it most definitely was. In order to move forward, she needed no more contact between them. Of course she didn't have the ability to forget him. She'd hate herself if she did, but she needed to start doing her best to put him on a mental shelf. And then to let that shelf collect dust. He'd been both her first love and her biggest mistake to date.

I should destroy this, she thought, while folding the note carefully and tucking it into the inside pocket of her robe. I should throw out this CD, she told herself, before walking over to her laptop and copying all the songs onto her hard drive.

CHAPTER NINETEEN

Sonny

Not knowing what else to do, he finished his pasta and bread and then began to clear the table.

"Come on, I've got this," he said, as Wendy stood up to help.

"I've got to do *something*. I'll go crazy if I sit here thinking of him storming out. And how he looked? Sonny, he's so angry. He has every right to be, but to see it up close? He feels dangerous." She sounded out of breath after taking just a few plates to the sink.

"You're exhausted from knocking out that meal. Seriously. Sit down." He poured her a glass of ice water, and she gave him a grateful look as she took it. He walked behind her and rubbed her shoulders. He winced a little at how frail she felt, her bones too sharp beneath his fingers.

"He'll come around." He smiled when he saw her close her eyes, accepting the comfort he offered.

"Everything's always so simple to you," she murmured. "You never worry, do you?"

"I accept what is. Thinking about what used to be or what might be down the line? I don't see the point." He put his mouth next to her ear. "Besides, now is working out pretty great for me," he said quietly, nibbling a little on her lobe before going back to the sink. He scraped what was left of Jake's pasta into the garbage disposal.

"What you tried to do, Wendy...It was nice."

"It was stupid."

Sonny laughed. "Maybe a little bit...too hopeful, but still...It *was* nice."

"Oh, Sonny, look."

He turned around to see her pointing to the chair Jake had been sitting in, his leather jacket still hanging from its back.

"He'll freeze out there. I'm guessing he doesn't have a spare coat?"

"You'd be right about that," said Sonny. "I'll head out now and try to catch up with him."

"Yeah, you'd better. I've already pissed him off enough. It's pretty clear he didn't like the way I tried to weasel my way back into his heart. It seems you can't mother somebody retroactively."

"You're way too hard on yourself. You were just trying to make a chink in the armor."

"Or a tear in the leather," she said, handing the jacket to Sonny. "I'll resist the urge to try to make you give him these leftovers again."

"Good thinking."

She gave him a little shove toward the door.

"Hurry back," she said, and Sonny responded to the warmth in her smile by pulling her into him.

"Yeah, I will," he said. "And leave those dishes alone."

Before heading out, he called Jake, but he wasn't picking up his cell. He hoped he could catch him before he got too far. He was uneasy leaving Wendy alone. Some of it was worry about the beer in the house, sure. He knew he needed to show her more support and get rid of it, but it was more than that. Yes, he finally had Wendy back, and she seemed as if she was really going to be better this time, but a part of him kept thinking she'd just leave him again. Despite his big talk all of five minutes ago about never worrying, he was just like everyone else when it came to his fears. His biggest ones tended to get stuck in his brain. Whenever he came home from work, he opened the door with a sinking feeling, with a certainty that the house would be empty and on the table would be a note explaining for the last time why he was better off alone. He wished trusting Wendy came as easily as loving her did.

"Really, I mean it," he said again, as Wendy started to wipe the table. "Stay put."

Vivian

She sat in a huge yellow building on the corner of Napoleon Avenue and Tchoupitoulas Street and reclaimed her dreams. Like everything else in New Orleans, the place had a history. It had once been a gambling house, then a gymnasium, and then a brothel. Since 1977, it had been Tipitina's, a music venue like no other. Bands as varied as The Radiators, Phish, and The Blind Boys of Alabama had recorded here. Local legend Dr. John made records at Tipitina's too and was one of its regular performers.

"It's all jazz tonight," her grandmother said, before handing Vivian her car keys. "You drive, baby. If you don't remember how to get there, I'll remind you."

She ended up needing some direction. It had simply been too long, but with a little guidance from Grand-mère, Vivian found their way. Hailey preferred alternative music; she'd once told Vivian, "Jazz is slippery-sounding stuff. Too many notes. Makes me anxious." But tonight she sat there with shining eyes, tapping her foot. For some reason, Ivy looked more like her New Jersey self, her mouth set in a grim line, but Vivian refused to let this put a sour note in her fun. She looked over at her grandmother instead, who was very still, her eyes closed, her hand on the wall. Vivian thought she looked as if she was drinking in the vibrations of the music through her open palm. The moonstone-and-sapphire ring she always wore on her pointer finger caught the stage lights. Vivian relished the sight of her grandmother's wrinkled hand with its ropey veins as blue as the sapphires on that flashing ring. She adored older people, their wisdom and their music. Her grandmother must have listened to these same songs when she was a very young girl.

The melodies washing over them were ones made famous by Artie Shaw: "Moonglow," "Gloomy Sunday," "Begin the Beguine," "Frenesi". The Martin Litton Sextet, a bunch of middle-aged guys possessing some of the most technically perfect skills Vivian had ever heard, played one difficult piece from the 1940s after another, helping her fall back through time. The clarinet, trumpet, guitar, piano, bass, and drums kept blending and then parting to give each of the players a chance to shine alone. And the instrument that shone the most at Tipitina's that evening was the clarinet.

Of course her grandmother had picked this show. Any Artie Shaw music meant lots of clarinet solos. When they performed one called "Scuttlebutt," Vivian stopped drumming her fingers on the table and bobbing her head along to the beat, sitting completely still until the final notes of that lively song had been played.

It was a moment of clarity she never forgot, because she caught a glimpse of her future in it. She was going to learn that song. She'd play it until calluses formed on her fingers, until she split her lip open with her reed from practicing the complicated runs until she nailed them. Until she mastered them. The college letters would be rolling in soon. Some of her top choices offered acceptance into their music programs on the condition that each student pass an audition. Hearing this piece, its youthfulness alive even though it was written almost seventy years ago, she knew this was the song that would make her. It was her ticket to Princeton. The one that would let her walk through the door she'd felt certain only a few weeks ago was closed and locked for good.

Wendy

Something was wrong. After Sonny left, all her energy did too. She'd been pretending to be an everyday mom rather than a middle-aged cocktail waitress wrapped up in a messy lawsuit. She'd been pretending that she'd never abandoned them, playing at what it would have been like if she'd only stuck around. That dinner was certifiable. It was weird how she'd felt possessed to make that meal. She couldn't blame Jake for wanting no part of it.

She wanted to have the kitchen cleaned up before Sonny got back, so they could go straight to bed. Sinking into Sonny's sheets was the most soothing thing she'd thought of all day. She had to admit that he was right about her being exhausted. She'd never felt a fatigue like this before, not even after hours on her feet at the Trop. She was starving too. She had a stomachache, probably from her nerves about seeing Jake, and hadn't been able to eat a bite. And she kept trying to ignore the fact that she was completely strung out and making choices any AA sponsor would gently reprimand her for. She was an addict only ten weeks in recovery doing what they always said she shouldn't. She was involved in a relationship when all her energy was supposed to be focused on getting, and staying, well.

She justified it to herself by noting that Sonny wasn't a new love. Even though the two of them being together should have been a complicated knot to unravel, she was continually floored by how easy it felt. She loved how he didn't need to talk about a damned thing. She was gone and now she was back. His arms were open wide, and she crawled into them with ease, the past slipping away. She thought of Sonny's cool sheets again and decided to finish up in the kitchen and crawl into them.

Standing up to finish wiping the table, she felt a crushing pain in her chest.

I'm glad no one's here to see this, she thought. Then she hit something cold and hard that her brain recognized as the kitchen tiles she and Sonny had picked out when she was twenty-two.

Jake

She was there on the floor, and she was gray—*gray*—and he'd forgotten his jacket. He was just there for his jacket. So cold outside. So cold. He couldn't keep driving without it, and now he was here, and she was on the floor, the color of an elephant or a rhinoceros at the Bronx Zoo. She'd taken him there when he was six? Seven? He blew on his cold-numbed hands until he could feel them again. He was going to need to use them now. He realized that he was running toward her. He was on the floor next to her. And she was so *still*.

"Mom?" He tried to rouse her, shaking her shoulder gently. "Mom?" He yelled it this time. Dialed 911. Gave his address and situation, words pouring from his mouth in a panic: *Idon'tthinkshe'sbreathing yesIknowCPRpleasehurry.* He placed the heel of his hand firmly in the middle of her chest and then his other hand on top of the first, interlacing his fingers. Thirty compressions. On the twenty-first, he heard something inside her pop.

"It's *normal*," he whispered to himself fiercely between clenched teeth. The instructor at Sister Celia's said not to be alarmed by the sounds of bones snapping:

If they aren't breathing, you're not going to make them any worse. Don't give up.

What she didn't tell the class was how horrifying it was to hear a bone break and to know that you were the breaker. He reached the thirtieth compression and then tilted her head back and lifted her chin. He pinched her nose gently and pressed his mouth firmly against hers to make the seal. He gave her two breaths big enough to watch her chest rise and fall. On the second, she gasped and her eyes fluttered open.

"Mom!" he yelled, shaking her. She stared right at him, but he wasn't sure if she saw him or not. She was looking beyond him somehow, as if she was gazing through a window.

He heard sirens in the distance. Her eyes slowly closed again. "Mom?...Mom?...*Mom...*?"

Wendy

She heard him say it. Before she dropped down into the well again, she heard him say it, and in the seconds before she felt nothing at all, she was flooded with peace.

Sonny

It was the longest winter of his life with unendurable moments of grief that he somehow did endure. He cleaned Saint Catherine's, sinking into the cool quiet of the church during weekday hours. The sunshine streaming through the stained-glass windows illuminated doves of peace, the outstretched hands of Jesus, Mary with her mysterious smile. But it was the deceptive sunlight of the cold months, shining brightly, warming no one.

So it turned out he'd have to spend the rest of his life without Wendy after all. There weren't words for how he felt, so he made one up as he polished the pews. *Wendyless*, he thought, rubbing Pledge into the seats until the deep cherry wood glowed brightly. He decided that being Wendyless was the worst feeling in the world. How hard it was to get used to her absence surprised him, considering all the years they'd spent apart. After her death, he realized that simply knowing she was in the world had meant a lot. Even when he was furious with her, knowing she was only a few exits away sustained him. He couldn't stand the fact that she was no more. How could she no longer exist?

"You couldn't have stopped it," the coroner told him after the paramedics who failed to revive her gave their condolences and left. "Your son did everything right, but the heart attack she had— it was massive." Sonny felt himself sinking into the memory of that day like a sponge being pushed into a murky bucket. He thought of her face...the lips he'd just kissed already looking cracked and dry. And her green eyes, no longer bright, staring at nothing. He was grateful when Jake leaned down and closed them. What was she seeing now, wherever she was? And where did she go? Even though she was still there, right in front of him, he couldn't feel her anymore. He couldn't feel a goddamned thing, until Jake put his arm around him.

"It's going to be OK, Dad. It sucks. So much. But it'll be OK. She's OK. I don't know how I know it, but I do." Sonny watched as his son walked back to where Wendy lay and kissed the cold cheek he'd tried hard to make warm and vital again. Sonny did the same before the coroner pulled up the blanket, and the quiet men who had arrived with him carried her body away.

Jake. That was what sustained Sonny now. In the weeks that followed that worst moment, he saw him enroll in the local community college and stick with his volunteering at the shelter, even after he'd completed his community service. Gratefully, he watched as Jake coped with his own grief by finally becoming a better man.

For his part, Sonny worked through the hard days by dreaming of flying again. Although the long winter felt as wretched as the turnpike at rush hour, he survived it. Spring did come, and he was so thankful to no longer be grounded that he surprised himself one morning in early May by walking into Saint Catherine's, sliding into a pew, and pulling down one of the kneelers. He sank to his knees, feeling the sun that poured through the stained-glass windows on his back. It was finally as warm as it was bright.

He didn't know who he was praying to, but he gave thanks for the summer days ahead, for the son who was growing into a man to be proud of, and for allowing him to have Wendy back, at least for a little bit. That was a miracle of sorts, wasn't it? The autopsy revealed that her heart had been severely damaged. From her years of heavy drinking, Sonny was sure. It could have easily given out long before they reconciled. On that spring morning, he found himself deeply thankful for the time he'd been granted with her, however brief. Then he squeezed his eyes even more tightly closed. Wherever she was, he wanted her to know that he loved her still, that he always had and always would, and that he was going to be OK.

CHAPTER TWENTY

Ivy

Of course she brought Vivian back for the funeral. It wasn't without effort, but she set aside her feelings and did the right thing. The boy's father got her contact information from the lawyer the Donnelys had sent to help Vivian. While she was getting ready to go with everyone to Tipitina's, her cell rang.

"I know we're not your favorite people, but my son could use a friend right now." Ivy heard a break in the strong-sounding voice when it said, "Please."

She called the airlines and made plans to leave the following afternoon, but she decided not to tell everyone until after they'd enjoyed the evening of jazz. She wanted to give her mother and the girls one more amazing night in New Orleans before she cut their trip short. She knew Vivian had been anxious to get out of Louisiana from the moment the plane had touched down, but Hailey had really come alive down here. Both Ivy and her mother had grown fond of her. Ivy had even promised Hailey that she'd work on her mother to let her apply to Ole Miss.

When they got home and picked up the mail, they found Vivian's acceptance letters. She'd gotten into every school she'd applied to, but of course the only one she cared about was Princeton. Playing for the director of music was the last hoop Vivian had to jump through, and then her daughter would be walking down the path she'd dreamed of since she was ten. Despite the frenzied tour of Southern schools, Ivy decided to take her mother's advice and let Vivian go to the audition. She nailed it, performing an Artie Shaw medley she'd put together, inspired by that night at Tipitina's.

It came as no surprise to Ivy that Vivian played each song beautifully. After attending the services for Jake's mother, all Vivian did was go to school and practice. Her playing "transcended her years," the director had said. And if she'd taken up with the Donnely boy again, there was no evidence of it. Whatever had happened between them when she paid her condolences, she refused to talk about, and Ivy had finally learned not to push so hard.

Besides, Vivian was like her old self again. Her final semester grades were stellar, and she practiced so much that Ivy started to feel the need to keep track of time for her. Even Einstein seemed concerned for Vivian, staying up past his usual bedtime, pacing and flicking his bushy tail, while Vivian practiced. Prior to the Princeton audition, she'd even forget to eat unless Ivy waved a plate of food in front of her, and she would only realize it was time for bed when Ivy pointed toward Will's crazy bird clock.

"I know, I know. When the hermit thrush starts singing, I need to call it a night."

Then they laughed together for the first time in months. Ivy had almost forgotten how it felt to get along with Vivian. She felt lighter and freer. Hopeful.

Before she knew it, she was dropping Vivian off at the dorms, all her belongings in bags, piled high and balanced precariously on a dolly. After Ivy helped Vivian put clean sheets on her bed, stacked her neatly folded sweaters on a shelf in the closet, and scattered a few plants around, it was time to leave. Vivian surprised her by putting her hands on either side of Ivy's face and looking in her eyes with something that could only be described as love.

"Thanks, Mom, for sticking by me." She let go of Ivy's face and walked to the window. Ivy went with her, and they both stared down at the mass of students with their personal belongings and family dynamics on public display. "I put you through hell, I know. And you still let me have this. I mean it: thank you."

Ivy was determined to hold it together in front of Vivian, even though she didn't know how she was going to leave her, to really leave her, as she was about to do.

"Thank *you*, Vivian, for understanding that I need to go home," she said, her voice shaking a little. "With you not stopping in for dinner every night, what do I have here?"

"Mom, it's better this way," Vivian said. "You in your natural environment, me in mine. You've gotta go where you feel the tug, you know?" She laughed. "Like Hailey. Man, I never dreamed she'd leave Jersey." Both Vivian's voice and laugh trailed off, and Ivy caught a sad expression in her eyes that clearly said, *I will miss my friend.* But when Vivian spoke again, her voice was strong. "I guess she can be your surrogate daughter, and I swear I'll visit you and Grand-mère for every holiday I can. Every summer too."

"Oh, I've already booked the Christmas and spring-break tickets, just to be sure. Don't you worry."

Ivy couldn't bear to drag out the good-bye any longer. Before she lost control of her emotions, she kissed her daughter, once on each cheek, gave a quick wave, and ran.

"Good luck!" she said, as she raced out the door in an uncharacteristically scattered and undignified manner.

"You too, Mom!" she heard Vivian call after her just as her feet hit the stairs. Ivy clattered down them, almost losing her footing once but still refusing to adjust her pace. She kept up her speed as she passed gorgeous buildings with gargoyles in the architecture and ivy climbing up the brown bricks. A breeze blew the branches of the stately trees, leaf patterns dappling the manicured grounds.

Unbidden, a memory of the day she hadn't been able to find Vivian in Central Park resurfaced. Her heart and breathing had been as fast as they were now, while the rest of the world seemed to be in slow motion. And she was running, running. Time dragged while she screamed at strangers, "Have you seen a little girl with dark curls and light brown eyes? Five years old? About this tall? No? *No?* Could you please help me look?" She cursed herself for taking Vivian into the city alone. New Orleans and New York were nothing alike. Losing Vivian here was like a hard slap. She was too far from home. So out of her element that it was dangerous. The panic made her lose her ability to think logically. All she could do was run and sweat and scream Vivian's name.

Something made her look up, and then she saw Vivian high above her, playing on the big rocks the park was famous for, only a short distance from the play area where Ivy had been watching her swing, her legs pumping, her head thrown back, the wild grin on her face showing the wide gap where her two front baby teeth used to be. Ivy had bent down for just a second to tie her shoelace, and when she looked up, Vivian was gone. Her life had been altered until she found her again, fears too terrible to name pounding inside her head until Vivian was safely back in her arms.

Ivy was shaking and crying and laughing all at once, and Vivian was wailing that Ivy had just swooped down and taken her off the rocks: "Right when I got to the *top!*" They were both basket cases, and people were staring, but she didn't care. She had her girl back, and that was all that mattered in the world.

In sight of the university's visitor parking lot at last, Ivy willed herself to slow down. Vivian was grown now, capable, and she no longer needed a guardian. That had been Ivy's biggest fault as a mother all along, forever treating Vivian as someone who would run away and come to harm at any moment. Always seeing her as the little girl who'd scrambled to the top of those slippery rocks, in danger of falling, of being snatched and lost forever. Since that day, Ivy's grip on Vivian had been so tight that she'd actually driven her toward the danger she feared.

Without a doubt, Ivy had just lost Vivian back in that dorm room, but if she could only let her daughter climb the boulders of her life in peace this time around, maybe the two of them would have a chance.

Jake

His mother was a celebrity. She won the case against the Tropicana posthumously, and that wasn't just big news in Jersey. It went national, his mother's image on every station. Sonny just kept shaking his head and answering phones.

"Unbelievable," he said, again and again. "I wish she were here to see this. It's really something, you know, this ball she got rolling."

And suddenly, Jake had mother figures everywhere. A warm and funny woman named Isabelle whom he recognized from the interviews kept showing up with pans of lasagna, mountains of salad, and even trays of sugar-free brownies for dessert.

"Don't think your mother never told me about you," Isabelle said, when he thanked her for making a dessert he could actually eat. The first thing Isabelle said she did after she heard of Wendy's passing was to organize a cooking schedule for all the waitresses who had been a part of the lawsuit, and the meals rolled in for a solid month.

"Your mom was amazing, young man. She made it so all of us would never have to worry about money or do embarrassing things to get it, ever again. Whipping up a few brownies is the least I could do."

And the motherly ladies kept stopping by. One came with sausage and peppers and soft bakery rolls to make sandwiches and told him how Wendy had loaned her a pair of boots and helped her keep the job she desperately needed until they won the suit. And it kept going on like that, cards and calls and condolences and stories about Wendy's kindness and bravery. It was nothing like the strange sympathy he and Sonny had received after she left them. Mothers Wendy had been friendly with, whose kids went to the same school as Jake, had stopped by with casseroles back then too. And a few of them put Post-it notes with their phone numbers on the tops of their containers. They looked at motherless Jake with pity they didn't try to mask, and they looked at Sonny with...something else...that Jake didn't understand until he was older. "Call me," one of them cooed, "and I can pick up the pan. You can call me for anything else you need too, you know." Sonny had cleared his throat uncomfortably, and Jake had been puzzled when he saw his dad throw out the entire pan without tasting the food inside.

What Jake had hated the most were the whispers about him and those looks of pity, but the women who kept stopping by now didn't try any of that stuff on Sonny, and they all looked at Jake with respect. He soon grew to understand that the strong women who kept checking in on him gave him that respect because he came from Wendy. He was a part of her, so they treated him as if he would one day do great things. They simply expected something of him. He didn't know what that some-thing was, but he decided he'd be damned if he didn't figure it out.

The way people were talking about his mother, who was so messed up in life, gave him a strange kind of hope. It was like she was Saint Wendy now, or something. And Jake thought that maybe all the saints, all those perfect people he'd been made to study in those religion classes Wendy used to drag him to, maybe they'd been big fuck-ups too. That's the part that usually got cut out of the stories they told kids. Maybe everyone always made a big mess of things, but the great ones kept trying anyway: well, I really screwed up *this,* but I can still do *that.* Maybe all anyone could ever do was to keep trying, wherever they were, with what-ever they had.

In the months after the casserole schedule ended and the visits became fewer, Jake took stock. One night in May, he looked through all the newspaper clippings he'd collected that told of his crimes. It was like reading about a person who no longer existed. Without hesitation, when he got to the last one he'd cut out about the fire he'd started at the drugstore, he ripped the paper into shreds. He did the same with each article until he had a pile of words that no longer fit together. Then he tossed the scraps into the recycle bin. A few hours after that, Jake pulled out over $3000 in cash from a compartment in the desk where he used to do his homework, and he drove to Sister Celia's.

"This should help feed the guests for a while," he told her.

"Jake, baby, where'd you get all *that?*"

He looked into the warmth of her brown eyes, felt her concern, and smiled. He never took it for granted that she'd learned his name at last, that he'd earned a spot in her memory. Another mother figure. He was collecting them now, welcoming them. He found he did better when he accepted the fact that they cared for him. It held him accountable.

"I'm trying to be a better person, but I'm not crazy enough to turn myself in. I went to jail once already, remember? Second chances, right?"

Sister Celia shook her head and embraced Jake warmly. "If this is the start of yours, then I won't turn it down."

That night, he and Sonny quietly ate the last of the vodka pasta that Wendy had made. Neither of them had had the heart to throw the container away, so Sonny had put it in the freezer. They thawed and reheated it, and there was just enough left for two. It was still rich and delicious. To Jake, it tasted like his childhood. There was nothing to say that wouldn't lessen the moment, so the two men sat in silence.

Jake couldn't allow himself to dwell on thoughts of his mother, so he let his mind jump to Vivian. To what she'd said to him when she came back from New Orleans to offer him comfort. To what she'd done. And to how she'd fixed him. He'd felt broken until he'd seen her, and somehow, just that little bit of time with her had been the beginning of his mending. He could feel the pieces of himself fusing back together. That had been January, and he hadn't seen Vivian since. She had major things to accomplish, and he had big changes of his own to make. It had been hard, but the months had flown by.

He put his hand in his pocket. There was a note in her handwriting. Just one line with a date on it: August 15. Three more months. He could hardly wait.

Hailey

She held the wonderfully fat letter from Ole Miss in her hands. Faulkner Land. Magnolia trees, armadillos, lizards, and tree frogs. Air thick enough to slow down and make her notice the fine nuances of life. Everything always moved so fast in Jersey, too fast. She hadn't realized until she'd gotten away that its racing pulse had never suited her. When she was in the South, the easier pace made her understand that every blessed second mattered, that life was something to be savored rather than endured.

And although she would be over a thousand miles from the only home she'd ever known, she would have the support of friends. Viv's mom and grandma weren't that far away. She had an invitation to visit them when she had her first school break over Labor Day for some home-cooked meals and conversation. And they lived in the city where *A Streetcar Named Desire* had been written, and *A Confederacy of Dunces*, and they said their door was always open to her, anytime. Inspiration was everywhere, hers for the taking, and she loved New Orleans as much as she loved Oxford, because her first trip there had meant more to her than even Vivian would ever know.

That meal at Commander's Palace had changed her life. Even though she'd been full to the point of bursting, after ridding herself of the bread basket, she kept the rest of her dinner down. Every dish from the turtle soup on had been art, and to throw it all up would have felt like a sin. It was the hardest night of her life, keeping that meal from hitting the toilet in the guest bathroom. And even though it was only one night of not throwing up, it was still a life-changing evening for Hailey because of what it inspired her to do.

When she got back to Jersey, with trembling hands, she looked up the number in the phone book: Overeaters Anonymous. She was shocked by how many chapters there were, how many meetings, from morning until late at night. She was not alone. She chose one far enough away that she doubted she'd bump into anyone she knew. She rode the bus north, to Toms River, and walked through the doors of their community center. She was a few minutes late, but no one stared at her when she walked in; she simply blended in with the others at the gathering. There was a paper on every chair. She took a seat in the back and picked one up, joined in with the others as they recited the words that slowly started to heal her:

> *Together we can do what we could never do alone. No longer is there a sense of hopelessness, no longer must we each depend upon our own unsteady willpower. We are all together now, reaching out our hands for power and strength greater than ours. As we join hands, we find love and understanding beyond our wildest dreams.*

She amazed herself by checking all of her snarky thoughts at the door. She didn't allow the editor in herself to mess with the words on the page. She realized that they were good words. Helpful words. As the room swelled with all the distinct voices reading as one, she caught sight of the hand next to her, extended, open. Still meeting no one's eyes, Hailey took the hand that was offered. Finding it comforting and warm, she accepted the understanding that she found there.

Vivian

It amused her to watch out the window as Ivy kept running as if a bear had somehow gotten on campus and was chasing her, all the way to the parking lot. That woman *is* nuts, Vivian thought. But of course she loved her mom. It was going to be a lot better from a distance, but she did love her all the same. And she finally understood that her mother loved her deeply too and that people who love each other that way tend to make all sorts of terrible mistakes. Love and madness often feel uncomfortably similar. Same coin, different sides—that was all.

Her eyes fell on the calendar she'd already hung up on her bulletin board. August 15. As soon as she got the letter with her dorm assignment, she'd texted him, and he'd known the date for many months now. Would he take her up on it? She hadn't understood, and still didn't understand, how she'd known all the right words to say to him after his mother passed, had known just what to do. Most people in somber situations like that freeze up or say stupid things about peace and light and being better off. Sure, she realized that she'd been through this with her dad, but it was more than that. It was more.

He'd stood there in his suit, outside the room where his mother lay. Vivian regretted never meeting her. She'd been in her cell, and Jake, in his. It really hadn't been the time for introductions. She'd seen the news reports, even read a blurb about her in *Time*. People were so complicated. A cocktail waitress in a too-tight costume, degrading herself for your spare change, could become a feminist icon. You never knew with anybody, really. At any given moment the most revered person on the planet could lose it, could come crashing down to earth, and the person you think of as nothing, as a loser, a waste, could sprout wings and fly.

She hadn't said a word of this to Jake, though. Was it wrong of her to have kissed him when his mother lay cold and still in the next room? Having buried her own father less than a year before, she could say firmly that it was not. Life was brief, and sometimes it got so damned boring that you held up a Dunkin' Donuts or two, just to rail against its sameness. Often, it was cruel. Jake was seeing it at its cruelest, and it was more than OK to kiss in the face of a death like that. To love and to feel and to move forward. Vivian knew that was all there was to hold onto in moments like these.

She'd written the date she was to move to Princeton on the back of one of Wendy's prayer cards and pressed it into Jake's hand.

"I have to go now. There's so much I need to do." She'd squeezed the hand that held the card. "Don't get stuck here. Think about taking some classes. And don't stop your work with Sister Celia. Keep moving. Feed your guests." She'd cupped his face in her hands, given him a final kiss. "Hope to see you." Then she'd left. She'd realized on the bus ride home that she hadn't given him a chance to say a word.

The dorm was thick with like-minded people. The university had offered her a room on a floor with other music majors, and she'd jumped at the opportunity. From her window, she watched the ones still arriving, their dollies loaded down with guitar cases and drum equipment. Trumpets and trombones were already making comical sounds in the hallways. She turned away from the window to listen. She heard the clash of cymbals on the stairs, heard people groaning as they dragged all their instruments up each flight. Her heart quickened with excitement. She couldn't wait to play. She looked forward to meeting everyone, but there was only one person she wanted to see right now.

As she listened to the cacophony outside her door, she realized at once that she could be both chaotic and controlled. She could be smart enough to see the risks but dumb enough to take them anyway. She could be deeply in love and still free. Some of the students outside stopped playing separately and started to work together, an informal jam session. It sounded great. Breaking through the music came the sound of the knock she'd been waiting for. She walked toward it, her hand on the door. She could have everything—*everything*—if she wanted it. Why not?

ACKNOWLEDGMENTS

First and foremost, my thanks go to my husband, C. J. Hilton, who has patiently waited for many years for me to believe in myself as much as he has always believed in me. His constant support and encouragement astonish and ground me. Most of all, he makes me profoundly happy, which makes me a more productive writer. In every way, I hit the marriage jackpot.

To my children, Matthew and Cordelia, my thanks for being the best kids on the planet and for being proud of me and cheering me on as I completed this book. From beginning to end, these two kept me writing. Clearly, I also hit the kid jackpot.

To my partner in crime and writing, Theresa Gibbons, my thanks for reading every word of the first draft of this book, for her wise critiques, and her sharp editorial eye. I am grateful for the writers' workshop breakfasts that lasted so long they turned into lunches, for the inspiration and insight she provided, and for all the laughs. It's a rare gift to have a colleague and friend who can make work feel like play.

To all the great teachers I've had throughout the years, my thanks, especially to Veronica Costello, Nancy Zafris, the late Lewis Nordan, Chuck Kinder, the late Belle Waring, Joanna Leake, Rick Barton, John Gery, and the late Jim Knudsen.

To my peers from the University of New Orleans Creative Writing Workshop, my thanks for helping me to learn my craft and for all your friendship and support, especially Paula Martin Morell, Allison Grace McNeil, Shana-Tara O'Toole, and Jocelyn Cady Spence.

To all my dear friends who know I spend my days dreaming up imaginary people and who still want to be my real friends anyway, especially Nicole Admire, Sheila Chillingworth, Erin Claypoole, Mandi and Rob Duffy, Donna Green, Kerry Libertucci, Carolyn Schussler, Al Terrononi, Helen Walter-Terrinoni, and Tammy Cummins Zeronis.

To Nancy Moffatt and Lori Lysiak, all my love and thanks for a lifetime of encouragement and inspiration. No one could ask for better sisters.

And finally, my thanks to my mom, Mildred Elliott, and to my late father, Paul G. Ratvasky, for not saying, "That's crazy," when I said I wanted to major in creative writing.

I am always in their debt.

2 1982 02919 3103

CPSIA information can be obtained
at www.ICGtesting.com
Printed in the USA
LVOW01s2009310816
502665LV00021B/1458/P